Published Aug. 2005

A10

£3·50

PUFFIN BOOKS

Zip's Apollo

Philip Ridley was born in the East End of London, where he still lives and works. He studied painting at St Martin's School of Art and by the time he graduated had exhibited widely throughout Europe and written his first novel. As well as three books for adults, and the screenplay for the award-winning feature film *The Krays*, he has written five adult stage plays: *The Pitchfork Disney*, *The Fastest Clock in the Universe*, *Ghost from a Perfect Place*, *Vincent River* and *Mercury Fur*, and five for young people: *Karamazoo*, *Fairytaleheart*, *Moonfleece*, *Sparkleshark* and *Brokenville*. He has also directed two films from his own screenplays: *The Reflecting Skin* – winner of eleven international awards – and *The Passion of Darkly Noon*. Philip Ridley has written eleven other books for children: *Mercedes Ice*, *Dakota of the White Flats*, *Krindlekrax* (winner of the Smarties Prize and the WHSmith Mind-Boggling Books Award), *Meteorite Spoon*, *Kasper in the Glitter* (nominated for the 1995 Whitbread Children's Book Award), *Dreamboat Zing*, *The Hooligan's Shampoo*, *Scribbleboy* (which was shortlisted for the Carnegie Medal and received a commendation at the NASEN Special Educational Needs Children's Book Awards 1997), *ZinderZunder*, *Vinegar Street* and *Mighty Fizz Chilla* (shortlisted for the Blue Peter Best Book Award).

D0280859

Books by Philip Ridley

MERCEDES ICE
DAKOTA OF THE WHITE FLATS
KRINDLEKRAX
METEORITE SPOON
KASPER IN THE GLITTER
SCRIBBLEBOY
ZINDERZUNDER
VINEGAR STREET
MIGHTY FIZZ CHILLA
ZIP'S APOLLO

For younger readers

DREAMBOAT ZING
THE HOOLIGAN'S SHAMPOO

Plays for young people

KARAMAZOO
FAIRYTALEHEART
MOONFLEECE
SPARKLESHARK
BROKENVILLE

Plays for children

KRINDLEKRAX
DAFFODIL SCISSORS

Zip's Apollo

PHILIP RIDLEY

PUFFIN

PUFFIN BOOKS

Published by the Penguin Group
Penguin Books Ltd, 80 Strand, London WC2R 0RL, England
Penguin Group (USA) Inc., 375 Hudson Street, New York, New York 10014, USA
Penguin Books Australia Ltd, 250 Camberwell Road, Camberwell, Victoria 3124, Australia
Penguin Books Canada Ltd, 10 Alcorn Avenue, Toronto, Ontario, Canada M4V 3B2
Penguin Books India (P) Ltd, 11 Community Centre, Panchsheel Park, New Delhi – 110 017, India
Penguin Group (NZ), cnr Airborne and Rosedale Roads, Albany, Auckland 1310, New Zealand
Penguin Books (South Africa) (Pty) Ltd, 24 Sturdee Avenue, Rosebank 2196, South Africa

Penguin Books Ltd, Registered Offices: 80 Strand, London WC2R 0RL, England

www.penguin.com

First published 2005
1

Copyright © Philip Ridley, 2005
All rights reserved

The moral right of the author has been asserted

Set in 11/12.75 pt Palatino
Typeset by Rowland Phototypesetting Ltd, Bury St Edmunds, Suffolk
Made and printed in England by Clays Ltd, St Ives plc

Except in the United States of America, this book is sold subject to the condition
that it shall not, by way of trade or otherwise, be lent, re-sold, hired out, or otherwise
circulated without the publisher's prior consent in any form of binding or cover other
than that in which it is published and without a similar condition including this
condition being imposed on the subsequent purchaser

British Library Cataloguing in Publication Data
A CIP catalogue record for this book is available from the British Library

ISBN 0–141–31384–6

For all the Friends of Apollo

'Love is the alchemy'
(Anonymous)

— PART ONE —

— 1 —

It is a winter's night in New Town.

The houses of New Town are square. The roads of New Town are straight. The trees of New Town, like the lawns, are plastic.

New Town is exactly what it says.

It is a town.

It is new.

So new, in fact, that proper street signs haven't been put up yet. Just makeshift placards declaring, 'Yet To Be Named'. So far, there are ten Yet To Be Named Roads, fifty Yet To Be Named Streets, and twenty-five Yet To Be Named Avenues. Some of these roads, streets and avenues are, like many of the houses, still under construction. So, perhaps, the more apt name for New Town should be Not Finished And Mostly Empty Town.

One house, however, is very much finished and not empty at all.

This is No. 1, Yet To Be Named Street.

Like all the others it's painted white and has a straight path leading up to the front door but, unlike the others, its windows are ablaze with light and, from somewhere inside, a television can be heard.

The door to No. 1 is opening now and two boys are stepping out.

'Glorious!' cries Zip. 'I *love* the cold! Look! You can see my breath! I'm a dragon! Rahhhhh!'

Zip Jingle is twelve years old, has an eruption of red dreadlocks, and is wearing layers of T-shirts, jumpers and jackets, all held together with scarves and a belt.

'Show me *your* breath, Newt! Let's see if you're a dragon too. Yesss! Can see it from here! Newt's a dragon too!'

Newt is Zip's younger brother and, cocooned in a silver puffa suit, resembles more a miniature spaceman than the two-and-a-half-year-old toddler he is.

'Come on, little brov, let's be on our way. Us dragons gotta fly.'

The brothers are going to the supermarket. It's the first time they've been there so, while Zip keeps hold of Newt with one hand, he's clutching a scrawled map in the other.

'We've got to walk down the main road, Newt ... Then we turn left along the motorway ... then we walk to the footbridge and use this to cross over the motorway and – Oh, ain't this exciting, Newt, eh?'

'...'

Oh, look at Newt, thinks Zip. *He don't think it's exciting at all. He don't think anything about New Town is exciting. I'll see if I can help.*

'Gosh! Look at those street lights, little brov! Bright orange! Know what I reckon? Night in New Town is brighter than day. Ain't that glorious! Eh? And look at the sky! Not a star in sight. Just orange clouds. It's the street lights reflecting off them that does it, you know. Glorious, eh? And – gosh! – listen to that traffic! What a comforting sound. Don't you think so, little brov?'

'...'

Will you ever smile again, Newt? I know how much you miss the forest, but ... it's over now.

Zip and Newt's parents had, until recently, been trying to save an area of woodland – which included a seven-hundred-year-old oak tree – from being chopped down. The Powers That Be were determined to build another terminal for a nearby airport and the forest, beautiful though it was, simply 'got in the way of progress'.

The Battle of Ancient Oak (as the local media dubbed it) had gone on for almost seven years.

That's over half Zip's life and, quite clearly, all of Newt's.

In fact, unlike Zip, forest life is the only life Newt has ever known.

Which is why, despite Zip's most valiant efforts, Newt finds it hard to get enthusiastic about orange nights, starless skies and traffic noise.

'Come on, Newt! We've just got to walk down the other side of the footbridge – Careful you don't slip, little brov! The metal slope of the footbridge is smooth as ice. Gosh! Can you see the light on the other side of this hill, Newt? Must be the supermarket. Shall we see if we can take a short cut over the hill? Yeah?'

Newt nods.

A reaction!

They start to climb the hill.

The light gets brighter.

'Exciting, eh, Newt?'

'Ya-ya!'

Words!

They reach the top of the hill and –

'Glorious!' gasps Zip.

'Ya-ya, Zi-Zi!'

Newt said my name!

Below them, on the other side of the car park, is the supermarket. Its glass front is radiant with neon and twinkling lights. What's not glass is the sleekest metal, polished to a silver sheen. All around is smooth, new concrete, shimmering like marble. Everything about the supermarket sparkles and gleams and shines. Across the top is a flashing sign declaring:

STARBUY'S

Newt says, 'Spish-hip.'

'Gosh, you're right! It *does* look like a spaceship – Hey! What you pulling my hand for? Oh, you want to run down the hill, eh?'

'Ya-ya, Zi-Zi!'

'Okey-dokey, but hold my hand tight!'

They run down the hill –

'YEEEEEHHHHH!!'

'YEEEEEHHHHH!!'

– and then walk across the car park.

'There's the doors, brov!'

'Ya-ya!'

Viiisssshhhhh!!

The doors open automatically.

'Gosh!'

'Gooosh!'

They go inside and –

It's huge! Aisles and aisles of food. And everything is wrapped in different kinds of shiny stuff. Shiny plastic. Shiny tin. Shiny foil – Hang on! Where's Newt gone? He was holding my hand a second ago –

Aha! There he is!

Newt has grabbed hold of the wire mesh of a shopping trolley and is pushing it recklessly towards the newspaper rack.

'Careful!' Zip dashes to Newt and takes the trolley from him. 'And *please* don't wander off like that, Newt.'

'I wanna push!'

'Tell you what,' says Zip, swinging Newt into the air

and putting him in the trolley, 'why don't you *ride* it? There! After all, you look like a spaceman so now you can be captain of your very own spaceship. How's that?'

'Ya-ya, Zi-Zi.'

'Okey-dokey! Now I'll push and . . . let's shop!'

Eeek-eek-clicka-click . . .

'Oh, you hear that, Newt? It's one of the trolley wheels. Trust us to choose the wonky trolley, eh? Never mind. You enjoying the ride in your spaceship?'

'Apple tin ta mooo!'

'Oh! Yeah! *Apollo 13* to the moon! What a clever boy you are. There was a film about that on telly last night, wasn't there. Astronauts tried to fly a spaceship called *Apollo 13* –'

'Ta mooo! Ta mooo!'

'Well, they *tried* to get to the moon, Newt, but they never made it. Their spaceship conked out and –'

'Apple-loo!'

'No, no, Newt, the spaceship wasn't called Apple-loo. It was Apollo!'

'Apple-loo!'

'No. Apollo! *Apollo! Ap-ol-lo!!*'

And within the metal mesh of the trolley something started to tingle and stir.

An energy, like the pulse of blood, seemed to beat from welded joint to welded joint, from rubber wheel to plastic push bar.

And a thought started to take shape within the trolley . . .

I . . . am . . . alive . . .

— 2 —

Although there are twenty-four checkouts in total, only one has the 'PAY HERE' sign illuminated.

Zip pushes the trolley over to it and says, 'Top of the evening to you,' to the person sitting at the till. She is about twenty years old, with long, blonde hair, blue eyes and a very round face.

'A friendly voice!' she gasps. 'And – Ooo, what a smile! Tell ya, customer, if scientists could find a way of bottling your smile, they'd make a fortune.' She indicates a badge on her uniform with the name 'ROSWELL SHEPHERD' printed on it. 'That's me! Labelled like a can of beans. Friends call me Roz. And who might you be, customer?'

'Zip Jingle.'

Roz claps her hands with delight. 'I can see it on the bottle now: "ZIP JINGLE'S SMILE POTION".' She indicates Newt. 'And who's ya little friend, Customer Zip?'

'My brother. Newt.'

'Hello, Customer Newt!'

'Hi-Hi!'

Roz starts checking the bar codes of Zip's shopping – Beep! goes the machine – then hands the items to Zip to put in plastic bags. 'You're the first customer I've seen all evening, Customer Zip. Trust The Powers That Be to build a supermarket in the middle of nowhere, eh? Ooo, your brother's having fun in that trolley, ain't he?'

'It's his spaceship. He's called it Apollo.'

'Tell me, Customer Newt, would you like to take Apollo home with you?'

'Ya-ya!'

'Can we, Roz? Really?'

'Of course, Customer Zip. After all, I don't suppose you've got your car waiting outside.'

'No,' chuckles Zip. 'I can't even drive.'

'There, that's all the shopping beeped!'

'We walked all the way from New Town – Here's the money, Roz.'

'New Town! That's where I live! We're neighbours!'

'I was beginning to think we were the only people there.'

'Well, now you know you're not alone.' She gives Zip his change. 'Goodbye, Customer Zip. Goodbye, Customer Newt. Thank you for shopping at Starbuy's.'

Viiissshhhhh!

I am . . . leaving . . . the supermarket . . .

It . . . different air . . . it cold air . . .

It . . . different . . . under me . . .

It rough and bumpy . . .

Where . . . roof gone?

Where . . . lights?

I'm not sure I like this!

'GRAN!' calls Zip, opening the front door and rushing into the house. 'WE'RE HOME!'

Gran – otherwise known as Holly – is sitting in an arm-chair wrapped in a bathrobe and wearing a baseball cap. She is sixty-seven years old and, for most of her life, has been a complete stranger to both injury and illness. But then, about three months ago, she suffered something called a stroke. A stroke is what happens when a clot of blood travels round the body and gets lodged in the brain. This clot, tiny though it is, can do a lot of damage. In Gran's case it left her with greatly impaired speech (hence 'Hi, Zip,' becoming 'Hiii, Zeee,') and half her body – her right side – paralysed. Walking, needless to say, is very difficult and, although Gran's tried several times (with the aid of a walking frame), a recent fall – in which she'd severely bruised her face – seems to have taken all the fight out of her.

'I hunnn-ree, Zeee.'

'I'm hungry too, Gran – Ouch!!' Zip stubs his toe on a cardboard box. 'We've got to start unpacking some of this lot, Gran! There's boxes all over the place. If you tell me where you want it all to go, I'll put it there. Okey-dokey?'

'Yeeeah, Zeee . . . buuu . . . I misss myy oll hoooos.'

'I know you miss your old house, Gran. But . . . well, none of us are where we used to be.' He gives Gran a kiss on her cheek. 'Now ... has Mum come down while I've been out?'

'Nooo.'

'Then Mum must be hungry too! I'll put the shopping away, then rustle up some food for all of us. How's that sound? Glorious or glorious? Hang on, let's just check on Newt!'

Zip rushes to the front door and –

There he is! Still playing with the trolley!

'Stay close to home, little brov. OK?'

'Ya-ya, Zi-Zi.'

LittleBrov!

So that is what this soft and warm thing playing with me is called.

So the other soft and warm thing ... must be ...

BigBrov!

And this place is ... Home.

I learn more and more about this new world all the time.

I soak it up.

But ... oh, I'm still not sure I like it here.

The supermarket — it felt so safe there.

Everything is different here.

Different things are so ... scary.

— **4** —

Rap, rap.

'Mum?'

Silence.

Rap, rap, rap.

'Mum! It's me! Zip!'

'. . . Come in, love.'

Slowly, balancing a tray of food in one hand, Zip opens the bedroom door and steps inside.

'Top of the evening, Mum – Gosh, it's so dark. Can I turn on the light?'

'Electric light gives me a migraine, love.'

'I'll pull the curtains, then.'

'And let that horrid street light in! No way!'

'But I can't *see*, Mum.'

'That's just the way I like it, Zip.'

'But I've brought you something to eat and if I can't see where to – Ouch!' Zip trips on a cardboard box. 'See?! I nearly dropped everything!'

'I'll light the candle,' she says with a weary sigh. 'Hang on, where're the matches . . .? Here!'

Striiikkke!

Zip's Mum – or Carol, as she's also known – is lying on the floor in a sleeping bag. There is a bed in the room (and Zip has told her many times this would be far more comfortable) but Mum won't use it. A sleeping bag on hard earth is what she got used to in the forest. A mattress is far too soft for her now.

'Where do you want the tray, Mum?'

'Put it beside me. I'll eat it later.'

'You should eat it *now*. While it's hot. You haven't eaten all day.'

'I had some walnuts and elderflower water earlier.'

'That's not enough! You're gonna make yourself ill. Then what am I going to do? Eh? Eh?'

'All right, love, all right.' She struggles into a sitting position. 'I'll eat it now.'

Zip's mum is thirty-eight years old. Her hair – which is long and red – is a mass of dreadlocks (decorated with ribbons and beads). Her eyes are large and very bloodshot and her face is so pale that, in the flickering twilight of the candle, it appears almost transparent.

'What you cooked, love?'

'Spaghetti with tomatoes and mushroom sauce.'

'Another microwave dinner?'

'Well . . . yeah.'

'Oh, the *chemicals*, Zip.' She sniffs the plate. 'Did you read the ingredients label? I bet there's nothing but artificial flavourings and preservatives.'

'The mushrooms and tomatoes are real!'

'Not *organic*!'

'Just *try* it, Mum. Please!'

Slowly, Mum forks some spaghetti into her mouth. She winces at first, as if several woodlice were crawling round her gums, then gradually her face relaxes and she starts chewing with more relish.

'Not bad, eh?' asks Zip.

'The trick . . .' replies Mum, forking some more into her mouth, 'is to forget chemicals and think yum.' She chuckles and shoots Zip a playful look.

Oh, that's her! That's Mum! Do it again, Mum. Please.

'Apollo ta moo . . . to moo . . . ha, ha, ha!'

'Listen to that!' Mum stops eating and looks towards the window. 'It's baby Newt. He's *laughing*!'

'He's playing with a supermarket trolley.'

'Oh, Zip,' sighs Mum. 'A . . . *trolley*?'

'So what? He's happy.'

'But *I'm* not! *You're* not!'

'I am!'

'Don't lie to me, Zip! How can you be? You loved the forest more than any of us.'

Oh, no, Mum! Don't go on about the oak tree again. Please!

'Remember how you used to sleep under the oak tree and –'

'COOO – EEE!!'

'That's Aunt Ivy!' cries Zip with relief. 'Best get down-stairs. See ya later, Mum.'

— 5 —

Auntie Ivy is checking her hair and make-up in the hallway mirror.

'Top of the evening, Auntie Ivy.'

'And the top of the evening to you, babycake.' She wipes some lipstick from her teeth. 'I've just closed the front door a little bit. Don't want to let all the heat out, do we?'

'But Newt –!'

'You can still hear him, babycake. Stop worrying so much.' She gives him a sloppy, wet kiss on each cheek. 'So you found the supermarket OK, did you?'

'Your map was spot on, Aunt Ivy. We even took a short cut over the hill on the other side of the footbridge.'

'And the shopping? You get it all?'

'Everything.'

'Bless ya heart!' She gives him another kiss. 'Now, where's that young gran of yours? I wanna show her my new hair colour. It takes twenty years off me, I swear it does. HOOLLYY! COOO-EEE!'

Aunt Ivy is Gran's sister, so – strictly speaking – that makes her Zip's *great*-aunt. But as that's a bit of a mouth-ful (and, as Aunt Ivy once said, 'Great? Me? Oh, that's far too grand for a bingo-and-chips girl like yours truly!') Zip just calls her plain and simple Aunt.

As Aunt Ivy's reference to 'young gran' implies, she is older than Holly by several years, although to look at them now, you'd never think it. Gran is all frail and colourless, like a black-and-white photo left in the sun, while Aunt Ivy, with her bright hair, clothes and earrings, is as vivid as a freshly printed Polaroid.

'Heeellloo . . . Iyyyy.'

'Wotcha, Sis.'

Look at them! They've probably always been like this. Even as girls. Big sister Ivy always asking little sister Holly, 'How do I look?' And little sister Holly always replying, 'You look beautiful, Ivy, beautiful.' Will it be like this with Newt and me? Will I always be looking out for him in the same way? Even when we're old? Will I still get worried when I can't hear – Hang on!

I can't hear him now!

Newt! Newt!

BigBrov is rushing out of Home.

BigBrov is worried about something.

BigBrov's worry . . . I can feel it –

'Newt? Newt?'

BigBrov is worried that he can't see LittleBrov.

We are in the shadows here, BigBrov!

'Where are you, Newt?'

BigBrov cannot see us. I will have to move –

Eeeka!

'There you are!'

Newt's asleep in the trolley. How calm and peaceful he looks. It's past his bedtime. I'll pick him up and – Wow! He's so warm! Hang on! The whole trolley is warm. How can that happen?

It is me! I would not let LittleBrov get cold.

Hang on! I'm sure . . . yes, I'm sure I heard the trolley move just now.

You did.

I thought Newt must have moved it but . . . if he's asleep . . .

I moved myself, BigBrov. Don't you see that?

*Wait! I . . . I've just realized something! I am doing more than just
feeling BigBrov's feelings!*

I . . . am reading BigBrov's mind!

'Whaaa . . . Zi-Zi . . .?'

'Oh! I didn't mean to wake you, little brov.'

'I . . . sleeepeee.'

'So I see. Say goodnight to Apollo.'

'Gooo . . . nighh . . . Apollo.'

Goodnight, LittleBrov.

Goodnight, BigBrov.

I think . . . Yes!

This new place don't seem so different any more.

It don't seem so scary.

— 6 —

*I'm lying flat on my back. I can feel grass underneath me and
smell wild flowers. I can hear insects buzzing. Sunlight shines
through my eyelids. I open my eyes and see – oh, the forest is all
around! I get to my feet and start walking. I walk into a field of
cornflowers. Bright blue. I am so happy – oh, look!*

The oak tree!

*It's so big. Its bark is all twisted and gnarled like ancient skin.
I walk round the tree. This is the heart of the forest. How safe I*

feel. No one and nothing can ever hurt me here. The oak tree will protect me – What's that?

A noise!

It's thunder!

And the sky is getting darker.

Clouds swirl over the sun. It's getting colder. I'm beginning to shiver.

The blue sky has gone. The wind blows stronger and stronger. Twigs and flowers whizz by me. I hang on to the tree for all I'm worth. Save me, tree. Save me! I feel the ancient oak begin to sway. A creaking sound like the sky ripping. The ancient oak is being uprooted –

'Don't go! Don't!'

That is BigBrov's voice! BigBrov is sitting up in bed. Sweat is trickling down his face. His heart is going thumpa-thumpa-thumpa.

It's that dream again!

What dream?

Every night it's the same.

Why?

I feel so scared!

Oh, BigBrov, what has happened to you to make you feel like this —?

He's getting out of bed.

Look! There he is!

BigBrov is looking out of the bedroom window.

BigBrov is looking up at the night sky.

'No stars . . . no stars . . .'

There is water coming out of his eyes. Why is that happening? Why are BigBrov's eyes leaking?

I don't know the answer to this yet.

But I will.

— 7 —

'You got the shopping list, babycake?'

'Yes, Aunt Ivy.'

'And the money?'

'Yes, Aunt Ivy.'

'And be sure to use the footbridge to cross the –'

'Cross the motorway. Of *course*.' Zip steps out of the house and on to the garden path. 'I'm always very careful. You know that.'

'Bless ya heart, of course you are!' Aunt Ivy ruffles Zip's dreadlocks, then looks at the grease on her hand. 'Get some shampoo while you're at the supermarket, babycake.'

'Dreadlocks shouldn't be washed, Aunt Ivy.'

'How'd ya clean them, then?'

'The body's natural oils keep them fresh.'

'Well, get the shampoo so it can remind the natural oils what fresh ought to feel like, eh?'

'IIIVVVYYY!' calls Gran from inside the house.

'ALL RIGHT, SIS!' Aunt Ivy calls back. Then she sighs deeply and rubs her temples. 'I've got one of my headaches coming on, I know it. Now ... where's that little brother of yours.'

'He's in the alleyway,' replies Zip, pointing to the gap between the house and the garage. 'He's playing – Listen!'

'Apple-loo ta mooo!'

'Bless him.' Ivy dashes to the corner of the house.

'Newt! Time to go to the supermarket with Zip. Come on, babycake!'

'Oh!' Zip rushes to Ivy. 'I told Newt he could stay here and play, Aunt Ivy.'

'I can't have Newt here, Zip. Your gran needs a bath this morning and –'

'IIIVVVYYY!'

'ALL. RIGHT, SIS! GIMME A CHANCE, WON'T YA!'

Zip says to Newt, 'It's all right, little brov. The trolley can wait here for you while we go and –'

'Oh, no, babycake. You've got to take the trolley back.'

Take me back? To the supermarket?

But — oh, you can't!

I've got used to this place now!

Don't take me back!

Please!

Please!

'Nahh!' cries Newt, clutching at the metal frame. 'Apple-loo is ma freeeend!'

I'm a friend to you all.

'But . . . but, Aunt Ivy . . . Newt has made friends with –'

'IIIVVVYYY!!'

'COMING, I SAID! COMING! – Oh, you'd think that mum of yours would do something – CAROL! GET UP AND MAKE YOURSELF USEFUL! Listen, Zip! These are stressful times for all of us. OK? You know The Powers That Be could pay us a visit at any time! You know what that means? Eh? If they think your mum can't cope with you and Newt and Gran they could . . . oh, they will take both of you away! You and Newt! Take you into care! You understand that, don't you, Zip?'

'I understand that, Aunt Ivy, but surely one trolley won't –'

'IIIVVVYYY!!'

'YES, SIS! YES!' She rushes back to the house, snapping back at Zip, 'Just do as you're told for once, babycake! I'm at the end of my tether! Honest I am!'

SLAM!

Do as I'm told for once! What's that supposed to mean? I always do what I'm told. I've done nothing but do what I'm told since I got here!

Zip grabs the trolley and starts pushing it.

Eeeka-eek-clicka-click –

no!

'Nooo, Zi-Zi!'

Cook dinner for your gran, Zip! Put Newt to bed, Zip! Go and talk to your mum, Zip! I never moan or complain. Not once!

Eeeka-eek-clicka-click –

no!

'Nooo, Zi-Zi!'

BigBrov is not listening. BigBrov is in such a bad mood. There is no smile on BigBrov's face. How strange to see him without that smile — NO! WE ARE CROSSING THE FOOTBRIDGE!

Eeeka-eeka-clicka-click –

STOP, BIGBROV!

'Stooop, Zi-Zi!'

WE ARE GOING ROUND THE HILL!

Eeeka-eeka-clicka-click –

STOP!

'Stooop!'

THERE IT IS! THE SUPERMARKET! I HAVE GOT NO CHOICE BUT TO —

Eeek –!

I've stopped!

'Oh, no!' cries Zip. 'That's *all* I need!' Zip kicks the trolley. 'Move!'

Ouch!

'Nooo, Zi-Zi!' shrieks Newt. 'NOOOOOOOO!'

LittleBrov is screaming so loud. His eyes are leaking so much.

And suddenly, Zip becomes very still, and he stares at the horror-filled face of Newt, and –

Oh, no! What have I done?

'Little brov! I'm sorry! I got all carried away and . . . oh, don't get upset, little brov. I can't stand it when you're upset. Please. Forgive your silly big brov.'

Give LittleBrov a big hug, BigBrov!

'Here, let me give you a big hug.' Zip wraps his arms round Newt. 'I just got annoyed with the silly wonky wheel –'

'Not wonnyy wheel,' says Newt. 'Apple-loo is scaaar-rree.'

'What's Apollo scared of?'

Newt points at the supermarket.

You tell him, LittleBrov.

'Apple-loo wanna stayyy wif usss.'

'Okey-dokey, tell you what we'll do. We'll take Apollo into the supermarket –'

I'm not sure I like this.

'– and then we'll take Apollo back home again.'

Home! Yes!

'Yessss!' cries Newt. 'But prom-eee, Zi-Zi.'

'I promise you, little –'

'Nooo. Prom-eee Apple-loo.'

That would be nice.

Zip hesitates a moment, then says, 'Apollo, I promise you – I give you my word – that I will not leave you in that supermarket. It must be terrible for you in there. Being pushed around all day. No one giving you a kind word. People treating you like a . . . like a slave. We're not like that, Apollo. We're grateful that you're helping us.'

Beautifully said. Let's shop!

— 8 —

'So many shampoos, Newt,' says Zip, gazing at shelves of the stuff. 'Who would've thought it? Medicated, anti-dandruff, with conditioner – Gosh, I've no idea what to choose . . . Hang on! Someone's kneeling on the floor over there. See? They're moving things on a shelf. They must work here. I'll ask for advice.'

Eeeka-eek-clicka –

'Top of the morning to you!'

'Eh? What?'

'My Aunt Ivy wants me to wash my hair. Of course, it's totally unnecessary as dreadlocks keep themselves clean but –'

'Why should any of this bother me?'

'Ain't you a supermarket person?'

'Do I *look* like a supermarket person?'

No.

The boy is thirteen years old and is wearing jeans, very worn trainers, black polo-neck jumper, a black furry coat (very shaggy and far too big for him) and has very, very short hair.

'I'm so sorry,' says Zip. 'I saw you on your hands and knees and thought –'

'Spare me, spare me.' The boy holds up his hands as if warding off the sound of Zip's voice. 'Just go away.' He crawls further along the floor.

This could be a friend for you, BigBrov. You need a friend. Talk to him. Go on.

'I hope your coat's not real fur?'

Not a good start.

'And why d'you hope that?'

'I don't think we should kill animals just for our vanity.'

'You know, that's *just* what I did. I went out one day and I saw this magnificent animal. A mammoth, to be precise. Unique specimen. That fur will make a beautiful coat, I thought. So I grabbed a spear and chased the mammoth all the way down the motorway. What a sight that was. Cars swerving out the way. Very dramatic. Finally, I caught up with it – down by the Dagenham fly-over, I seem to remember – and the result is what you see me wearing. Happy now? Goodbye.' He crawls further along the floor.

Don't let him go! Talk!

'You're lying.'

'Nah? Really?'

'It's not right to tell lies.'

'It's not right to bug people when they don't want to be bugged!'

'All I want to know is –'

'*No!* It's *not* real fur. It's man-made fibre.' He turns his back on Zip. 'Goodbye. Have a good life. Get married. Have lots of children. Watch telly. Die. Don't invite me to your funeral.'

More questions, BigBrov.

'Are you from New Town?'

No response.

'Are you from –?'

'Yes!'

'What a coincidence! Me too!'

'Holy macaroni, what ya talking about, *coincidence*? It's

the only place for a zillion miles. Now I'm gonna say this one more time: Good – bye.'

Don't let him go! He needs a new friend as much as you. I know he does! Don't be fooled by the way he acts.

'Are you looking for something?'

Much better.

'Me? *Looking* for something? Course not. I just noticed the floor was a bit dirty so I decided to get on my hands and knees and lick it clean.'

He's joking again.

'You're joking again, ain't you?'

'It was *sarcasm* actually.'

'Why be sarcastic?'

'Cos you keep asking dingbat questions.'

'I'm just trying to make conversation, that's all.'

'Why?'

'Because . . . it's friendly.'

'*Friendly!* Listen, I know you mean well, in your misguided and totally irritating fashion, but you . . . you are a happy 'n' clappy sort of person. I'm surprised you ain't banging a tambourine and giving me a few choruses of "Kumbaya". But me – oh, me, on the other hand – I'm not your happy 'n' clappy type at all. If any-thing, I'm gloomy 'n' doomy. And it's one of the great laws of the universe that happy 'n' clappy and gloomy 'n' doomy do not mix. They're like sausages and custard. Both totally scrumptious on their own. But together . . . a pile of puke. So, in light of that, please watch my lips and read them very, very carefully . . . *Good – bye – you – dingbat.*'

Don't be put off! Follow him and —

'Listen!' says Zip firmly. 'I'm not going away until you tell me what you're doing on the floor! If I go away without knowing, it will bug me all day. And I've got a little brother to keep an eye on. And a mum who never gets out of bed. And a gran who's not very well. And an aunt who's at the end of her tether. And all of them need me to keep their spirits up. And if my mind's full of wondering about you, then I won't be able to do it. Their spirits will sink. And if their spirits sink – especially the spirits of my little brov – then my spirits will sink too and who knows what dark pit of endless despair we might all find ourselves in, and all because you won't blooming answer a blooming civil question!'

I'm proud of you, BigBrov!

The boy's dark eyes glint and a faint smile puckers his lips. 'You know something, Happy Clappy, I'm beginning to like the way you think. So here's the deal. I'm looking for my pet. His name is Rudi. Now they don't allow pets into this here supermarket, so I've got to find Rudi before someone –'

'AAAHHHHH!!'

'Too late!'

He's rushed off!

Someone's found his pet!

'Looks like someone found his pet, eh, Newt?'

'Ya-ya!'

'What a shame. I felt we were just beginning to experience some good energy between the two of us ... Now, what was I doing?'

Shampoo.

'The shampoo! That's it! ... Oh, I still don't know what to choose.'

Try herbal.

'I'll try herbal.'

'Top of the morning to you, Roz.'

'Oh! What a lovely surprise! Good morning, Customer Zip – Ooo, what's all that hullabaloo over there?'

'Some boy brought his pet inside.'

'Well, animals of any description ain't allowed. The management is very clear about that sort of thing – Ooo, there goes Guard Krick. Hear his boots?'

Klack!

Klack!

Klack!

'Who's Guard Krick?'

'Security.'

'I ain't seen him.'

'Well, you can bet ya life he's seen you. Guard Krick notices everything. The supermarket's security cameras ain't up and running yet, so Guard Krick thinks he's fully entitled to boss and bully. Thinks he owns the joint, he does. Even sleeps in the basement.'

'Sleeps in the basement!'

'I know! It's pathetic! – Ooo, Customer Newt certainly likes playing with trolleys, don't he?'

'Oh, gosh, yes . . . I suppose so.'

'That's not the *same* trolley as he was playing with yesterday by any chance, is it?'

She suspects something!

She suspects something.

'Oh . . . gosh . . . I shouldn't think so, Roz.'

'Be honest with me, Customer Zip! Is that . . . *Apollo*?'

Oh, no!

Oh, no!

'Did you keep Apollo at your home all night?'

Oh, no!

Oh, no!

'And do you intend to take Apollo back home again now?'

Oh, no!

Oh, no!

'Well, if you do,' continues Roz, 'then it's a good thing Guard Krick is on the other side of the supermarket, ain't it. Because he wouldn't take very kindly to you treating a supermarket trolley like your own personal property –!'

Get out quick, BigBrov.

I best get out quick!

'I'm in a bit of a rush, Roz, so . . . here's the money.'

'Apple-loo myy freend!'

Shut up, LittleBrov.

Viiissshhhhh!

— 10 —

Zip pushes Apollo across the car park as quickly as possible.

Eeeka-eeka-clicka-click –

'That was close, Newt! All my promises to Apollo

would've counted for nothing if that Guard Krick had got his claws into –'

Wait! Did you see that, BigBrov?

'Gosh! Did you see that, Newt?'

'Wha, Zi-Zi?'

A tiny animal just ran under that parked car.

'Something ran under that parked car. A little animal. About the size of a – gosh! There it is again! You see? It's pure white and got a long body. Short legs and – oh, look at those jet black eyes, Newt. It's a ferret! Gosh, what's a ferret doing in a supermarket car park?'

It's that boy's pet.

'It's that boy's pet, little brov! Of *course*.'

It must have run out of the supermarket as we rushed out!

'It must've run out of the supermarket as we rushed out. Oh, I hope it doesn't run to the motorway! Those cars will – oh, I don't even want to think of it. Perhaps I can catch it . . . Come here, nice ferret. I won't hurt you. Come here and – oh, it's running away. Towards the motorway! Oh, Newt! What can we do?'

Let me see if I can help —

'STOP, FERRET!'

STOP!!

The ferret stops and twitches its nose.

'Gosh, Newt! Did you see that? I called out "Stop, ferret!" and it stopped! – COME HERE, FERRET!'

Come here, ferret!

Twitch!

'Look, Newt! The ferret's doing everything I say!'

Jump up into me.

Twitch!

'Into the trolley, ferret!'

The ferret jumps into the trolley.

'Look, Newt! It's in the trolley. Gosh, I never knew I had such control over animals.'

Sorry, BigBrov, but it's me, not you.

Viiissshhhhh!

'Look! That boy's being thrown out of the supermarket by – oh, gosh! That must be Guard Krick! Look at him, Newt!'

Guard Krick is wearing black leather trousers, a black jacket, and the darkest dark glasses Zip has ever seen. His front teeth glint with gold fillings and his head is shaved completely bald.

'You're banished, mister!'

'I'm not going without my pet!'

'SHUT GOB, MISTER!' screeches Guard Krick, with a voice like nails being chucked in a tin bucket. 'You think everything is here for your benefit, don't you? You think life is a playground. You make me sick. If I keep talking to you I will be sick; I will puke all over my shiny leather boots and that would never do! Now ... I'm gonna go back inside and find that pet of yours. And when I do, I'm gonna put it in the microwave! Alive!'

'I'm a customer. I know my rights.'

'Kids ain't got no rights, mister!'

Go to him, BigBrov! Quick!

'I'm going to him, Newt. Wait here.'

Zip runs across the car park and tugs at the boy's sleeve.

'Not now, Happy Clappy. I'm doing battle with the imperious face of the capitalist establishment!' He glares at the security guard and shouts, 'If you hurt so much as a whisker of my Rudi I'll sue you and the whole Starbuy's empire for cruelty.'

'SHUT GOB, MISTER! I'm going to find your rat and kill it! NOW CLEAR OFF!!'

Viiissshhhhh!

'COME BACK OUT HERE, YOU CAPITALIST PIG! I'M GONNA ALERT THE MEDIA ABOUT THIS! I

CAN SEE THE HEADLINES NOW! "SUPER-MARKET KIDNAPS BOY'S HARMLESS PET!" AND IT'S NOT A RAT!'

'Of course not,' says Zip calmly. 'It's a ferret.'

The boy's mouth drops open and he stares at Zip.

'A black-eyed, white ferret, to be precise,' Zip continues. 'The most beautiful black-eyed white I've ever seen. Not that I've seen that many. They're not that common in the wild. Your Rudi is in our shopping trolley over there!'

'RUDI!' The boy darts to the trolley and scoops the ferret up in his hands. 'Oh, Rudi!' he coos. 'Little baby! Oh, ya tickle. Oh, baby, baby. Give Papa a kiss. I thought I'd lost ya, baby.'

Twitch! Twitch!

Zip strolls over and watches the boy for a moment, then says, 'People tend to think anything rat-sized is a rat. It's a terrible problem. You know the poor water vole has been hunted to near extinction because of it.' He gives the animal a kiss. 'You're safe here, little one.'

'You . . . you *kissed* Rudi!' gasps the boy.

'Gosh, sorry. I didn't mean to –'

'Holy macaroni! Don't apologize! Happy Clappy, I think I'm beginning to almost probably, perhaps possibly, maybe, like you. Oh, sure, you're a bit smiley and shiny for my tastes, but . . . well, you kissed Rudi so there must be some sense in ya somewhere. I'm Nabil. Nabil Brazil.'

'Zip,' says Zip. 'Zip Jingle.'

'Zip, I think this is the beginning of a beautiful friendship.'

So do I!

— 11 —

'Zombie cathedral!'

'Wh-What, Nabil?'

I like the way BigBrov is pushing me across the car park. His grip on my push bar is so firm. It feels so safe.

'The supermarket!' explodes Nabil. 'A cathedral for zombies. Ain't ya noticed what happens to people as soon as they step through those glass doors? Their faces go all blank. Eyes dead. Like this ...' He shuffles and mimes putting things into a shopping basket. 'Ohhhh, half-price marmalade. Ohhh, buy one, get one free. I am a shopping zombie.' He stomps his foot angrily. 'GET A LIFE, SHOPPING ZOMBIES! GET A LIFE!'

'You're funny, Nabil.'

'*Funny!* You think I'm doing this for your *amusement*, Happy Clappy? Well, let me shatter that comforting, but totally incorrect assumption. I am serious. *Deadly* serious. Big business wants to turn us all into shopping zombies. How else can they keep flogging us their new cars? New computers. New mobile phones –'

'Well, I think mobile phones are a glorious invention,' comments Zip. 'Without them my gran would lose one of her main means of communications. Gran's had a stroke, you see. But her left hand works perfectly so she can text me all she wants. Or text anyone for that matter. So long as they have a mobile phone.'

'Holy macaroni, you are so ... so ... *positive*.'

'What's wrong with being positive?'

'It's boring! And it makes you sound . . . affable.'

'What's "affable" mean?'

'Easy to get on with. I hate it!'

'Well, I want to be easy to get on with. The whole world should be easy to get on with. Then there would be less people in it that are . . . hard to get on with.'

'Holy macaroni, Happy Clappy, with a world view as complicated as that, you should apply for a job presenting kids' telly. And talking of telly – oh, don't get me started! Telly's another conspiracy to turn us all into zombies.'

I've never heard anyone who can just talk and talk like him. And he's so angry with it. Hope Newt ain't being disturbed by all the – No! He's too busy playing with Rudi. Aha! Here's the ramp up to the footbridge.

I will be able to see Home from the top of the footbridge.

'Ya-ya! See hooom, Apple-loo.'

LittleBrov said what I was thinking! Can LittleBrov hear my thoughts so clearly? Try again . . . I want to go, LittleBrov!

'Gooo hooom, Apple-loo!'

Listen to Newt chattering away to the troll– Hang on! The trolley! It . . . it seems to be pulling me. Pulling me up the slope of the footbridge. Pulling me across the top. Oh, this is stupid. It can't be. It's just not possible. But . . . let's see what happens if I take my hands off the push bar –

Eeeka-eek-clicka-click . . .

It's moving!

'Nabil! Look! The trolley!'

'Trolleys!' explodes Nabil, stomping his foot. 'That's another plot of the global empire of capitalism! They make the trolleys far too big so we feel compelled to fill them up and buy more food than we will ever eat, while millions starve –'

'No! Look! I ain't holding it!'

Ooops! My mistake! I'll stop!

'Stoop!'

'So?' wonders Nabil. 'You ain't holding it. It ain't moving. Is there some law of physics I'm missing?'

'But I wasn't pushing it a moment ago and ... and ...'

'Mmm?'

'You're gonna think I'm crazy.'

'I think that already.'

'Well ... the trolley kept moving.'

Nabil gives Zip a long hard look, then says flatly, 'You interrupted me in full flourishing rant to tell me this gibberish, you dingbat.'

'It's *not* gibberish!' insists Zip. 'And *I'm* not a dingbat. Whatever that is. I felt the trolley *pulling* me up the slope. When we got to the top I ... I took my hands away and –'

'It carried on moving?'

'Yeah!'

'Apple-loo wans get hooom!'

'You see!' cries Zip. 'Newt believes me!'

'Holy macaroni, Happy Clappy, Newt's an ankle-biter or ain't ya noticed? He still believes in the tooth fairy and beasties under the bed! But you ... you're – what? Twelve?'

'Twelve and a half.'

'Holy macaroni, you should be suitably bitter and twisted by now.'

'I am! I mean, I'm not bitter and twisted, but I know what you mean. It's just that ...'

'Mmm?'

'Well, lots of odd things have been happening lately. The trolley ...'

'Mmm?'

'Well ... last night Newt fell asleep in the trolley outside the house and when I went to pick him up he was warm as roasted chestnuts, as if –'

'Don't tell me. As if the trolley was keeping him warm.'

'Well ... yeah.'

Precisely.

'Listen, Happy Clappy, I guessed by the way you look you're one of these New Age traveller types and you've probably spent your whole life worshipping pebbles and eating raw dandelions, but ... oh, please, *please*, if you're about to tell me the supermarket trolley is alive, I'll stick my head in a washing machine and set it to fast spin.' He takes a deep breath, grabs hold of Zip's shoulders and stares him in the eyes. 'Zip! *Zip! Amigo!* Don't let me down. Please! I thought we were gonna be friends.'

'We are!'

'Then dig down deep inside you! Dig down deep and find that cynical and twisted soul I know lurks in you somewhere. I beg of you. For the sake of our potentially fruitful friendship ... STOP BEING A DINGBAT!!'

Zip starts to wither under Nabil's fervent words and glare. 'You're right ... It was silly of me. What was I thinking of? Come on, let's get home. Of course I don't think the trolley is alive.'

But you will, BigBrov.

— 12 —

'Fake grass!' explodes Nabil as they turn off the motorway and on to the main road of New Town. 'You notice that, Zip?'

'Yeah. It's plastic. As I said to Newt the day we arrived, at least the lawns won't need cutting, eh?'

'Holy macaroni, you're the kind of person who could suck joy from a stick of chalk, ain't ya.'

'All right, all right. Fake grass is crackers.'

'I prefer the word doolally myself.'

'All right, all right, it's doolally.'

'Not as doolally as fake trees! Look at them. All planted the same distance apart. All the same height. Same number of plastic branches. Same number of plastic twigs on each plastic branch. *Plastic* trees for a *plastic* town they want to fill with *plastic* people.'

'I ain't plastic!'

'Well, nor am I. But you know what that means, don't ya? Everyone else who comes here – all the plastic people who're *happy* being plastic, who *want* to be plastic, who *yearn* to be plastic – they'll take one look at us and yell, "Outcasts!".'

'They won't!'

'They will! We'll be as welcome as farts in a spacesuit – Hang on! What's that coming towards us?'

'Looks like a vehicle of some kind.'

'Well, I gathered *that* much, Happy Clappy, but what's it doing here? Hang on! It's a removal van. That means –'

'New neighbours!'

'New plastic!'

The removal van comes to a halt beside them. A man in a white overall (one of the removal men) is in the driver's seat and beside him (the side nearest the kerb) is –

A girl! About my age. Gosh! She's got dazzling eyes. Hang on! There's big muscles in those arms. It's a boy. Yeah, look, he's wearing a button-up shirt with the sleeves rolled up. Nah, wait! The face is so pretty. A girl. Wait! Look at that hair. Jet black and styled in a . . . a . . . oh, what's it called?

'Quiffs are pure dingbat,' mutters Nabil.

Quiff! That's it! Must be a boy. And yet . . . look at those eye-lashes. So long and thick. Girl! But . . . look! Armpit scratching. Boy!

The kid winds down the window and says, 'Wotcha, mates!'

Boy! Definitely!

'Top of the morning to you,' says Zip, stepping forward. 'Welcome to New Town.'

'You're being affable again,' mutters Nabil.

'I'm looking for number twenty-seven, Yet To Be Named Avenue, mates. Any chance of a friendly point in the right direction, mates?'

'Holy macaroni, it's a conspiracy of affability!'

'None of the street signs have been put up yet,' explains Zip, stepping in front of Nabil to mask his muttering. 'So there might be a few twenty-seven, Yet To Be Named Avenues. You'll just have to check each one until you find the house –'

'That can be opened with this,' says the kid, holding up a street door key and grinning. 'You know, I'm really gonna enjoy this. It's like a kinda game, ain't it, mates?'

'Gosh, yes, it is!'

'Spare me, spare me!'

'Looks like we're all gonna be neighbours, mates.'

'Gosh, yes, it does.'

Nabil murmurs, 'We buzz in the same sterile hive, if that's what you mean.'

'You know something,' says the kid, leaning out of the window and pointing at Nabil, '*you* are *not* a matey mate. But *you*' – pointing at Zip – 'are a *very* matey mate. Me name's Memphis, mates. Memphis Lemonique.'

'I'm Zip. Zip Jingle. This is my brother, Newt.'

'Newt the cute, eh?'

'Oh, spare me, spare me.'

'You gonna make nasty noises or tell me your name?'

'Let me think ... Yeah! Make nasty noises.'

'His name's Nabil Brazil.'

'Well, Zip, Newt, Nabil, when me and Missy have settled into our new house you must all pay us a neighbourly visit, mates.'

'Who's Missy?' asks Zip.

'Missy's me mum, mate. She's in the back of the van reading one of her educational books.' The kid reaches out and thumps the back of the van. 'MISSY! WE HAVE A MATEY NEW MATE HERE AND A NOT-SO-MATEY NEW MATE HERE. WANNA SAY "PLEASED TO KNOW YA"?'

A voice yells, 'PLEASED TO KNOW YOU, LAMBS!' from inside the van.

Zip calls back, 'PLEASED TO KNOW YOU TOO, MRS LEMONIQUE!'

'OH, CALL ME MISSY, LAMB. EVERYONE DOES!'

'THANK YOU, MISSY!'

'Oh, spare me, spare me.'

'Well, mates, it's been a joy getting to know you, mates, but now me and Missy best be off to find –'

'Before you go,' says Nabil, stepping forward, 'can I ask you a question?'

'Sure, mate.'

'Are you a boy or a girl?'

'Nabil!' gasps Zip. 'Don't be rude.'

'I ain't being rude!'

Memphis smiles. 'He's right, Zip, mate. He ain't being rude at all, mate. I bet you were thinking the same thing, mate. I'm not offended in the least. OK. See you mates soon, mates.'

'Hang on!' yells Nabil. 'You ain't answered the question. Boy or girl?'

'That's right,' calls Memphis as the van drives away. 'I am a boy or a girl.'

— 13 —

I am in the gap between Home and the garage. This is where I stay when BigBrov and LittleBrov do other things. I can feel them inside Home. When I touch my metal against the wall I can hear them. I do not understand everything they say. But I will understand. Every moment I am understanding more and more.

'. . . brother still asleep?'

'Yeah, Aunt Ivy.'

After BigBrov and LittleBrov got back from the supermarket LittleBrov played with me for a while. Then BigBrov took LittleBrov into Home for a . . . oh, what was the word . . .? Nap! That's it!

'Put the saucepans in that cupboard, babycake.'

'Sure thing, Aunt Ivy.'

Boxes are being opened and things taken from them and put in cupboards and on shelves —

Oh, I can feel something coming from my BigBrov!

Want to . . . get out . . . get out of the house . . .

Do it, BigBrov! Get out! Now! Visit Nabil!

'Aunt Ivy? Do you mind if I visit Nabil? He gave me his address and . . . well, he said I could visit any time. Of course, if you want me to stay here and help you –'

'No, no, babycake, you go. Have a laugh with your new friend. You deserve all the fun you can get after all you've been through.'

All BigBrov's been through? What does Aunt Ivy mean? Not living in the forest any more? Is that what 'all you've been through' means?

'Thanks, Aunt Ivy. See you later. Bye.'

'Bye, babycake.'

No! 'All you've been through' means more than that.
Something much worse has happened to my BigBrov!
BigBrov is leaving the house.

SLAM!

Gosh, I don't know the way!
Phone Nabil for directions.

I'll phone Nabil for directions. Where's my mobile? Here! Oh, I'm looking forward to seeing Nabil and – oh, what about Newt? What if he wakes up and I'm not there? He might think I've gone for good. He might panic. He might cry. I can't bear it when Newt cries –

Don't worry about LittleBrov. I am here.

Oh, I'm sure little brov will be all right. He can play with the trolley.

I've got a name, you know! Now … dial Nabil's number.

I'm dialling Nabil's number …

He's going to answer … Now!

'Who's this?'

'Nabil, it's me.'

'Who's "me"?'

'Zip.'

'Holy macaroni, Happy Clappy, we only said goodbye a few hours ago. Miss me already, eh?'

'Well, it's just that … well, I thought I'd visit and –'

'Where are ya now?'

'I'm walking down the main road.'

'You see the first big crossroads yet?'

'Just at it now.'

'Keep walking straight. Go two houses up and you should see a big hole in the road. It's where The Powers That Be are gonna put some gas pipes or cable telly or some such global conspiracy. See it yet?'

'Errr … Yeah!'

'Turn left.'

'Okey-dokey.'

'Now keep walking. Stick to the right. You'll see another hole in the road any second.'

'Aha! Another hole, Nab!'

'Good. Turn left.'

'Okey-dokey.'

'I should see you from my bedroom window any minute now. Tell me when you come to the cement mixer and a pile of those plastic trees –'

'It's getting dark, Nab.'

'The street lights'll come on in a second.'

'I'm just coming up to what looks like … Yep! Plastic trees. Gosh, they've got a block of cement where roots should be.'

'That's evolution for ya – What else d'ya see?'

'A row of houses. All empty.'

'Look at the end of the row.'

'A house with lights on! And … someone's at one of the windows.'

'I bet that someone's waving, right?'

'How d'ya know?'

'Cos it's me, you dingbat! Now, hurry up before ya fingers get frostbite. I'll rush down and …' Crackle, crackle.

'What d'ya say, Nab? I'm losing you.'

Crackle, hiss, crackle.

The front door to Nabil's house swings open.

'Welcome, my shivering amigo!'

— 14 —

Nab's house looks just like mine. Same hallway. Same colour paint. Same floorboards. And he's got boxes of unpacked stuff too –

Bang! Bang!

'What's that, Nab?'

'It's me dad.'

'What's he doing?'

'Putting some shelves up in the living room.'

More hammering is heard from behind the closed door, plus the sound of a man muttering, 'Got to be perfect ... got to be perfect ...'

Zip asks, 'Who's he talking to?'

'Himself,' replies Nab, heading for the stairs. 'Come on, let's go up to me room. Rudi's in a playful mood and –'

'But ...' Zip hesitates in the hallway '... shouldn't I say hello?'

'Who to?'

'Your dad.'

'Why?'

'Well ... ain't it polite?'

'*Polite?* Listen, Happy Clappy, we don't stand on ceremony here.'

'But ... I feel a bit rude just walking past your dad without introducing myself.'

'Holy macaroni! Suit yourself.' Nab pushes gruffly past

Nab and opens the living-room door to the front room. 'Dad, this is me new friend, Zip.'

Nabil's dad has got wispy hair. Like a spiders' web. And he's wearing grey trousers and a dark green cardigan and brown slippers and ... oh, he needs a bit of a shave and his eyes are rimmed with red, like they've been near stinging nettles. And there's plasters all over his hands. And he seems to be covered with a layer of pollen ... no, it's not pollen. It's sawdust!

'Top of the afternoon to you, Mr Brazil.'

'Can you see the sandpaper? Hmm? I don't want anyone to get a splinter from this shelf –' His eyes come to rest on Zip for the first time. 'You're not my son.'

'No, I'm here,' says Nabil, waving his arms. 'Hello? Remember me?'

'Then who's this?'

'I told you. He's my friend, Zip. He wants to introduce himself for some totally obscure reason.'

'Oh, I see, I see. Hmm. Hello, Zip. What do you think of the shelf I've just put up? Hmm?' He indicates a wall with several shelves fixed to it but, judging by the pile of wood on the floor, many, many more have yet to be affixed.

'They look quite glorious, Mr Brazil.'

'Glorious! Really?' Mr Brazil looks at Nabil. 'You hear that, son? Hmm? Your friend thinks the shelf looks jolly glorious.' He beckons Zip to have a closer look. 'Take a peek at the grain on this wood here, Zip. You see? Hmm? Isn't it jolly beautiful? And you notice how it fits against the wall. Hmm? Jolly flush, eh?'

'Very impressive, Mr Brazil.'

'You've no idea how I've worked and worked. No, no. Mmm. If a shelf ain't absolutely perfect, then I jolly well take it down and – hmm, yes, hmm – start from scratch. I've had this up and down more times than you've had hot dinners. Oh yes. And I'm still not satisfied. Oh, no. Hmm. I might have to jolly well buy a new piece of wood altogether. Oh yes. Hmm. What's your opinion, Zip?'

'Well, I'm not an expert, but it looks just fine to me.'

'But "just fine" ain't good enough! No, no, no. They have to be *perfect*. Only *perfect* shelves will please her.'

'Come on, Zip.' Nab grabs Zip's arm and pulls him towards the door. 'Best let Dad get on with this work – Aha! The sandpaper's here, Dad. Under the box of plasters. See?'

'Oh, joy! Joy. Now I can make the wood smooth as silk – Ouch!' Mr Brazil gets a splinter from the shelf.

'A pleasure meeting you, Mr Brazil.'

'Can you see the plasters?'

— 15 —

'What did your dad mean?' asks Zip as he follows Nabil up the stairs. 'About only perfect shelves pleasing her? Who's "*her*"?'

'Me mum.'

'She's ... not here?'

'Nah.'

'She ... out visiting someone?'

'Nah.'

'Has she ... left you?'

'You could say that, yeah.'

'And your dad thinks if he puts perfect shelves up it will persuade her to come back? '

'Doolally, I know. I keep telling him it's doolally. Mum

ain't coming back whether Dad puts perfect shelves up or not.'

'Don't be so gloomy all the time. Nothing's impossible.'

'Believe me, Mum coming back *is* impossible.'

'She can't dislike your dad that much.'

'She didn't dislike Dad at all. She loved him. She loved me. But when you're a popped clog you don't come back no matter how many perfect shelves are made for you.'

'What's a ... "popped clog"?'

'Holy macaroni, Zip, ain't ya ever heard the expression, "Someone's popped their clogs"?'

'I ... I don't think so, no.'

'Where you been living? A cave?'

'No. A forest. And I don't want to talk about it.'

'Suits me. I ain't gonna ask about it. Except to say surely – *surely* – something must've popped its clogs in the forest! Eh? A deer? A fox? A duck-billed platypus?'

'There ain't any duck-billed ... whatever in the forest. And if you blooming told me what "popped your clogs" means I might be able to answer the blooming question!'

'It means *dead*!'

'... Dead?'

'Yeah.'

'Your mum's ... *dead*?'

'A popped clog, if you please. Come on, here's me room.'

'Wait! When ... when did she die – I mean, pop her clogs?'

'... Recently.'

'How recently?'

'Seven weeks. You coming in me room or what?'

'What she die of, Nab?'

'What popped her –?'

'All right, all right, what popped her clog?'

'An argument.'

'What? You can't pop your clogs because of an argument!'

'Look, I ain't standing here holding me bedroom door open for you all day.'

'Then blooming tell me about your mum!'

Nabil takes a deep breath and says, 'It was like this: the one thing Mum and Dad always argued about was Dad saying he was gonna do things around the house and then not doing it. You know the kind of thing. Mum would say, "Oh, the toilet has got a leak." And Dad would say, "Hmm? Yes. I'll jolly well fix it." Only he wouldn't. Mum would ask him and ask him and still Dad would do nothing. So for months, every time we went to the toilet, we'd get soggy socks. You with me, amigo?'

'Yeah, Nab. Go on.'

'The longest-running thing Dad never got round to doing was the shelves. Mum wanted shelves to put family photos on. Dad, as usual, said, "Hmm? I'll jolly well put the shelves up." Dad, as usual, did nothing. One Saturday night they had a big row about it. Holy macaroni, right screaming match it was. I was up in me room, playing with Rudi. Later that night Mum said she had a bellyache. She said, "It was that argument with ya dad brought this on. Arguments always give me a bellyache."'

'Me too!'

'Small world, eh? Anyway, Mum's bellyache kept getting worse and worse. She started to throw up and stuff. She went to see the doctor and the doctor sent her to the hospital and the hospital said Mum had a sort of blockage or something in her abdomen. Now, I ain't no medical man, so I don't know any of the technical jargon, but the way I understood it, whatever was doing the blocking had to be unblocked. You with me, amigo?'

'Yeah, Nab. Go on.'

'A routine operation, they said. Know what that means?'

'Nothing to worry about.'

'Exactamundo! No danger. Like having ya tooth filled or something. So Mum went into the operating theatre saying, "See ya soon, Nabby." I waited with Dad in the television room. A game show was on. Someone had just won a million quid. The contestant was jumping up and down and screaming and lights were flashing and the audience was clapping. Next thing I know a doctor was coming over to us. He asked to have a word with me dad. They went outside to the corridor. I watched them talking through the glass. Couldn't hear what they were saying. All I could hear was the cheering on the telly. Then I saw Dad fall down. He'd fainted. I rushed out to him. Turns out Mum had had a heart attack while they were doing this so-called routine operation. And so, to cut a long story short, Mum and Dad had an argument. Result: popped clogs.'

'I'm sorry, Nab.'

'Yeah, well, bad luck happens.'

'But ain't you ever asked *why*?'

'Course I have. Lots of times. And you know what answer always comes back?'

'What?'

'"Why *not*?" Now ... you coming in me room or staying out in the hallway?'

'I'm coming in your room, Nab.'

'After you, amigo.'

— 16 —

Dirty clothes all over the place. Empty Coke bottles. A half-eaten hamburger. His bed is an explosion of sheets and blankets. Books everywhere and – cardboard tubes! Look at them! All Sellotaped together to make long and twisting pipes. Wonder what they're for –?

'Where's my Rudi, baby? Come to Papa, Rudi. Come on!'

The ferret pops his head out of one of the pipes.

'There you are, my little baby! Did you miss ya papa, eh?'

The ferret runs into Nabil's hands.

They're for Rudi! Of course! Ferrets love to explore and rummage in all sorts of things and –

'Oh, nah!' laughs Nabil, flopping on to his bed. 'Rudi is going up me sleeve! Ha, ha, ha! Look, Zip. Ya see? Ha, ha, ha!'

Zip flops beside Nabil. 'Gosh! Bet it tickles, eh?'

'Yeah! It – ha, ha, ha – tickles all right. Oh, nah! He's nibbling me armpit. I can't – ha, ha, ha – bear it!'

'Shall I pull him out?'

'Yeah! See if you can grab – Nah, wait!'

'What?'

'Rudi's moving!'

'Where?'

'Down me back . . . oh, nah!'

'I see him!'

'Ha, ha, ha, ha, ha, ha – oh, I love playing with Rudi! I forget – ha, ha, ha – everything when I'm – ha, ha, ha – playing with him . . . oh, nah! Nah!'

'He's moving to your belly, Nab!'

'My most ticklish place! Ha, ha, ha . . . oh, get him out, Zip.'

'Lift your shirt!'

'He's tickling me to death, ha, ha, ha!'

'I'll just grab him gently like this and – oh, no!'

'What's happened?'

'Rudi's run up *my* sleeve now – oh, no!'

'Ha! Now it's your turn!'

'Ha, ha, ha – oh, it tickles!'

'Make him suffer, Rudi!'

'He's at my armpit – ha, ha, ha!'

'Ha, ha, ha!'

'Stop laughing, Nab, and – ha, ha, ha – help me!'

'Where is he?'

'On my belly!'

'Ha, ha – it looks like you're gonna explode!'

'Just get him out!'

'OK, OK – ha, ha, ha – Holy macaroni, amigo, how many shirts ya wearing?' He lifts the shirts one by one, then reveals Rudi sniffing Zip's belly button. 'There's me baby! Come here, you rascal!' He picks the ferret up and kisses its nose. Then, looking at Zip, adds, 'Wait, Zip! What's that on ya chest?'

'Oh . . . it's nothing.'

'Let me see.'

'It's only a . . . scar.'

'A scar! I *love* scars!'

'Why does that not surprise me.'

'Holy macaroni, it's big.'

'Compared to what?'

'Other scars I've seen.'

'Oh! A scar specialist now, are we?'

'I've read books on the subject.'

'They write books about *scars*?'

'Holy macaroni . . . it feels odd.'

'How d'you mean?'

'It's like a . . . a worm of cool Plasticine on your chest.'

'Well, thanks for the compliment.'

'Nah, don't pull ya shirt down. I ain't finished feeling it yet!'

'Finished *insulting* it, you mean.'

'It's just a scar.'

'It's still part of me.'

'You're too touchy, that's your problem.'

'Well, you're too . . . too . . .'

'Mmm?'

'*Not* touchy!'

'*Not* touchy. Holy macaroni, Happy Clappy, you need a crash course in how to insult someone.'

'I don't *want* to insult someone. I don't want to insult *any*one. I want to be nice to people.'

'An admirable, if misguided, ambition.'

'I bet if you saw a scar on Rudi it'd be all, "Ooo, poor little baby. How'd that happen? Did it hurt?" But with me it's just, "Ugh, it feels like a worm."'

'I didn't go, "Ugh".'

'It's what you meant!'

'It's not!'

'It is!'

'Not!'

'Is!'

'Holy macaroni, is this our first argument?'

'Oh, shut up!'

'All I'm saying is –'

'You don't know how to be friends with someone. I don't know why. You just don't. But me . . . I do know how. I was friends with lots of people in the forest. We'd help each other. We'd all sit around the campfire and sing songs and tell stories –'

'I'm gonna puke in a minute.'

'It was glorious!'

'It was doolally!'

'You don't know what you're talking about . . . Gloomy Doomy!'

BigBrov is upset. All the way on the other side of town I can feel it.

Something is bothering him . . .

And Nabil too . . .

And — yes! Look! I can see them!

They are sitting next to each other on the bed. They are not talking . . . Oh, one of you must start to talk again.

Please . . . one of you break the silence.

Please . . . one of you talk.

— 17 —

'Perhaps . . .' says Nabil softly, 'I don't know how to treat a friend because . . . well, I've never really had one before.'

'You . . . haven't?'

'When Mum married Dad . . . there was a lot of trouble between her family and Dad's. Mum's family weren't from this country. They didn't want her to marry someone like Dad. You know? Different religion. Different skin. Different taste in wallpaper. And Dad's family felt exactly the same about Mum. But Mum and Dad loved each other. So they ran away.'

'Oh, that's really romantic!'

'Don't get all soppy about it, amigo, else I won't carry on.'

'Sorry, Nab.'

'So ... well, I grew up not knowing anyone from Dad's family – cos they wouldn't speak to us because of Mum – and no one from Mum's family would speak to us –'

'Because of your dad.'

'Exactamundo.'

'But what's this got to do with you –'

'Having no friends?'

'Yeah.'

'Cos I grew up in an area where my colour face ain't supposed to chat with your colour face. Know what I'm saying? And me ... well, I was right in the middle, weren't I? Not dark enough to be dark. Not white enough to be white. Know what that means? Not the right colour no matter where I was!'

'I'm sorry, Nab.'

'Stop saying "Sorry, Nab," all the time. I'm not after sympathy! I'm *glad* no one wanted to be my friend. Most of them had as much sense as knickers on a pineapple. Besides ... Mum had bought me Rudi here. And Rudi was all the company I needed.'

'I hope ... I hope you don't think *I'm* knickers on a pineapple.'

'No. I don't think that. At least ... not *all* the time.'

Zip gives Nabil a playful shove.

That's it, BigBrov.

'Now, Zip, my friend, my good friend, my best friend –'

'Your *only* friend!'

'My one and only, totally not doolally friend ... tell me about the scar.'

Tell him, BigBrov.

'Okey-dokey, I'll tell you. But ... well, I feel a bit awkward doing it. You see, it's to do with my heart. And after what happened to your mum ... well, I feel a bit awkward talking about it now.'

'Nah, nah, don't worry. Tell me, amigo.'

Tell him!

'Well ...' says Zip softly, 'the moment I was born the doctors knew there was ... well, something not quite right with me.'

'How d'ya mean?'

'I was breathing all funny. My heart wasn't beating right. So they put me in this incubator thing. The doctors carried out these tests. They said to Mum, "We have to operate as soon as possible. He has a hole in his heart." You ... you sure you want to hear this, Nab?'

'Yeah, yeah, Zip, go on.'

'They operated on me. Put me back in the incubator. It was touch-and-go. Mum said she cried for seven days non-stop. It's how I got my name.'

'What is, Zip?'

'The *scar*. From the operation. Dad said it looked like a zip in my chest. Dad always said he didn't like the heart I was born with cos it didn't have enough love in. So Dad unzipped my chest, put in a new heart brimful with love, then zipped me up again.'

'Your *dad* said that?'

'Yeah.'

'And your *dad* was there from the beginning? When you were born? Comforting your mum when she cried for seven days?'

'Yeah. Why so surprised?'

'I'm sounding so surprised, my baffled amigo, because this is the first time I've heard you mention your dad.'

'So?'

'So ... *why*?'

'Oh, look! Rudi's trying to climb up my jeans –'

'Don't change the subject!'

'I'm not!'

BigBrov is getting upset again!

'Was he in the forest with you?'

'Who?'

'Your *dad*!'

'Yes, he was – Oh, look at Rudi!'

'But this *dad* ain't with ya now?'

'What? In this bedroom?'

'In *New Town*. And don't be a dingbat.'

'Why you so bothered?'

BigBrov wants to run away.

'Cos it takes one to know one, my in-denial amigo.'

'What does "in denial" mean?'

'It means you're not admitting something to yourself.'

'Like what?'

'You're the child of a popped clog!'

Zip jumps to his feet. 'I've had enough!'

BigBrov wants to run and keep running.

'Why can't you talk about it, Zip?'

'I *can* talk about it!'

'Then talk! I'm all ears!'

'Why should I? Just because *you* say, "Talk!" I'm supposed to jump to attention, eh? Well. No! I won't! I'm not your pet, you know! I ain't your blooming ferret!'

'You wanted to be treated like my ferret a second ago!'

'Stop trying to be so blooming clever all the time! Listen! It's up to me what I talk about! I'm grown up now!' Zip clutches his stomach. 'See what you've done! I'm all tensed up and – I'M GOING HOME!'

Zip storms out of the bedroom and rushes down the stairs.

'Zip!' Nabil rushes after him. 'I'm sorry. OK? Let's phone for a pizza to be delivered. They do a brilliant sausage-and-baked-bean special at that place down the motorway.'

'I don't eat sausage! Or bacon! I'm a vegetarian. And even if I wasn't, a sausage-and-baked-bean pizza sounds like the most disgusting thing I've ever heard!'

'Lots of things that sound disgusting are brilliant once you try 'em.'

'You're trying to be clever again.'

'I don't have to *try*! It just comes *natural*!'

'Oh ... SHUT UP!'

Mr Brazil comes out of the living room, pulling yet another splinter from one of his fingers. 'What's all the noise, boys? Hmm?'

'Ask your son!' cries Zip. 'He thinks he's an undercover cop for Get People To Talk About Their Family Branch!'

'*Now* who's trying to be clever, Happy Clappy?!'

'I'm sorry for the noise, Mr Brazil.'

'Well ... hmm ... that's fine ...'

'Goodbye, Gloomy Doomy. Have a good life. Hope I never see you again!'

'That's my line!'

'Ahhhhh!' screams Zip in frustration and, still clutching his stomach, opens the front door and –

SLAM!

– marches away from the house.

— 54 —

Gosh! I'm glad I'm out of there! Who does Nabil think he is?

Nothing but questions, questions, questions!

BigBrov is walking very fast.

BigBrov is not looking where he is going.

I'm sorry I spoke to him in the first place. I was better off without him.

I'm going to take his number off my mobile and never walk near this part of New Town ever again.

What's that stuff that is falling from the sky?

It is the size of cornflakes.

But white and fluffy . . .

It's started to snow!

Snow?

I've never seen snow fall in a town before.

BigBrov has stopped walking.

BigBrov is calming down.

BigBrov looks at the snow.

It looks like orange feathers in the glow of the street lights.

And there's so much of it.

So much snow . . .

So much snow . . .

So much snow . . .

So much snow . . .

So much snow . . .

snow, snow, snow . . .

Come back Home, BigBrov!
Come back!
Come back!

I best get home as soon as possible . . .

Hang on!

Where

am

I?

I should've looked where I was going!

I should have thought about where I was going!

I shouldn't've got so angry!

I best phone Aunt Ivy so she can –

Oh, no!

The battery's dead!

I think I'll . . . turn left here.

No.

Wrong!

I think I'll . . . turn right here.

Wrong again!

The snow is getting in my eyes.
The snow is getting up my nose.
The snow goes in my mouth.
And the snow . . .
it's settling now.

No chance of seeing the yellow crosses.

I am so cold.

And my feet are –
Squinch!
Squinch!
– in the snow.

My lips are freezing.
My hands are burning with cold.
Breathing is like swallowing ice cubes.
Oh, I'm lost!
Help!
'HELP!!'

No one is here.
All houses dark.
Empty homes.

'HELP!'

I might freeze to death out here.
If Aunt Ivy is busy with Gran and Newt is still asleep . . .
why, they won't even think of me.
And Mum is probably asleep . . .

'HELP!'

Eeeka-
Eek-
click-a
click.

What's that?

Eeeka-
Eek . . .

It's the trolley!
Who's pushing it all the way out here?
Can't see because of the . . .

Eeeka-
Eek . . .

Wait!
No!
It can't be.
It can't!

NO ONE IS PUSHING THE TROLLEY!!

What's going on?
How can this . . .?
How can this . . .?
Eeeka . . .

'Ap . . . Apo . . . Apollo?'

Eeeka-eek!

'You've . . . come to find me?'

Eeeka-eek!

The trolley has come right up to me.
Oh . . . it feels so warm.
I grab hold of the push bar.

Oh, my hands!
They're defrosting!

Eeeka!

Now it's pulling me –

Bzzz.

The mobile's working again!

It must be Gran!
Yes. There's a text message.

I am taking you home.

No! It can't be!

'Apollo . . . is this you?'

The trolley is moving . . . but not saying
anything on the mobile –

Wait!

Perhaps I have to touch the mobile to the trolley.
That's what happened just now!
The mobile was in my hand when –

Touch!

Yes.
It is me!

Oh, gosh, oh, gosh, oh, gosh!

'But ... how, Apollo?'
Touch!

I do not know, BigBrov.

BigBrov?

All I know is it's happening.
And I want to take you Home.

'Well ... I want to go home.'

Hold on to me.

'Okey-dokey ... whatever you say.'

Eeeka-eek-clicka-click.

Squinch!
Squinch!
Squinch!
Eeeka-
eeka-
clicka-
click ...

I feel . . . I feel so safe.
Holding on to the trolley . . . it feels so natural.
The sound of its wheels is as comforting as a lullaby.

'Apollo . . . this is so odd and yet . . .'

It feels right, BigBrov?

'Gosh, yes! Gloriously right!'

I know, BigBrov.

'Apollo . . . how did you know where to find me?'

I could see you.

'What do you mean?'

I can see . . . other places.

'Sort of . . . mind travel?'

I suppose so.

'Can you see my little brov?'

Yes.

'He's not worried about me, is he?'

No. He's asleep.

'What about Gran?'

Aunt Ivy's just putting her to bed.

'And Mum?'

Asleep.

'They don't know it's snowing yet then, do they?'

No.

'Apollo . . . have you seen snow before?'

No, BigBrov.

'It's beautiful, ain't it?'

Yes, BigBrov.

'How did . . . how did you know I was lost?'

I just . . . felt it, BigBrov.

'How can that happen?'

I do not know, BigBrov.

'Is it like a . . . sort of animal instinct?'

I suppose it must be, BigBrov.

'Gosh!'

Gosh, indeed, BigBrov.

Squinch.
Squinch.
Eeeka!
Eek!

'Apollo ...?'

Yes, BigBrov?

'You know ... I had a feeling that you were ...
you were ...'

Alive, BigBrov?

'Yes. But I couldn't ... oh, I just couldn't understand
how that could be.'

It be, BigBrov.

'Oh, yeah. It be all right. It be in a big way – Oh,
gosh! Look! It's our house coming up. We're home,
Apollo. We're home! And look! There's Aunt Ivy
opening the door!'

Don't tell her about me, BigBrov.

'Aunt Ivy wouldn't believe it anyway.'

No grown-ups must know about me.

'Okey-dokey, Apollo.'

None. None.

'Yes, yes, I understand – Apollo!
You've stopped moving by yourself!'

**It appears ... I cannot move in the presence of
a grown-up.**

'What? Not at all?'

No. It's like I'm ... frozen.

'Frozen! Gosh!'

'COOO-EEE, BABYCAKE!'

'TOP OF THE NIGHT, AUNT IVY!'

Squinch!

Squinch!

Squinch!

'Oh, babycake! Snow! Snow!'

'It's beginning to settle, I think, Aunt –'

'Babycake! What on earth are you doing with that
trolley?'

Don't say anything, BigBrov!

'Oh ... it was on the street, Aunt Ivy. The ... wind
must've blown it. I'm just ... wheeling it back.'

'Just shove it in the alleyway.'

'No, Aunt Ivy, I'll put it in the garage. The trolley will
be more comfortable – I mean, *safer* – there. After all, it's
not our property. We don't want anything to happen to it
in weather like this, do we?'

'Whatever you say, babycake. You'll have to use the

back door to get in, though. There's supposed to be a remote to open the garage from outside but Lord knows where it is. Once you're inside the garage there's a button that'll open the door. As for me ...' She yawns. 'Oh, I'm going to have an early night.' Aunt Ivy heads for her house next door. 'Everyone's all tucked up in bed. An early night. Gran's taken her medication so she'll sleep right through. Goodnight, babycake.'

— 19 —

I am waiting for BigBrov outside the garage. BigBrov is in the garage trying to find the button that will open the door.

'Gosh, where can it be? I've only got this torch to search with, Apollo. I can't find the light switch either – Aha! What's this?'

Vvvmmmmm ...

'Yesss!'

I am watching the garage door open. It looks very dark inside the garage. I can see my BigBrov's boots ... his hand holding the torch ... his face —

'Welcome to the garage, Apollo.'

Eeeka-eek-clicka-click ...

'Bet you're wondering what all this furniture is doing here. It's Gran's. From her old house. She bought lots of new stuff when she knew she was moving, but ... well, she couldn't seem to chuck the old stuff out. All the boxes

you can see – well, that's our stuff from the forest. Brrrr!
Wish I could find one of the oil heaters we used in the
forest. I'm chilled to the bone –'

Eeeka!

'What, Apollo?'

Touch!

I will heat it.

'You! What? The whole garage?'

If you like.

'Well, yes, of course I'd like ... but I don't think you're
going to be able to get rid of this cold. Coming to rescue
me from the snow is one thing, but – Gosh! Hang on! It ...
it *is* warming up. I'm feeling quite toasty. But – look,
Apollo. The door's still wide open. How can it be *warm* in
here when it's *freezing* out there?'

I do not know.

'I'm going to take my jacket off and relax a little ...
That's better. Now, let's see if I can find a lamp so we can
have some light. I'm sure I saw a – Yes! This is Gran's old
upright lamp – Oh, where's the plug socket?'

Eeeka!

Touch!

I will light it.

'Oh, honestly, Apollo, the heating's one thing, but
I'm sure there's no way you can – Hang on! Look! The
lamp's flickering. And now – it's alight! So bright too!
Okey-dokey, I'll move this armchair over like this – There!
I'm going to sit down and take my boots off and ...
oh yesss!! I'm really comfy now. Ooops! I forgot to shut
the –'

Vvvmmmmm ...

'Thanks, Apollo.'

Tell me, BigBrov, have you met others like me?

'How d'you mean?'

Trolleys? Alive?

'Oh! Well ... no. But, to be honest, I haven't met that many supermarket trolleys at all. What about you, though? In the supermarket? Were any of the other trolleys ... like you?'

My memories of the supermarket are very vague, BigBrov. More and more memories come back to me as time passes, but ... I have no memory of others like me.

'Perhaps you're unique?'

Unique?

'The only one?'

Oh, that's terrible to think of, BigBrov.

'Is it?'

Of course. A world full of supermarkets. And every super-market full of trolleys. And none of them ... like me. Why me, BigBrov? Why am I alive, BigBrov? Why am I here?

I wish I knew what to say. If I was in the forest ... oh yes, if I was there someone would know what to do. Whenever I got into a state or was confused, we'd all sit around the campfire and someone would tell a story to help make sense of things and –

Are you still a bit cold, BigBrov?

'What? Oh. No, Apollo. I'm just fine.'

Then why are you thinking about fire?

'Oh! I was just remembering – Hang on! How did you know I was thinking about fire? Can you read my mind?'

Yes. In the beginning I just felt what you were feeling. But that has grown stronger and stronger. And now ... yes, I hear your thoughts.

'Telepathy! That's what it's called! One mind reading another. Or talking to another. Someone in the forest said she could talk telepathically to the animals.'

I can do that.

'You can?'

Yes, BigBrov. I made the ferret stop and run into me.

'Gosh, I thought it was me. What a let-down.'

Sorry, BigBrov.

'Have you made me . . . *do* things?'

Oh, it's not like that, BigBrov. All I do is . . . advise you. Help you make the right decisions about things. I say the things –

'Like any friend would?'

Exactly, BigBrov.

'Do it now, Apollo!'

What?

'Make me do something.'

It's not a game, BigBrov.

'Oh, please, Apollo. I want to experience it.'

You've already experienced it.

'Yes, but I want to *know* I'm experiencing it.'

Phone Nabil. Say you are sorry for rushing out of his house in anger. He is your friend. Think of how upset he must have been. Phone Nabil. Phone Nabil –

'Hang on, Apollo. Before you do anything in my mind, I'll just give Nabil a quick ring. I feel bad about rushing out of his house in anger like that. He's my friend, after all. Just think of how upset he must have been – Oh, he's not answering.'

Leave a message.

'I'll leave a message . . . Top of the night to you, Nab. You're probably asleep or playing with Rudi or something. Anyway, just wanted to say sorry I got all hysterical and stuff earlier. I hope we're still friends. Cos . . . well, I think we're meant to be friends. Why don't you pop round and see me in the morning. OK. Bye for now . . . Gosh, I'm glad I did that, Apollo.'

I know you are.

'So . . . come on! Make me do something.'

I have.

'What do you mean? I've been on the phone to Nabil ever since . . . Oh, hang on. Oh, gosh. Oh, goshy-gosh. You *advised* me to make that call, didn't you?'

I did, BigBrov.

'Apollo . . . you're glorious!'
So are you, BigBrov.

— **20** —

BigBrov is sleeping now. He is curled in the armchair. I have covered him with a blanket of warm air. I have turned the lights down very low. I am watching him.

'. . . cornflowers . . .'

BigBrov is dreaming. He is gently kicking his legs as if walking. He likes what he is seeing in his dream.

'. . . tree . . .'

BigBrov has seen a tree in his dream. This tree in the dream is so important to BigBrov. How BigBrov loves this tree. Look! BigBrov is arching his back as if looking up at the tree.

'. . . clouds!'

BigBrov's mood has changed. He is worried now. He is frowning. His muscles are becoming very tense. There is a trickle of sweat on his forehead. He is writhing in the chair as if in pain —

'No! I thought I could save you, tree.'

Calm down, BigBrov!

'. . .'

Calm . . .

Calm . . .

BigBrov is calm.

He is no longer worried. The frown is going.

Poor BigBrov. There are so many worries inside him. And I want to help . . .

Is that why I'm alive?

Alive and here?

Am I alive and here to help BigBrov?

Yes ... it must be!

I feel it in every atom of my metal frame and rubber wheels and plastic push bar.

BigBrov ... I am here to do for you what you couldn't do for the tree.

I'm here to keep you safe!

— **PART TWO** —

PART TWO

— 21 —

'Apollo ta moo . . .'

Eeeka-eeka–

Zip's eyes click open –

Wh-What . . .? Where . . .? Oh, gosh. It's morning! I must've fallen asleep in the armchair and – There's Newt! He's playing with Apollo. Little brov looks really happy. So does Apollo – Hang on! How can a supermarket trolley look happy?

'Top of the morning to you, Apollo.'

Eeeka-eeka.

Touch!

And to you, BigBrov. Sleep well?

'Yes, thank you. Has Newt been here long?'

LittleBrov got here about ten minutes ago. LittleBrov woke up and saw you weren't in the bed and guessed where you might be.

'With a little help from you, of course.'

I . . . advised him of the most likely option, yes. I hope we didn't disturb you, BigBrov.

'Well, if you did, I'm glad. I've gotta get breakfast started before Aunt Ivy turns up or –'

Wait!

'What?'

Too late.

'She's here?'

This very second.

'Oh, no! She's going to wonder why Newt's still in his

pyjamas and we're both out in the garage and I haven't even put the kettle on –'

'COOO-EEE!!'

Answer her, BigBrov! Before she worries!

'WE'RE IN HERE, AUNT IVY!! THE GARAGE!!'

The back door opens and Aunt Ivy pops her head in. 'Rummaging in the boxes for your sledge, are you, baby-cakes?'

Sledge?

Sledge?

'Have you *got* a sledge? Probably not. Perhaps it's a thing of the past. It's just that a sledge is the first thing I used to hunt out in weather like this. Oh, listen to me. Prattling on like a silly cabbage. It's just that I'm *so* excited. Thick, thick snow is just the tonic we needed!'

Thickthicksnow?

'IIIVVVYYY!!'

'COMING, SIS!' Aunt Ivy closes the door and rushes back into the house.

'The snow! Of course! It must've settled! Oh, Newt, you've never seen settled snow before, have you?'

'Ni-ni, Zi-Zi.'

'Can you open the garage door, please, Apollo?'

Vvvmmmmm . . .

'Oh . . . glorious!'

'Glor-rushh!'

A glory rush indeed.

New Town is all . . . sparkle and white. The snow – it's taken away all the hard edges. It's a soft world. A spotless world. A quieter world. Muffled. That's it! It's like . . . like pulling blankets up over your ears. A tucked-up-in-bed safeness. Snow has made everything feel . . . like someone's living room –

'Cold enough for ya, Happy Clappy?'

— 22 —

'Nab!'

'Got your message, amigo.'

'Message? Oh, on your mobile. I forgot.'

'Charming! I traipse all the way across this wasteland and you –'

'Wasteland! But it's glorious and –'

'Stop it right there. If I hear one more word of happy, clappy cutesieness I'm liable to puke right here. Right on your garden path. This puke'll freeze. Someone'll come rushing out of your house and slip over on it. They might break their neck. Instant popped clog. Is that what you want on a loved-one's death certificate? Eh? Cause of death: slipped in frozen sick!?'

'Er . . . I guess not, Nab, no.'

'So cut out the cute stuff! Holy macaroni, I'm so cold my snot's turned into a lethal weapon.'

'Where Ru-Ru?' asks Newt.

'Eh? What?'

'Little brov wants to know where Rudi is.'

'Oh! Left him at home. Didn't know if these sub-zero temperatures were safe for a ferret. A popped-clog parent is one thing. But a popped-clog pet – no way!'

'Oh, Rudi should be safe in the snow, Nab. As far as I know, anyway. After all, they're wild creatures and it must snow in the wild.'

'Well, I'll try him for a few minutes at a time when I get

back home. I don't want anything to happen to my little baby – Ouch!'

'What's wrong, Nab?'

'My feet! They're so cold they're burning.'

'Well, you ain't wearing the right sort of shoes, are you?'

'Only ones I've got, my correctly booted amigo.'

'There's some spare boots in one of the boxes over there. Why don't you put them on?'

'Because I'm not after charity, Happy Clappy – Hey! How'd that happen?'

'How'd *what* happen, Gloomy Doomy?'

'It's ... so *warm* in here. Even with the garage door open. I step here ...' Nab takes a step back outside. 'Arctic! I step here ...' Forward. 'Sahara! It's like when you walk into a supermarket and the hot air suddenly blows on ya. But ... there's no hot air here. In fact ...' Nab looks all round '... there's no heating in here at all. So ... how come?'

Zip looks at Apollo and asks, 'He's a friend, Apollo. Can I tell him the truth?'

'Holy macaroni, Happy Clappy, what ya doing?'

Touch!

Tell him the truth, BigBrov.

'I'm talking to Apollo.'

'The trolley?'

'It's worse than I thought.' Nabil grabs Zip by the shoulders. 'Listen, amigo! I'm sorry I kept asking questions about ya dad yesterday. I know popped-clog stuff is stressful malarkey. But believing the trolley is alive is just too doolally –'

'I don't *believe* the trolley is alive.'

'You don't?'

'Of course not. I *know* it!'

'What?'

'It's *true*, Nab. Right, little brov?'

'Ya-ya, Zi-Zi.'

'Zip! Stop it now before the men in white coats come and take you away.'

Eeeka-eek.

Apollo nudges Nab.

'Not now, Newt.'

Eeeka.

Nudge.

'I said not now, Newt.'

'It's not Newt, Nab. Newt's sitting on the armchair over there. See?'

'Then who –?'

Eeeka.

Nudge.

'HEY!' Zip jumps back from Apollo. 'How . . .? How . . .?'

'Nab, this is Apollo.'

Eeeka-eeka-clicka–

'Stay back!'

'There's no need to be scared, Nab. Is there, little brov?'

'Ni-ni, Zi-Zi.'

Eeeka –

'Stop! Wait! Hang on! Slow down! Cool it! Let me think . . .' Nabil gazes at Apollo for a while, then at Zip, then at Newt. Slowly, he approaches the trolley and, grinning and nodding, says, 'Oh, OK, I get it. Yeah. This is some kind of joke, right? A trick. Well, it's very well done, amigo, I'll give ya that.' He waves his arms around Apollo as if checking for strings.

'It's not a trick, Nab.'

'Remote control! Must be!'

'Touch Apollo with your phone.'

'Eh?'

'Your *mobile*. Touch it to the metal frame.'

'OK, OK. If you've gone to this much trouble it would be bad manners of me not to –'

Touch!

You had it all the time.

'OK, OK. Neat trick.'

'What did Apollo say?'

'You *know* what it says. You did it!'

'I didn't, Nab.'

'You *did*! And, for your information, I've no idea what "You had it all the time" is supposed to mean.'

'Touch Apollo again, Nab.'

Nabil chuckles, 'You're a good actor, I'll give ya that. I suppose you planted something in my phone yesterday when I wasn't looking, eh? OK, OK, I'll humour you.'

Touch!

It's in the lining of the coat.

'OK, Zip. Joke over. It's getting boring now and –'

It fell through a hole.

'– so don't push it –'

Left pocket. Look there. It's what you've been searching for.

Nabil becomes very still and gazes at Apollo. 'Nah,' he says softly, 'it … *can't* be … It *can't* be –' And, suddenly, he's taking off his coat and spreading it out on the floor and feeling every inch of the lining. 'It *can't* be! It just … *can't*!'

'What, Nab? What?'

'Hang on, Happy Clappy … I'm just trying to – Wait! I feel something! In the lining of my coat.' Nabil reaches down through a hole in the left pocket. 'I can … I can … feel it! Yes! Oh yes!'

'What *is* it, Nab?'

'Holy macaroni, amigo!'

'What?'

Nabil brings his hand out of the pocket and thrusts something small and gold into the air. 'It's Mum's ring!' he cries. 'Mum's ring!'

'And . . . you thought you'd lost it?'

'Dad gave it to me just after Mum popped her clogs! Dad said, "She would've wanted you to have this, Nabby." And then, in the move, I lost it. Holy macaroni, I've looked everywhere. Drove me doolally. Thought it was gone for good. I was dreading telling Dad. But . . . oh, look! It was here all the time!'

'Just like Apollo said, Nab.'

Nabil gazes at the supermarket trolley. 'It . . . can't . . . be . . .'

Eeeka.

'Your mobile, Nab, your mobile.'

Touch!

Hello, NabBrov.

'NabBrov! The trolley called me NabBrov!'

'And I'm BigBrov. Newt is LittleBrov.'

And my name is Apollo.

'Ho-ly ma-car-ro-ni!'

No. Apollo.

'Ha! Apollo's got a great sense of humour, don't you think, Nab?'

'I . . . er . . . yeah . . .'

'Say hello back, then, Nab. Go on!'

'Hello . . . Apollo.'

Now the introductions are over with . . . may I suggest something?

'Gosh, sure, Apollo. What?'

Exploration.

'Of what, amigo?'

Snow, of course.

— 23 —

'Gosh, ain't it glorious to walk through New Town in weather like this? Even the plastic trees look glorious – Look! Icicles on the branches! That big space over there was just flat earth waiting to be dug up yesterday. But now ... oh, it's an ocean of pure white. Not a footprint. You know what that means? The snow's kept all the workmen away. Don't suppose they can do much when the weather's like this. Look! Not a soul in sight! Glorious! You see, Apollo? You see, Nab?'

'Glor-rush!'

Glory rush, BigBrov.

'...'

'Oh, come on, Nab. You're not so bitter and twisted you can't enjoy the snow, are you?'

'It's me feet, amigo – ouch!'

'We forgot to find you proper boots!'

'Every footstep – ouch! – hurts.'

Climb in me.

'Gosh, Apollo, what a good idea. Get in with Newt, Nab.'

'Ya-ya, Ni-Ni!' says Newt, making room. 'Apple-loo warrrm.'

'Nah, nah – ouch!'

'Why not, Nab?'

'Cos I'm thirteen years old and I'm *not* riding in a supermarket trolley – no offence, Apollo – with a two-year-old toddler. No offence, Newt.'

'But you can't walk in those shoes.'

'I can. It's just – ouch! – very painful.'

Please let me help you.

'This is doolally, Nab! No one can see you. There's just us. You're amongst friends. So stop being stubborn and get in!'

'Ya-ya, Ni-Ni!'

Get in, NabBrov.

'All right, all right, spare me!' Nabil swings one leg into the trolley, then fixes Zip with a firm stare. 'But this ain't gonna be a regular occurrence. Ya hear? This is just until I can get some proper boots and – Hey! It's ... it's really *comfortable* in here.'

Thank you.

'Told you!' says Zip, pushing the trolley once more. 'Nice and warm.'

'It's more than just *warm*, amigo. It's ... it's like there's invisible cushions all round me. I can't feel the metal frame at all. It's like ... the most comfortable place I've ever sat in my whole life.'

How kind.

'You've gotta try it, amigo.'

'There's not enough room.'

'Sure there is! If I tuck myself in the middle ... Like this! And, Newt – you tuck yourself between my legs ... That's it. Like we're paddling a canoe or something.'

'Ya-ya, Zi-Zi!'

'Come on, amigo! Sit behind me. Put your feet inside the trolley and park ya bum on the push bar. Then we'll all be facing the same direction and – oh, come on, amigo! Do it!'

'Doo tit, Zi-Zi!'

Do it, BigBrov.

'Listen, you three, I'd love to feel comfortable and warm too. That goes without saying. But – if I get in – who's gonna push?'

I don't need pushing, BigBrov. Remember?

'I *know* that, Apollo, but what if someone *sees* you moving all by yourself?'

No one is here.

'Apollo's right, my many-worried amigo. Not a soul for as far as the eye can see. As you said yourself, not a footprint anywhere. Now ... get in!'

I'm climbing into the metal frame and –

'Gosh!'

'Ya see, Zip?'

'Comfyy, Zi-Zi!'

It's like floating in a bath of warm water. The push bar feels like the edge of a mattress. And something is supporting my back. I'm being held in place. Oh, if I could curl up in a cat purr it would feel just like this.

Eeeka-eek-clicka-click.

'Gosh!'

'Go for it, Apollo!'

'Ta moon.'

We're moving down the street! Oh, it's so smooth. Not a jolt. Not a bump. Not even when we go up and down kerbs – Oh, I love this!

'Faster, Apollo!' cries Zip. 'Faster!'

'That's the way, amigo – Faster, Apollo!'

'Fasser, fasser.'

So ... faster –

'Gooossh!!'

'Hoollyy macoorooonii!!'

'Haa, haa, haa, haa!!'

Faster –

'Gooooossssshhhhh!!'

'Hooooolllyyymacooooorrrooooonnnniiiiii!!'

'Hahahahahahahahahahahahahahahahahahahaha!!'

Fasterfasterfasterfasterfasterfasterfaster!!

Eeekaeekclickaclickeekaeekclickaclickeekaeekclick clickaclickeekaeekclickaclickeekaeekaclick . . .

The houses are whizzing by! And when we go round corners . . . oh, there's no sensation of turning. Nothing forcing us left when Apollo turns right. Nothing forcing us right when Apollo turns left. Nothing forcing us back when Apollo speeds up. Nothing forcing us forward when Apollo slows down. There's nothing. Not even wind in my face. Oh, this is glorious! Truly glor–

♩ Tender ♩ ♩

What's that?

I can hear something!

'I can hear something!' cries Zip. 'Can you stop, Apollo, please?'

Of course.

Eeeka-eek –!

♩ ♩ love ♩ ♩

'Music!' cries Zip.

— 24 —

Yes . . . it's a song, BigBrov!

'Where's it coming from, Apollo? Can you tell?'

Let me see.

Where is the music coming from? Where is the music coming from? Where is the music —?

Yes!

'Can you take us to it?' asks Zip.

Of course.

Eeek-eek . . .

We're going down a road . . . round a corner . . . down another road . . . another road . . . Gosh! No idea where I am, but —

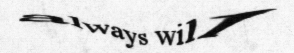

'We're getting closer.'

'We certainly are, amigo.'

'Ya-ya!'

'I'm sure I've heard this song somewhere before, Nab.'

'Me too, amigo. And the singer – Oh, who is it? On the tip of my tongue. He's a popped clog, I know that much.'

'The music's from that house! There! Stop, Apollo, please!'

Of course.

'ELVIS!' cries Nab. 'That's who's singing! It's Elvis Presley!'

'Who's Elvis Presley?'

'Holy macaroni, amigo, where you been living? A cave?'

'No. A forest. I keep blooming telling you.'

'Well, I would've thought even in a forest you would've heard of Elvis Presley. He's only like one of the most famous singers to have lived and popped clogs –'

'Wotcha, mates!' says a voice from behind.

They turn to see –

'Memphis!' gasps Zip.

'You!' cries Nabil.

'Mi-Mi!' says Newt.

'Just been down to the supermarket, mates.' Memphis indicates two bags of shopping in each hand. 'This stuff weighs a tonne, mates.'

'You should've put it in a trolley and wheeled it home,' says Zip.

'You're not allowed to do that, mate.'

'You are! That's how we got Apoll– I mean, this trolley here.'

'Well, you must've got it before today, mate.'

'What d'you mean?'

'The management of the supermarket has just changed its policy. You ain't allowed to take trolleys beyond the car park any more.'

'What!'

Oh, no!

'It's true, mate. Mind you, no hardship for me. I've got muscles enough for twice as many bags. I can see how it might be difficult for wimps like you, though, mates.'

'Wimps!'

'Wimps!'

'Ha!'

I agree, LittleBrov. Very amusing!

'Don't deny it, mates! After all, why else you sitting in the trolley? Don't want to get your poor little tootsies cold, eh?'

I forgot! We're still in Apollo!

Zip and Newt scramble out so fast they trip over each other and fall face first into the snow –

Splat!

Splat!

'Get out me way, Happy Clappy!'

'You're in *my* way, Gloomy Doomy!'

'Your scarves are lethal weapons!'

'Well, your coat made me slip.'

'Stop all the bickering, mates.'

'Well, it was *his* fault,' mutters Zip.

'It was *his* fault,' mutters Nabil.

'NO BICKERING, MATES!! You need to take a leaf out of Elvis's book. Elvis had lots of mates around him. They played music. They practised kung fu. They had fun. That's what mates are for. Fun! Not friction! Get me?'

'Yeah, yeah,' murmurs Zip, brushing snow from his scarves.

'Yeah, yeah,' murmurs Nabil, brushing snow from his fur coat.

'If you ever have any doubts about how to behave in life, mates, just think of the King. He will give you all the answers.'

'The King?' asks Zip. 'Who's the King?'

'That's what Elvis is called, mate. Where you been living, mate? A cave, mate?'

'A forest, actually!' says Nabil. 'But he don't like to talk about it.'

'Gosh!' says Zip, looking towards the house. 'So ... that's *your* music blaring out like this!'

'I phoned Missy to play it like this so I could find my way home, mate. It's a bit unneighbourly, I know. So I

— 86 —

sincerely apologize for that – Hey, why don't ya all come home with me and meet Missy? There's nothing she enjoys more than being hospitable to neighbours.'

'We'd love to . . . Right, Nab?'

'Why not? But I still wanna know if you're a boy or a girl.'

'Of course you do, mate,' says Memphis, striding towards the house. 'Only natural.'

— 25 —

I will concentrate very hard and — Yes! I can see my Brovs in the house. Memphis is introducing them to a woman. This must be Missy.

'Let me make you a nice cup of tea, lambs. You must need warming up after those sub-zero conditions. And I'll get you some of my home-made mince pies. How does that sound?'

'Glorious, Mrs Lemonique – Sorry, Missy.'

'Yeah, great, amigo.'

'Elvissy, Missy.'

'Ya!'

Missy is small and wearing a dress. The dress is . . . bright pink. The dress has . . . little ribbons tied in bows. There are ribbons in Missy's hair too. And Missy is . . . oh, what's the word? Pregnant! That's it! Her belly is huge!!

'Your mum is very affable, Mem.'

'She's *always* affable, Zip, mate. Missy is very community-spirited. Where we lived before, our house

— 87 —

was always full. Anyone with a problem, they'd come to Missy and Missy would make a cup of tea and help them sort their problems out.'

'Don't worry, mate. I don't think you're the kind of person someone'd go to *with* a problem.'

'Nah, Mem. They'd go to Nab to *get* one.'

'Ha-ha, very good, mate!'

'Thanks, Mem! Ha-ha! Oh, laugh, Nab, it was a joke.'

'Oh? *That's* what it was, eh? I did wonder.'

Missy has returned with tea and a plate of her home-made mince pies. Missy is indicating a table covered in books at the back of the living room —

'I'm educating myself, lambs. I decided a little while ago that I've gone through life with blinkers on. I just believed everything everyone told me without questioning a single thing. So I'm having a complete life change. Ain't that so, Trix – I mean, Memphis?'

'Yes, that's true, Missy.'

NabBrov is shooting BigBrov a look. BigBrov shoots NabBrov a look back. And now NabBrov is whispering in BigBrov's ear —

'Trix?'

'Shhh!'

'I'm studying science now, lambs. I'm just reading about the birth of the universe. The way everything started. The Big Bang, they call it. Oh, how thrilling and inspiring it is. The Big Bang happened about fourteen million years ago. BOOOM!! Everything in the universe, my lambs, absolutely *everything*, comes from that boom. Us. The planets. The moon. So . . . so, when you look up at the stars, you're looking at part of us. Now ain't that a truly inspirational thought, eh – More mince pies, lambs?'

'No thank you, Mrs Lemonique.'

'Oh, no, lamb! Call me Missy. Everyone calls me Missy! And what about you, Nabil, lamb? Another mince pie?'

'No thanks, amigo.'

'And what about you, Trixabelle – I mean, Memphis?'

'*Trixabelle! Amigo!* Ya real name's *Trixabelle!* Ha!'

'Shut up, mate! Oh, Missy, *now* see what you've done?'

'Oh, no! I'm sorry, Trix– I mean, Memphis!! I do *try* to remember. Honest I do! Lambs, listen to me, please call her Memphis – I mean *him* Memphis! Oh dear!'

'*Her!* Zip, I told ya! Ha! Memphis – I mean Trixabelle – is a girl! Ha! Ha! Ha! Ha! Ha!'

Memphis is standing now. Memphis looks very, very angry. Memphis is pointing at the stairs.

'My room, mates! NOW!!'

— **26** —

Memphis is pacing up and down in front of us. We are sitting on the bed. Posters of . . . yes, that must be Elvis Presley all over the place!

'Right, mates,' says Memphis, coming to a halt in front of them. 'I'm gonna ask you a series of simple, oh so simple, questions. The answers to these questions is either 'boy' or 'girl'. That OK with you, mates?'

'Okey-dokey.'

'Whatever, yeah.'

'Ya-ya.'

'Look at my hair, mates. A quiff. Made famous by the one and only Elvis Presley. If you saw someone with this hairstyle at the front of a queue in a burger bar, would you think the next person to get served is a boy or girl?'

'Er . . . boy.'

'Er . . . boy.'

'Er . . . boo.'

'And look at this, mates! The way I walk. Study that swagger! If you saw this walk swaggering towards ya on a dark night would you think that's a boy coming home from visiting his macho mates or a girl coming home from visiting her girlie mates?'

'. . . Boy.'

'. . . Boy.'

'. . . Boo.'

'Now the most important question, mates.' Memphis kneels in front of them. 'In here . . .' – tapping head – '. . . in me skull. For as far back as I can remember – from the moment I was born probably – I've thought of myself as a boy. I wanted to climb trees and play football and play with other boys and wear trousers and talk in a deep voice and grow whiskers and shave and fart out loud and . . . and . . . oh, listen, mates, I can't say it any plainer, any clearer. I am a boy, mates. My name is Memphis, mates. So look at me, mates . . . boy or girl?'

'Boy.'

'Boy.'

'Boo.'

'Thank you, mates.'

Oh, I'm so proud of you all.

'And now, mates,' says Memphis, 'let me explain something else. This' – pointing at a photo of Elvis – 'is the King. Why he's called the King is clear for all to see. Look at that kingish face, mates. Look at that kingish physique, mates. Look at the kingish clothes.'

'I think the word is "regal" actually,' corrects Nabil.

'Glad you agree, mate. But please don't interrupt when I'm spreading the word about Elvis, mate.' Memphis takes a deep breath. 'The word "star" was invented for Elvis. He is the brightest star there is. Ever was. Ever will be. He shines in the dark cosmos of contemporary pop –'

'Enough, enough,' says Nabil, standing, 'we get your point.'

'My *point*,' says Memphis, pushing him back down again, 'is *this*: you and me cannot be mates – in fact it would be impossible for me to remain in your company – unless you agree with me on the most important thing about the King.'

'And what's that, amigo?'

'*Elvis is not dead!*'

'Holy macaroni!' gasps Nabil. 'I don't believe I'm hearing this! Of *course* he's a popped clog. *Everyone* knows he's a popped clog!'

'*I* didn't know, Nab.'

'You didn't know he was *alive* to begin with!'

'I did!'

'Didn't!'

'Did! Did!'

'NO BICKERING, MATES!' Memphis points to a blurred photo of a man with a quiff standing against the sunset. 'Look at this, mates! It's the King standing in the Arizona desert. It was taken seven weeks ago. So you see? Elvis is alive and well.'

'It could be anyone!' cries Nabil. 'You can't even see his face.'

'It's Elvis, mate! It's *got* to be, mate!'

'Why?'

'Because the King was the greatest talent the world has ever known. His voice changed the world. He was loved by millions and millions of people. For him to die like he did makes no sense –'

'*Sense!*' explodes Nabil, stamping his foot. 'Holy macaroni, why do people expect things to make *sense*? Things just happen. There's no rhyme or reason. The San

— 91 —

Francisco earthquake. The *Titanic*! Pompeii. Exploding space shuttles. Where's the sense in all of those things, eh? So don't stand there and tell me the death of some fat, sentimental, spoilt, overweight singer – with horrendous taste in clothes in later life – makes no sense, because in the light of all the tragedies I've just mentioned, and a million more we haven't got time for, it makes more sense than ... than ...' Nabil comes to a halt and looks round at the faces staring at him. All the energy seems to drain out of him now and he slumps back on the bed with a loud sigh. 'Lots of things don't make sense,' he says softly. 'That's all I'm saying.'

NabBrov is feeling embarrassed at saying too much. BigBrov puts his arm round NabBrov's shoulders. Memphis is smiling at them both. Oh, what a bunch of good friends they are —

Hang on!

Someone is walking across the snow towards me!

Someone with a limp. Someone with a walking stick —

Oh, no! It is Roz! The girl from the supermarket!

She has seen me!

BigBrov! Get down here!

BigBrov!

BigBrov!

BigBrov!

'Hang on ... I need to look out of the window ...'

There is BigBrov!

'GOSH!'

BigBrov has seen!

'Nab! Downstairs! Quick!'

'What's up, amigo?'

'Yeah, mate. What's up?'

'Er ... snow, Mem! Let's play out in the snow. Now! Very quickly!' He picks up Newt, then whispers in Nab's ear, 'Supermarket person approaching! Apollo in danger! Quick!'

'Holy macaroni! Yeah! Snow! Downstairs! Quick!'

'Hey, mates ... wait for me! I need to put my jacket on. And I'll bring my radio. I've found a station that finds non-stop Elvis. Pure heaven. We can listen to Elvis in the snow.'

'Elvissnowy!' Nabil calls back.

'No time for jokes, Nab!' snaps Zip.

'Sorry, amigo!'

— 27 —

She is touching my push bar.

'Hello, there, trolley ...'

Leave me alone!

Zip, carrying Newt, and Nabil come rushing out of the house.

'Top of the morning, Roz.'

'Customer Zip! And Customer Newt! And Customer ... what's your name?'

'I am not a customer, I am a free man.'

'Wotcha, mate.' Memphis rushes out of the house, buttoning a coat and clutching a radio. 'You work at the checkout, don't ya, mate?'

'That's me!' Roz grabs the trolley. 'Now, listen, customers, I need to talk to you about this.'

Gosh, no!

no!

'Sorry, Roz,' says Zip, picking up Newt and putting him

in the trolley. 'We'd really love to natter but we . . . we really are in a rush and –'

'It's the same trolley, ain't it, Customer Zip?'

'Wh – What?'

'Is it *Apollo*?'

'Apollo! Gosh, no!'

'Holy macaroni, course it's not Apollo!'

'So you *know* about Apollo, do you, Customer . . .?'

'Er . . . nah, course not. All I meant was –'

'Yes? What *did* you mean, Customer . . .?'

'What's this all about, mates?'

'Customer Newt, is this trolley your Apollo?'

'Leave my brother out of this!'

'Pick on someone your own size, you capitalist!'

'Customer Newt,' continues Roz, leaning very close to the trolley, 'this is the same trolley you've always had. Ain't it? Eh? You took it out of the supermarket and you think it's your friend and you do not intend to take it back to the supermarket. *Not ever!*'

'We've really got to go, Roz, so . . . Gosh, will you let go of Apoll– I mean, the trolley?'

'*Apollo!* You see! I *knew* it!'

'I . . . I . . . oh, gosh, I . . . I . . . Nab?'

'Well, I . . . holy macaroni . . . this trolley . . .'

'This trolley is *mine*, mates!'

'*Yours*, Customer . . .?'

'The name's Memphis! And yes. It's mine!' Memphis puts the radio inside the trolley. 'I got it this morning when I was at the supermarket!'

'But . . . I watched you leave, Customer Memphis.'

'Fancy me, did ya, mate?'

'You did *not* have a trolley with you!'

'Not in the supermarket, no, mate. But I got halfway across the supermarket and the plastic bags started to cut right into my hands. Now I'm a big strong boy with big strong boy's hands, but even I couldn't stand the pain. Then I saw a supermarket trolley in the car park. So I put me plastic bags in the trolley – oh, what a relief that was, mates – and I wheeled it all the way home. And this' – indicating the house – 'is my home. And this' – indicating Apollo – 'is the trolley. Now, if you will excuse us ...' Memphis removes Roz's hand from Apollo. 'Me and my good mates have got very important things to attend to. Namely, Elvis in the snow. Ready, mates?'

'Ready, Mem.'

'Ready, Mem.'

'Ree-dee, Mi-Mi.'

Never readier!

'Then we will be on our way, mates.' Memphis starts pushing the trolley away. 'Goodbye, checkout person.'

'If Guard Krick sees you with that trolley, he'll take it!' Roz calls after them. 'He's got a van to go out searching for trolleys, you know! Security Guard Krick treats the trolleys terribly. He'll find you! Listen to me –'

'Listen, mates. On the count of three ... we run. OK?'

'OK.'

'OK.'

'Okee!'

'One, mates ... two, mates ... ruuuunnn!'

Eeekaeekaclickaclickeekaeekaclickaclickeeekaeekaclick-aclickeekaeekaclickaclickeeekaeekaclickaclickeeekaeeka clickaclickeeekaeekaclickaclickeeekaeekaclickaclickeeek aeekaclickaclickeeka –

— 28 —

'Gosh . . . you can run so fast, Mem!'

'It's the strong-boy muscles in me legs, mates. Now, where are me big strong-boy muscles running us all to, mates?'

Home!

'To my place, Mem.'

'And where's that, mate?'

'I . . . gosh, I don't know . . . how to get back. Do you remember the way, Nab?'

'Ouch . . . ouch . . . nah.'

'What's wrong, mate?'

'I've got – ouch! – holes in me shoes.'

'Get in the trolley, mate.'

'But – ouch!'

'Get in, Nab!'

Get in, NabBro!

'Ouch . . . OK! Shove over, Newt!'

'Ya-ya, Ni-Ni!'

'Why don't you get in, mate?' Memphis asks Zip. 'I'm strong enough to push all of you!'

Get in, BigBro!

'I'll get in, Mem – Move over, Newt. Move over, Nab.'

'Ya-ya, Zi-Zi!'

'Sit here, amigo.'

'Listen, mates. I still don't know where I'm going, mates. Does anyone know how to get to Zip's house?'

'No, Mem.'

'Nah, Mem.'

'Ni-ni, Mi-Mi.'

'I bet the trolley knows, don't it, mates?'

Have you guessed I'm alive?

'Listen, mates, I ain't stupid. I heard the way that check-out person was talking about the trolley, mates. And when I saw you all near the house earlier ... there were trolley tracks in the snow. But no footprints. The trolley can move by itself, can't it, mates. It's alive, ain't it, mates? You call it Apollo, don't you, mates?'

You have guessed!

'Listen, mates, I've been reading about stuff like this most of my life, mates. And I remember once ... I read somewhere ... about a trolley that came alive.'

'What?!' gasps Zip. 'Where?'

'On the Internet, I think, mate.'

'No, no, amigo. He means where did this trolley come alive.'

'Oh, somewhere in Africa, I seem to remember. A lorry was delivering trolleys. It was way out in the wilderness. The lorry wasn't in the jungle. But it was pretty wild country. And the lorry got a flat tyre. And a boy from a nearby village helped the lorry driver change the tyre. And the driver gave the boy a trolley as a gift. And the boy took the trolley back to his village and he started to play with it and stuff and ... well, according to the boy, this trolley came alive. The boy's grown up now. He's a doctor in some big city. He put his story on the Web. Just one of the things I've come across in my search for mysterious stuff. You see, mates, I believe in flying saucers. I believe in sea monsters. I believe in ghosts. All I've wanted – all my life – is just some kind of proof, mates. Because if I get proof about one ... why, *anything* could be true, mates. Elvis could really be alive.

So tell me the truth, mates. Please. Is this trolley alive?'

Zip touches his mobile to Apollo –

Tell the truth, BigBrov!

'It's alive, Mem.'

'Yeah, amigo, the trolley's alive.'

'Ya-ya!'

Hello.

'Apollo says hello, Mem!'

'Oh, Apollo, mate, I'm so pleased to meet ya, mate! So, mates, I take it that Apollo can move without me having to push. Correct?'

'Correct, Mem. So long as there's no grown-ups around.'

'What happens when a grown-up's around, amigo?'

'Apollo freezes.'

'Holy macaroni, ya learn something new every day.'

'Well, there's no grown-ups around now, mates. So what about I hop in and Apollo can take us all the way back to your place, Zip, mate? How about it Apollo, mate? You up for that, mate?'

Get in!

'Apollo says get in, Mem!'

'Oh, really, mate, oh, mate, oh, mate ... I'm jumping in, mates, and ... oh, it's so comfy, mates, and I don't need comfort cos I'm a big strong boy, mates, and liking comfort can be girlie, mates, but ... oh, it feels like I'm sitting on cushions, mate, and we're moving faster and faster, mates. Oh, I'm so happy, mates. Anything is possible, mates – yeahhh!!'

'Gosh, yeah, anything is possible – yeahhh!!'

'Anything is possible, amigos – yeahhh!!'

'Anyy tinggg tisss poss bubble – yeahhh!!'

Anything is possible!!

— 29 —

Vvvmmmmm . . .

'So this is ya hideout, eh, mates?'

'Gosh, I guess it is, yes.'

'Yeah, amigo.'

'Ya-ya.'

'Oh, mates, that's just what I've always wanted. To be with mates in a hideout for mates, mates. A place where mates tell mates lots of matey secrets, mates.'

'Well, we've only got one secret in this hideout, Mem,' says Zip, taking off his coat. 'And it's the best secret of all: Apollo!'

Thank you kindly, BigBrov.

'Holy macaroni, amigos, all that escaping from the clutches of the global conspiracy supermarket police is thirsty work . . . ya got anything to drink, Zip?'

'There's a bottle of spring water in the house –'

'Spring water!' splutters Nab. 'You trying to poison me? Ain't you got anything sweet 'n' fizzy and flavoured with chemicals?'

'Afraid not, Nab.'

Eeka–

'What is it, amigo?'

Touch!

Watch!

'Gosh! Apollo, you're shaking!'

'Vibrating, I'd say, amigo.'

'No, mates! Rock 'n' rolling!'

'Gosh! Look! A bottle is appearing inside Apollo!'

'The bottle's filling up with something, amigos!'

'It's bubbling, mates!'

For you!

'Holy macaroni!' Nabil picks up the bottle and takes a swig. 'Lemonade! Apollo has made us a bottle of the most refreshing lemonade I've ever tasted! And it's ice cold – taste!'

'Thanks, mate.' Memphis takes a swig. 'Chilled to perfection. Have a gulp, Newt the cute.'

'Hang on, little brov! Oh, no! You know Mum doesn't like us to drink things with artificial flavourings and chemicals and –'

Eeeka!

Touch!

The lemonade has only natural ingredients, BigBrov. One hundred per cent organic, I assure you.

'Well ... gosh! In that case' – Zip takes the bottle Newt is offering – 'Cheers, everyone!'

'Cheers, amigo.'

'Cheers, mate.'

'Choos, Zi-Zi.'

'Cheers, BigBrov.'

'Apollo!' splutters Zip. 'You ... you ... you *spoke*!'

— 30 —

'Yes, I did, didn't I? And I'm still doing it now. Hello, BigBrov. Hello, LittleBrov. Hello, MemBrov.'

'MemBrov, mate!'

'Yes. You are a Brov to me now.'

'But, Apollo, your *voice* ... gosh ... where's it coming from? Where's your ... *mouth*, so to speak?'

'Mates! Look! It's the radio, mates. I left it in Apollo and ... well, somehow, mates, Apollo is talking through me radio! And that's not all, mates. Cos unless I'm very much mistaken ... Apollo is speaking with the voice of Elvis Presley!!'

'Gosh! You *are* talking like Elvis, Apollo. And – here! I'll get some string and tie the radio to the front of you ... like this ... now you can talk whenever you want. How's that feel, eh? Not too tight?'

'No. And look — MemBrov is busy.'

Memphis is rearranging the armchairs and moving that coffee table from the back of the garage and putting it in front of the chairs and ... Gosh! Where'd Memphis dig out that old rug? The roses on it have almost faded away.

'You're making it very homely in here, Mem.'

'That's what a mates' hideout should be, mates. After all, mate, we wanna be relaxed and comfortable while we're here, don't we, mates. Stars 'n' bars! Is that a sofa over there, mate?'

'Yes, Mem.'

'Mates, we need a sofa! A sofa is the perfect thing for good mates to slumber on while they – Mates! Shush! Listen!'

'What, Mem?'

'What, amigo?'

'Voices, mates!'

Zip and Nabil fall silent and hear –

'. . . You've got to learn to use your walking frame!'

That's Aunt Ivy!

'Nooooo!'

That's Gran!

'But you'll fall over without it!'

'Nooooo!'

'Oh, I give up!'

'Then gooo!'

'Go where, you silly, sick, old woman?'

'Awayyy from meee!'

Aunt Ivy is at the front door. Gran is in the front room by the sound of it. Both of them are crying.

'I can't go away from you, you selfish old woman! Not now. Not ever. Look at you. Helpless! I'm stuck with you for the rest of my life. So . . . walk in the snow! Go on! Fall over and break ya blooming neck. See if I care!'

SLAM!

'Gosh!'

'Holy macaroni!'

'Stars 'n' bars!'

'Ya-ya!'

'Aunt Ivy is sitting on the doorstep, BigBrov. She is so sad. She needs someone to talk to, BigBrov.'

'Yeah, of course, Apollo.' Zip looks at Nabil and Memphis. 'Listen, everyone, I've got a bit of a family crisis and so . . . if you don't mind . . .'

'Say no more, mate. We'll see you later, mate.'

'Yeah, amigo. I should be getting back to my little Rudi

anyway. I'm sure he's wondering where I've got to. See ya later, amigo. And ... well, good luck.'

'I'll get the door for you, NabBrov and MemBrov.'

Vvvmmmmm ...

— 31 —

'Top of the afternoon to you, Aunt Ivy.'

'Oh ... hello, babycake!' Aunt Ivy dabs the tears from her face with a tissue. 'Were ... were those your two friends I just saw leaving?'

'The new one's Memphis.'

'He looks a handsome boy.'

'Yeah, I know.'

'I bet they both wondered what all the screaming and shouting was about, didn't they ...?' She wipes away some more tears. 'And I bet they thought, What's that silly old woman doing sitting on a freezing-cold doorstep?' She starts sobbing again. 'Oh, I don't seem to be able to stop these waterworks.'

Ask her into the hideout, BigBrov.

'Do you want to come into the hideout – I mean garage, Aunt Ivy? It's warmer in there.'

'Oh ... thank you, babycake.'

Help her up, BigBrov.

'I'll help you up, Aunt Ivy.'

'Oh, thank you, babycake.'

'Be careful of the ice ... Now, here we are.'

Sit her on the sofa, BigBrov.

'Sit here, Aunt Ivy.'

'Oh, babycake, how homely you've made it! And you've made use of that old rug, I see. Luverducks, that's donkey's years old. Your mum used to love playing on that when she was a little baby. It's all so worn now you can barely make out a thing.'

Ask if she wants something to drink, BigBrov.

'Do you want some lemonade, Aunt Ivy?'

'A gin and tonic would be more like it, but – oh yes, thank you, babycake. I'd love some lemonade.'

The bottle's full again! And chilled to perfection. I'm looking at Apollo but, of course, Apollo can't speak or move. Not with Aunt Ivy in the room. But Apollo knows what I'm thinking. Thank you, Apollo.

You're welcome, BigBrov.

'You and Gran love each other so much, don't you, Aunt Ivy?' says Zip, sitting next to her on the sofa.

'That we do, babycake.'

'Did you ... always argue like you do now?'

'Well, we argued. Of course we did. Families always argue. But our arguments were ... never quite like they are now, no.'

'Is that because you never had a walking frame to argue over before?'

'Oh, you heard it all that clearly, did you? Oh, baby-cake ...' She gives Zip a big hug and a kiss. 'Us grown-ups can be blooming embarrassing sometimes, can't we?'

'You could never be embarrassing, Aunt Ivy.'

'Well ... perhaps I am and perhaps I'm not. I certainly don't mean to be. And, to answer your question, yes, your gran and me were shouting at each other because of that blooming walking frame, but ... well, that wasn't what the argument was about. Not really.'

'Then ... what *was* it about?'

Ivy sighs deep and long and gazes through the open garage door at the snow outside. 'You know, babycake, every time it snows like this ... it makes me think of all the other times in my life it's done the same. Oh, I know what you're thinking. That's stupid! There must be lots and lots – hundreds! – of snows like this in a lifetime. How can you possibly remember them all? But, you see, snow like this ... thick, thick snow, snow that makes the whole world look different ... *that* kind of snow don't happen often at all. I heard on the radio that we ain't seen snow this thick for ten years. *Ten years.* Just think of it, babycake. So let's say someone lives to be ... what? Ninety years old. Heck, let's make it a round hundred. Why, a person who makes it to a century might only live through a snow like this *ten times*. And, well, let's say, for argument's sake, that for one of those times this person is too young to remember. And let's say, again for argument's sake, that another couple of times this person is either too ill, or too busy, or out of the country on holiday. Or, luverducks, they might just be too blooming old. Then that leaves only seven times. Oh, babycake, just ponder that for a moment. Only seven times in your whole life – even if you're lucky enough to get to a hundred – might you experience the world as magical as this.'

'... Gosh.'

Gosh indeed, BigBrov.

'And so I've been thinking ... it snowed like this when I was nineteen years old. I worked in a pub, then. The Mistletoe and Firkin it was called.'

'You were a barmaid, weren't you.'

'That's right, babycake. I was a barmaid. And ... oh, I loved that job. And what made it even more perfect was your gran worked there too. She wasn't a barmaid, though. She sang. Every Friday and Saturday night. There was a little stage in the pub – Stage! Ha! Just a couple of beer crates covered with a tablecloth – and a piano so out of tune it set my teeth on edge, but . . . oh, when your gran started to sing, I tell you, that stage was the London Palladium and the piano sounded like . . . like Chopin.'

'What's Chopin?'

'Piano that sounds like fluffy clouds.'

'Gosh.'

Gosh.

'One Saturday night . . . oh, babycake, I remember it so well. Me and your Gran were just leaving the pub – it was just gone midnight – when it started to snow. Your gran squeezed my hand and said, "Ain't it pretty, Sis?" And I said, "Very pretty, Sis." The snow settled so quick. We were giggling and larking about. Mind you, we'd probably knocked back one or two Babychams as well, truth told.'

'What's Babychams?'

'Bubbly drink that makes you giggle.' Aunt Ivy puts an arm round Zip and continues, 'Anyway, to cut a long story short, your gran and me, we got lost. Don't ask how we did it. After all, the pub weren't that far from where we lived. And we'd done the journey hundreds of times. But . . . well, the snow made everything look so different. And street lights weren't too good in those days. We linked arms and held each other very tight. We walked and walked. But still we recognized nothing. Not a single building. Your gran started to cry. I started to cry. Our tears froze on our cheeks. And then . . . then we see them!'

'Who?'

'Two figures are walking towards us out of the snow. Two young men. I feel your gran grab my arm tighter and tighter. And then one of the men calls out, "Hello, there! You two pretty young ladies all right?" And . . . oh, it's the safest-sounding voice I've ever heard. I call back, "Me and my sister are lost." And the two men come over to us. How good-looking they are! We ask them for their names. They tell us Dasher and Dancer!'

'Dasher! That was ... that was Grandad's nickname, wasn't it?'

'That's right. And you could see why. He was so, so dashing. Anyway, Dasher takes your gran's arm and Dancer takes my arm and I take your gran's and, all of us, arm in arm, walk through the snow. Dasher and Dancer take us home. I'd never felt so safe as I felt that night.' She gives Zip another affectionate squeeze. 'Now, I bet you're wondering why I'm telling you all this when the question you asked was about me and your gran shrieking at each other like wildcats. Well ... in a way, this *is* the answer. Our argument wasn't about walking frames. Not really. It was about ... it's about how one day you're nineteen and you're deeply in love, everything in the world gobsmacks you with wonder and then – Bam! You're eighty and love has gone and you know nothing will ever gobsmack you again.'

'Oh, Aunt Ivy, don't say that!' Zip wraps his arms round her. 'There's lots of things to be gobsmacked about. Honest! And I love you. And Newt loves you. And Mum loves you.'

Well said, BigBrov.

'IVVVYYY!! PLEEESS!!'

'That's ya gran, babycake! She wants to make up! I can tell – I'M COMING, HOLLY!! I'M COMING!!'

And Ivy gives Zip a big wet kiss on both cheeks, then rushes out of the hideout and into the house.

Eeeka-eek-clicka-click.

'You helped her a lot, BigBrov.'

'But I didn't *do* anything.'

'You listened. You made her feel her stories were worth telling. That's the most precious gift you can give anyone.'

'But I wish I could've given her more, Apollo. I wish I could've . . . oh, never mind.'

'I know what you were going to say, BigBrov. You wish you could tell Aunt Ivy about me.'

'Well . . . yes!'

'I wish that too, BigBrov. But . . . it cannot be. There is something in me that freezes when an adult is near. I cannot move. All I can do is . . . be pushed — Wait!'

'What, Apollo?'

'I've just had another idea. About how I can help.'

'How?'

'Listen, BigBrov, go to your gran and tell her . . .'

— 32 —

'The trolleee?'

'Gosh, yes, Gran! Don't you see? Use the trolley like it is a walking frame. Let it support you. No one who sees you will think that's what you're doing. They'll just think you're doing the shopping.'

'Oh, babycake, that's a marvellous idea.'

'I wannn do it noowww!'

'Okey-dokey, Gran. But let's get you in some warm clothes first. It's freezing out there.'

'Babycake's right, Sis. Let's get your overcoat on . . . Here!'

'Wannn do it now!'

'And your big boots, Gran . . . Here!'

'And your scarf, Sis ... Here!'

'Nowwww!'

'Okey-dokey, Gran! You're wrapped up snug as a bug in a rug! Let's hit that snow!'

BigBrov and Aunt Ivy are helping Gran out of Home. BigBrov is holding Gran's right arm. Aunt Ivy is holding Gran's left arm. Gran is wrapped up very warm.

'Everything soo boofull inn snooo.'

'Yes, Gran. But please, be careful where you're putting your feet. There're lots of slippery patches.'

'I knowww, Zeee. I not stoopidd.'

'Gosh, Gran, I know that.'

'The boy's just trying to help, Sis.'

'Look, Gran, here's Apoll– I mean, the supermarket trolley. I'll just pop Newt in like this ...'

'Ya!'

'Now, Gran, you grab hold of the push bar ... That's it!'

'Well done, Sis.'

'You got your balance, Gran?'

'Yeahhh, gooo balnce.'

'Okey-dokey. Let's go forward.'

Eeeka ... eek ...

I am moving very slowly and carefully. Gran is holding on to me as best she can. Her feet drag along —

'Remberr songg.'

'What's that, Sis?'

'Gran says she remembers a song.'

'What song, Sis?'

'Abooo snooo.'

'About snow, eh, Gran? I'd like to hear that.'

'Ya-ya, Gri-Gri!'

Eeeka ... eek ... clicka ... click ...

Gran wants to sing it for BigBrov. She wants to sing it so much. She is concentrating so hard. But she can't seem to get the song up through her throat and out of her mouth —

'You don't have to sing, Sis.'

'I wannn singgg!'

Eeeka . . . eek . . . clicka-click . . .

The song begins 'Pretty snowflake'. I can hear it in Gran's head. It was sung to her by . . . by a man . . . A man she loved . . . Her husband. Yes. It was sung to her by Dasher.

'Preettee snowwflarr . . .'

Oh, BigBrov, you must hear this song. Your mum used to hear it when she was a child. It is so beautiful. I will try to help your gran.

'Preettee *snowflake* . . .'

'You said *snowflake*, Gran!'

'I heard it too, Sis.'

'Clear as a bell, Gran!'

'Oh, well done, Sis.'

'Ya-ya, Gri-Gri!'

More, Gran! Come on!

Eeeka-eeka . . . clicka-click . . .

'Pretty snowflake . . .'

'Clearer and clearer, Gran.'

'Keep going, Sis!'

'Ya-ya, Gri-Gri!'

More, Gran!

Eeeka-eeka-clicka-click . . .

'Pretty snowflake, pretty snowflake, you fell to me . . .'

'Gosh! A real tune now.'

Eeekaeekaclickaclick . . .

More, Gran! Come on! You can do it! That's it!

SING!!

> *'Pretty snowflake,*
> *Pretty snowflake,*
> *You fell to me*
> *From high above.*
> *Fluffy, frosty,*
> *Small and gentle*

In my palm,
You're safe, my love.

Pretty snowflake,
Pretty snowflake,
You change your shape
As I look on.
Water now
Is all I'm holding.
All your snowiness
Has gone.

Pretty snowflake,
Pretty snowflake,
Mine for only
A blink of an eye.
I'll miss you so,
My pretty snowflake.
A love like ours
will never die.

— 33 —

Vvvmmmmm . . .

'Glorious!' cries Zip, flopping into an armchair and kicking off his boots. 'And can you hear that, Apollo?'

'Gran and Aunt Ivy are going back into the house with LittleBrov.'

'But they're all *laughing*, Apollo! *Laughing!* Gosh, I never thought I'd hear them laugh like that again.'

'It certainly is a glory rush sound, BigBrov.'

'They've been so unhappy since they left their old houses. They never really wanted to move.'

'Why did they, then, BigBrov?'

'Their rent – it just kept going up and up. And then they were offered money if they came to live here and so ... well, they both said yes. And then Gran had her stroke. And then my dad ... well, let's just say everything went doolally and all the laughter went out of their lives. Until now. And it's all because of you, Apollo.'

'I suppose it is.'

'What do you mean suppose? Gran touched you and you ... made her better.'

'Yes ... I did.'

'But ... how did you do it, Apollo?'

'I don't know, BigBrov. I could feel little broken bits inside Gran. And I just concentrated on these broken bits and then ... they weren't broken any more.'

'Gran's speaking again.'

'And walking!'

'Gosh, Apollo, I wish ... I wish ...'

'What?'

'Oh ... nothing.'

'No, it's not nothing, BigBrov. I know what you were about to say. It's about Mum. Am I right?'

'Yeah.'

'You're wondering if I can help her too.'

'Well, can you?'

'I don't think I can, BigBrov. You see, with Gran there were broken bits that could be healed. Broken bits of her body. But with Mum ...'

'It's different.'

'Yes. With Mum, it's not her body. It's her ... feelings.'

'So ... you can't help at all.'

'Well ... perhaps ... Oh, I wonder!'

'What?'

'Perhaps ... perhaps I *can* do something.'

'What? What?'

Apollo wheels back off the rug. 'Watch!'

'You're rocking 'n' rolling again, Apollo! Gosh, what's going to happen? Hang on! The rug! The rug is ... it's changing colour. The pattern on the carpet is becoming stronger. Roses are turning redder. The leaves are turning greener. All the frayed bits of wool are going – oh, Apollo, the rug is looking as good as new. It looks glorious!'

'I ain't finished yet, BigBrov!'

Gosh!

A green leaf is moving.

A green leaf is moving on the carpet and –

A green leaf is growing up from the carpet.

And another green leaf.

Another.

A stalk.

And –

Gosh!

A bud appears at the top of the stalk.

The bud gets bigger and bigger.

The bud starts to open.

The bud blooms.

And –

Gosh!

Petals start to uncurl.

Petals, petals, petals.

Bright red petals.

And then –

'It's a rose, Apollo. Mum loves roses. I'm going to take it to her now. Oh, thank you, Apollo.'

'You're welcome, BigBrov.'

'Oh, love ... *where*?'

'In the back garden.'

'The back garden *here*?'

'Yes, Mum. *Our* garden.'

'But ... just a single red rose?'

'Yes, Mum. No bush or anything.'

'Just this ... in all the snow. How, love, *how*?'

'No idea, Mum. It was just there ... growing.'

'And you picked it for me and – oh, it smells so wonderful.'

'I know, Mum. And look at the colour. It's so bright. The brightest red!'

'Oh yes, love. I'd forgotten anything could be this bright.' Carol smells it again and feels the petals. 'Soft as velvet. How I love roses. Have done ever since I was a child. Put it in some water for me, love.'

'It needs light too, Mum.' Zip looks round the gloomy room. 'It'll die in here.'

'What's the brightest room in the house?'

'The living room.'

'Then put it there.'

'But ... you can't see it if you're up here.'

'I ... I know what you're trying to do, Zip, but ... I can't get up yet. I want to but ... I can't ... I can't ... Everything is just too painful for me now, Zip. The slightest glimmer of light hurts my eyes. The slightest sound makes my ears ring. It's like I've had a layer of skin removed. Like when you got sunburnt last summer. Remember?'

'Gosh, yes, my shoulders were so sore it hurt if a . . . if a ladybird walked on them.'

'That's what I feel like now, Zip. It feels like even a ladybird could hurt me . . . oh, Zip, Zip.'

'It's all right, Mum.'

'No! It's *not* all right. The Powers That Be could turn up at any minute. And if they see me like this –'

'Don't worry, Mum!'

'But I've *got* to worry. The Powers That Be could take you away from me. You and Newt. And if they did that there'd be nothing left to live for. Nothing!'

'They won't take me from you, Mum!' Zip kneels beside his mum and wraps his arms around her. 'I won't let them! I won't!'

BigBrov is getting upset. I can feel it all the way down here in the garage. He is holding Mum very tight. He doesn't know what to do — BigBrov! Can you hear me, BigBrov! BigBrov!

. . . Apollo?

It's me, BigBrov!

I . . . I can hear you so very clearly now.

And I can hear you so very clearly too.

You're . . . you're talking to my mind.

And you're talking to mine.

Gosh!

Gosh, indeed.

Apollo! Mum is so upset. She wants to get up but she can't. I want to help but . . . I don't know what to do.

What you are doing now is exactly right, BigBrov. Let her know you love her. And . . . put the rose by the window in her room.

Really?

Yes. Long journeys are made up of lots of little steps. So, perhaps Mum's first small step might be to get up and smell the rose.

Okey-dokey, Apollo, whatever you say.

And . . . one more bit of advice, if I may, BigBrov.

Of course. Anything.

It's been a long and emotional day. I suggest you have an early night.

I will, Apollo. And thank you.

For what?

For being me in my head just when I needed you.

I'll always be here, BigBrov. Always.

Goodnight, Apollo.

Sweet dreams, BigBrov.

— 35 —

I'm lying flat on my back. I can feel grass underneath me and smell wild flowers. I can hear insects buzzing. Sunlight shines through my eyelids. I open my eyes and see – oh, the forest is all around me! I get to my feet and start walking. I walk into a field of cornflowers. Bright blue. I am so happy. Oh, look!

The oak tree!

It's so big. Its bark is all twisted and gnarled like ancient –

Wait!

What's happened to it?

The tree's a different shape.

It's . . . it's like it's been pulled in two. One half of the trunk has separated from the other. The branches join the two halves of the trunk like a . . . like a bridge.

Oh, what's going on?

What's happened to the oak tree?

What's happened to the oak tree?

What's happened to the –?

Zip gasps himself awake.

*Oh, gosh! What a dream. More like a nightmare. I hope I
haven't disturbed little brov . . .*

Zip looks down at Newt in the bed beside him.

No. Still sleeping peacefully. That's good.

Zip sits on the edge of the mattress and wipes sweat
from his face with the corner of a sheet.

*Oh, what was that dream all about? The oak tree has never
looked like that before. It's like some giant has come along and
sawn it clean in half – Hang on! I best draw it! You know what
dreams are like. You wake up in the middle of the night and you
think, Oh, that dream was so bizarre I'll never forget it in a
million years. And then, by breakfast, you can't remember anything about it at all . . . Now, I'm sure my sketchbook is under
the bed somewhere.*

Zip feels in the dark until –

*Aha! There it is! And my box of pencils and crayons . . . Aha!
There!*

Zip sits by the window.

It's a good job Dad taught me how to draw.

Zip smudges some of his drawing now.

*That's it! And I mustn't forget the way all the branches
sort of weaved together at the top. Oh, I'm not doing this very
good, but . . . well, at least I won't forget what I saw . . . Bit
more shading along the trunks here . . . Bit more smudging . . .
That's it!*

I wonder if Apollo will know what it means . . .
  BigBrov to Apollo! Can you hear me, Apollo?
  Zzzzzzzz . . .
  Gosh! I can feel Apollo there but all I get is a sort of –
  Zzzz . . .
  Asleep! Well, who would've thought that? Trolleys sleep!
  Zip gets back into bed.
  I won't disturb Apollo now. It can wait. There's still a few hours to go before it's time to get up. I'll ask Apollo after breakfast.
  Zip kisses Newt on the forehead.
  Pleasant dreams, little brov.
  Zip pulls the sheets and blankets up to his chin.
  I wonder what trolleys dream of . . .

— 36 —

'I dreamed it too, BigBrov!'

'You . . . *what*?'

'The oak tree. In the forest.'

'Like in this drawing?'

'Exactly!'

'But . . . how?'

'I don't know. I didn't even know I could sleep until last night. It's never happened before. But perhaps . . . well, perhaps I'm picking habits up from you.'

'Well, it's from me you got the memory of the oak tree.'

'Yes, BigBrov, undoubtedly.'

'Then if the *oak tree* comes from *my* mind –'

'Then the *shape* of it . . . well, that must come from *mine*.'

'Gosh! You're changing the shape of my dreams, Apollo.'

'I don't mean to, BigBrov.'

'Oh, I don't mind at all. Not at all. But the question is . . . *why*?'

'Again, I don't know.'

'You have *no* idea what the oak tree shaped like this means?'

'No. No idea at all — One moment! NabBrov is approaching.'

'Open the door for him, please, Apollo.'

Vvvmmmmm . . .

'Morning, amigos.'

'Top of the morning, Nab.'

'Top of the morning, NabBrov.'

'Hi-hi, Ni-Ni. Whooo Ru-Ru?'

'Rudi's right here, amigo. You wanna play with him?'

'Ya!'

Twitch!

'You see, Nab? I said he'd be safe in the snow.'

'Safe? My baby loves it! – Hey! Don't close the door yet, amigos. I can see Mem heading this way – Morning, Mem!'

'Wotcha, mate. You're here bright and early.'

'So are you.'

'I couldn't wait to get here, mate. Never had mates before, mate. Don't wanna miss a moment of all this mateyness, mates – Wotcha, other mates.'

'Top of the morning, Mem.'

'Top of the morning, MemBrov.'

'Hi-Hi, Mi-Mi.'

'Why you frowning, Zip, mate? Not bad news, I hope, mate.'

'I was about to ask the same question, amigo. What's up?'

MemBrov is putting his arm round NabBrov's shoulders as my BigBrov explains about the dream. And now NabBrov is putting his arm around MemBrov's shoulders. I feel such friendship between these soft and warm things. It is such a safe feeling –

'So, Apollo, amigo, let's get this thing straight … You have *no* idea what made your half of the dream turn the oak tree a doolally shape?'

'None at all, NabBrov.'

'But it must've done it for a reason, mate.'

'I agree, MemBrov. All I can say for sure is … well, when I saw the oak tree shaped like this I had an overwhelming desire to … go through it.'

'Go through it, Apollo?'

'Yes, BigBrov. I can't explain it any better than that. It was as if the shape was … calling me almost. I wanted to wheel forward and … well, as I say, go through. Under the arch of branches.'

'Mates! It's a mystery! Oh, this is just too Elvissy for words. A mystery for a gang of mates to sort out, mates. This is what gangs of mates do, mates. I've seen it in movies, mates. They investigate and – Oh! Mates!'

'What, Mem?'

'What, amigo?'

'What, MemBrov?'

'Whaa, Mi-Mi?'

'We should *call* ourselves something. Don't ya think, mates? All gangs have names, don't they, mates? And we're the most special gang of mates there ever was. I bet no other gang of mates has ever been brought together because of a supermarket trolley. It's made us really close, mates. It's made us more like brothers than – Oh, mates! Mates! That's what we should call ourselves, mates. The Brotherhood of Apollo! Elvissy or what?'

'Sounds a bit secret handshake, global conspiracy to me, amigo.'

'And don't you think it's a bit . . . *male*-based, Mem?'

'What d'ya mean, mate?'

'What our tangle-headed amigo means, my rigorously quiffed amigo, is if we call ourselves The *Brother*hood of Apollo, the *male-based* quality of that name seems to imply that all members have to be . . . well, male! Boys!'

'Stars 'n' bars, that's what we *want*, ain't it, mates? We don't want any soppy, wishy-washy girlies in the gang, do we?'

'But, Mem . . . it shouldn't matter what gender or race or religion anyone is. The only thing that matters is that we are all friends –'

'*That's* what we should call ourselves, amigos.'

'What, Nab?'

'What, mate?'

'Friends of Apollo.'

'Oh, gosh . . . That's glorious!'

'Stars 'n' bars, yeah.'

'Ya-ya.'

'I'm deeply touched, my Brovs.'

THUDDD!

The back door has just crashed open and – Look! There's Aunt Ivy. Her hair looks brighter than ever. And her lipstick is the reddest I've ever seen it. And that blouse is very sparkly –

Hang on! It's . . . it's not Aunt Ivy! It's –

'GRAN!'

'GRI-GRI!'

'That's right, sugarplums! Your Aunt Ivy has given me one of her makeover specials. What d'ya think? Pretty good, eh? Now come on outside! I want to build a snowman! And I want you all to help me! What d'ya say?'

'Oh yes, Gran!'

'Ya-ya, Gri-Gri!'

'Why not, amigo!'

'Sure thing, mate!'

A snowman?

— 37 —

My family is outside in the snow. They are building a snowman. I want to wheel out of the garage and join them so much, but it is not possible. Aunt Ivy and Gran are enjoying themselves. Where's Mum? Oh, there she is! — Apollo to BigBrov! Can you hear me, BigBrov?

Hear you, Apollo!

Look at Mum's window.

She's there!
She got up to smell the rose.
She's made that first step just like you said.
And now she's watching you make the snowman.
Shall I wave or something?
No. Just let Mum watch — NabBrov is about to say something to you.

'Take ya scarf off, amigo!'

'What for, Nab?'

'We'll wrap it round the snowman.'

'Good thinking, mate.'

'It'd suit the snowman, babycake.'

'It would, sugarplum.'

Gran is throwing a snowball at Aunt Ivy. Oh, how similar Gran and Aunt Ivy look. Their hair is so bright against the whiteness of the snow. Now Memphis is throwing a snowball at NabBrov. LittleBrov is playing with Rudi. Oh, how Rudi loves the snow. Everyone is laughing. Even Mum is laughing.

'What shall we use for the snowman's eyes, sugarplum?'

'Two boiled sweets, Sis.'

'Gosh! Perfect, Aunt Ivy!'

'Ya-ya!'

'What shall we use for a mouth, mates?'

'We could try drawing a mouth on, Mem.'

'Here, babycake, use my blusher.'

'Thanks, Auntie – Oh, it's a lovely colour.'

'Cranberry Crush, babycake – Now rub it into the snow! That's it! Luverducks, don't worry about how much you use. Just make sure that snowman gets lips . . .! Very good! Lips luscious enough to kiss. And now – a nose!'

'Gosh, yes! The snowman needs a nose.'

'What we gonna use for that, amigo?'

'What about one of my earrings, babycake?'

'But your earrings are the wrong shape, Aunt Ivy.'

'And a nose should stick out, not dangle, Sis.'

'Well, I've seen a few dangling noses in my time, Sis.'

'But we don't want one on our snowman. Do we, little brov?'

'Ni-ni, Zi-Zi.'

I will help my family. I cannot wheel out there but . . . Yes! I can help them from here. And I will . . .

'Gosh! Look!'

'The snowman, amigos!'

'It's growing a nose, mates!'

'Gro-gro, ya-ya!'

'But, babycakes . . . how?'

'But, sugarplums . . . how?'

BigBrov is looking over in my direction. So is NabBrov and MemBrov and . . . yes! Now LittleBrov. Even Rudi is looking at me! They all know it is me. Perhaps I shouldn't have done it. Look at Aunt Ivy's face. And Gran's. And Mum's. They can't believe what they are seeing.

'Well . . . gosh . . . I . . . I . . .'

Oh, Apollo to BigBrov!

Hearing you, Apollo.

I got carried away. I shouldn't have done it really. It's just that I wanted to be part of building the snowman so much. I couldn't stand being left out. Think of an explanation.

I can't think of anything, Apollo!

Nor can I — Wait! Something's about to happen!

What?

Listen!

'WHERE IS SHE? HMM?'

Where's that voice coming from, Apollo?

It's Mr Brazil, BigBrov.

'I'M MAKING SHELVES FOR HER!'

Mr Brazil is coming back from the supermarket. Look! He has a bag of shopping in each hand. They look very heavy.

He's put too much in each of them.

The plastic is beginning to split —

'SHE MUST COME BACK TO ME!'

'Dad!' cries Nabil, rushing over. 'Dad! Dad!'

'Oh, that poor man, Sis.'

'What a state he's in, Sis.'

'He looks a little . . . well, tipsy, Sis.'

'Tipsy? He's as drunk as a skunk, Sis!'

'His wife died, Auntie and Gran!'

Mr Brazil's shopping bags split and the contents spill all over the icy road.

'He needs help, sugarplums.' Gran rushes over. 'Come on, Sis!'

'Of course, babycake!'

'Zi-Zi? Zi-Zi?'

'Oh, don't worry, little brov,' says Zip, scooping Newt up in his arms. 'Nab's poor dad has . . . has . . .'

'He's spent too much at the supermarket, mate. That's all. Right, mate?'

'Gosh, that's right, Mem. Thank you. Poor Mr Brazil has spent too much at the supermarket and he's just thought of all the money he's spent. But he'll be fine in a couple of minutes. Look, Gran and Aunt Ivy are taking him into the house for a nice cup of tea. And Nab's picked up all the shopping. This is why you must always be careful not to get carried away when you're in a supermarket, little brov – Hey, Mem! Who you phoning?'

'Missy,' replies Memphis. 'In an emergency situation like this we need an emergency rescue, mate, and – MISSY! ME! COULD YOU COME OVER TO MY MATE ZIP'S PLACE, MISSY? THERE'S A BROKEN THING NEEDS A BIT OF STICKING TOGETHER AGAIN!'

— 38 —

Missy is talking to Mr Brazil. I can hear their hushed voices coming from Home. BigBrov and LittleBrov and NabBrov and MemBrov are all in the hideout with me. NabBrov looks very distressed. He is sitting on the sofa stroking Rudi ... BigBrov and MemBrov are sitting on either side of him. They are trying to cheer him up —

'Your dad'll be fine, Nab, you'll see.'

'If anyone can sort him out, mate, Missy can, mate.'

'Listen, amigos! Stop it! I know what you're trying to do. And I'm grateful. But ... oh, holy macaroni, that was my dad out there. My *dad*. Staggering all over the place and making a total idiot of himself –'

'He wasn't making an idiot of himself, Nab.'

'No way, mate. He was just ... distressed.'

'He was *sozzled*! Don't pussyfoot round the subject. *You* know it. *I* know it. We *all* know it.' Nab sighs deeply and gazes at the floor. 'Dad's been drinking like a fish since Mum popped her clogs. At first he used to hide the bottles but since we moved here he don't even bother doing that – Oh, I wish I knew what was being said in there!'

I can feel NabBrov's sadness. It is like too much heavy shopping crushing my rubber wheels. I must try to help —

'I can ... let you hear inside Home, NabBrov.'

'Wh ... What d'ya mean, amigo?'

'I will bring their voices to you through the radio.'

'Gosh! Can you do that, Apollo?'

Crackle, Crackle. '... all lose things, babycake ...'
Crackle, crackle.

'Holy macaroni, Apollo! You did it. Hang on! My dad's talking!'

'It ... it would have been easier ...' – Mr Brazil's voice comes through loud and clear – '... if I hadn't felt I had to deal ... with the loss ... alone.'

'What do you mean *alone*, babycake?'

'You have your *son*, sugarplum.'

'And surely your son is a great comfort, Mr Brazil. Certainly my little Trix– I mean, Memphis – is a comfort to me.'

'I wish Missy would stop getting my name wrong, mates.'

'She's trying her best, Mem.'

'Shush, amigos! It's Dad.'

'But ... Hmm? ... It would have been easier for me if I had to comfort him, you see. If ... if Nabby had been ... upset and ... oh, comforting him would have helped me. Don't you see that?'

'Of course I do, lamb,' says Missy. 'But I can't believe your son didn't need lots of hugs and cuddles and –'

'No!' says Mr Brazil. 'He didn't. He just went on with his life as if nothing had happened –'

'Nothing happened! Holy macaroni! I tried to be strong for you, Dad! For you!'

Crackle, crackle. 'All he does is lock himself in his room and play with Rudolph.'

'Rudolph, lamb?'

'Oh! That's his ferret. Rudi. It was the last thing his mum bought for him before she ... she ... The ferret had such a red nose when she got it home. Must've had a chill or something. I called it Rudolph and the name stuck.'

'Oh, that's lovely, babycake.'

'You know what I think? I think my son's more

interested in playing with that ferret than me ... or remembering his mum –'

'Turn it off, Apollo! Now! I don't wanna hear another blooming word!'

'NabBrov, I'm sorry if I –'

'It ain't your fault, amigo. You didn't know what he was going to say. Oh, holy macaroni, I hate feeling like this. Hate it! Look at me. Tears coming and stuff! It's like ... like a big, prickly thing is opening up in me skull and it's making me – Listen! Apollo! Can you zoom us somewhere else?'

'Where, NabBrov?'

'Anywhere ... so long as it's away from here and there's no one else around.'

'The edge of town, mates!'

'Holy macaroni, yeah!' exclaims Nabil, climbing into the trolley and tucking Rudi into his fur coat. 'The edge. The very edge. The edgier the better.'

'Gosh, let me check the coast is clear first – Apollo! The door, please.'

Vvvmmmmm ...

'Clear, mate?'

'Totally clear. Everyone's too engrossed in the house to notice anything and ... not a soul in sight anywhere. That the way you feel it too, Apollo?'

'It is, BigBrov. But I will move as fast as possible just in case.'

'How fast can you move, mate?' asks Memphis, climbing in.

'That,' says Apollo, 'is what we're about to find out. Everybody ready?'

'Yes, Apollo.'

'Yeah, amigo.'

'Yeah, mate.'

'Ya-ya, Apple-loo!'

'Then let's rock 'n' roll!'

Everything around them turns white!
A radiant white!
A blinding flash!
And –
'GOOOOOSSSSSSHHHHH –'
'HOLYYMACOORRONII –'
'STAARSSNNBAARRSS –'
'YAAAYAAAYAAAYAA –'

— **39** —

'– HHHHHHHHHH!!'
   '– IIIIIIIIIIIIIIIIII!!'
   '– SSSSSSSSSSSS!!'
   '– AAAAAAAAAA!!'
'The edge of town, my Brovs. See? The nearest completed house
is way over there . . . or should I say *down* there.'
   'Gosh, yes. We're on a hill.'
   'We can see for miles and miles, mates.'
   'Look at the motorway, amigos! It's like a . . . a snake of
twinkling lights going on forever.'
   'The snow as well, mate. That goes on forever too,
mate.'
   'Climb out of me, my Brovs, and have a look around.'
   'Gosh!'
   'Holy macaroni!'
   'Stars 'n' bars!'
   'Ya!'

My Family is gazing at the view now. BigBrov is holding LittleBrov in his arms. NabBrov is holding Rudi. MemBrov is gently humming a song. The sun is setting. And — oh, look! All the street lights in New Town have come on. My Brovs have all gasped at such a sight. Oh, how wonderful to be here with them like this.

'You know what I've been wondering, mates?'

'What, Mem?'

'The trees! Look at them. No leaves. Nothing.'

'Well, it *is* winter, Mem.'

'But what's gonna happen in spring, mate? These are *plastic* trees. They ain't gonna blossom in May and have green leaves by June and red leaves in October. Are they? Eh?'

'Their tops unscrew.'

'What's that, Nab?'

'Ain't you read the "New Town Brochure"? It explains everything. What we're looking at now, amigos, are trees with their winter tops on. When spring comes along The Powers That Be come round and unscrew the winter tops and replace them with tops that have leaves on. We keep the leaves until November when –'

'The winter tops are screwed back on, mate.'

'Exactamundo. In other words we're living in a place where spring and autumn no longer exist. Just winter and summer. And if that ain't the most doolally thing you've ever heard, then I don't know what is.'

'Yeah . . . it's doolally, mate.'

'Gosh, yes, Nab. Doolally.'

'Doolly-lally! Ya!'

How relaxed my Brovs are with each other. It's like they've known each other all their lives. I'm so lucky to be here with such soft and warm things.

'No, Apollo,' says Zip, snuggling close to Apollo's metal frame. 'It's *us* who are lucky to be here with *you*.'

'Aha! You read my mind, did you, BigBrov?'

'What's this?' says Nabil, leaning on Apollo's push bar and looking at Zip. 'Mind-reading?'

'Yeah . . . me and Apollo – we can do it, Nab.'

'When did this start, mate?'

'Almost from the beginning, I guess, Mem. We started feeling each other's feelings. Then that got stronger and stronger. And now we –'

'Trollepathy!' exclaims Nabil. 'That's what it is!'

'Oh, very good, NabBrov.'

'Can you trollepathize with me, mate?'

'I don't think so, MemBrov, no.'

'What about me, amigo?'

'No, NabBrov. Not you either. I don't know why. LittleBrov can hear my thoughts. And I can trollepathize with Rudi too.'

'My baby!'

'Watch!'

Hello, Rudi.

Twitch!

'Elvissy!'

Zip, Nabil, Memphis, Newt and Rudi all snuggle up close to Apollo.

'Oh, BigBrov . . . I wish this moment could go on forever and ever. Like the snow.'

'Gosh, me too, Apollo. Forever like the snow.'

And, for a few minutes, they remain silent and still, gazing at the snow all round and feeling the warmth of their friendship pulse between them.

'Amigos . . . I'm just thinking – we're now up here. And we were down there. Right?'

'Yes, Nab.'

'Yeah, mate.'

'Ya-ya, Ni-Ni.'

'That's correct, NabBrov.'

'And we got up here from down there, not just very quick, but without feeling a single jolt or bump. So . . .

— 131 —

Apollo, you must be gliding a little above the ground to avoid all these jolts and bumps. Right?'

'I suppose I must, NabBrov.'

'So you're . . . hovering.'

'I suppose so, NabBrov.'

'What you getting at, Nab?'

'What I'm getting at, amigo, is this! If Apollo hovers higher . . . then higher . . . then higher still . . . then surely the hovering will become . . . *flying*!'

'Flying!' gasps Apollo. Then, after a moment, adds, 'Well . . . yes. I suppose I *must* be able to fly. I had just never thought about it in that way before . . . Get in me! All of you. Quick! Come on. Now!'

'Gosh! You mean –?'

'I do!'

'Amigo! You're gonna –?'

'I am!'

'With us inside, mate?'

'Of course!'

'Glorious! But –'

'But what, BigBrov?'

'Well, hovering's one thing –'

'But flying?'

'That's another, Apollo.'

'It's *better*, amigo!'

'It's *higher*, Nab!'

'Don't be nervous, mate.'

'I'm not nervous! I'm worried about –'

'LittleBrov, BigBrov?'

'Gosh, yes.'

'I wanna flyy!'

'Newt wants to fly, amigo!'

'I'm *responsible* for him, Nab!'

'So am I, BigBrov.'

'Yes, I know but –'

'Come on, amigo!'

'Come on, mate!'
'Ya-ya, Zi-Zi.'
'Gosh, I don't know –'
'Holy macaroni, I'm getting in!'
'Me too, mate!'
'Pleess, Zi-Zi!'
'You will all be safe, BigBrov!'
'Of course we will, amigo!'
'Trust me, BigBrov.'
'. . . Okey-dokey, little brov! Come on! In you get!'
'. . . You all comfortable, my Brovs?'
'Yes.'
'Yeah.'
'Yeah.'
'Ya-ya!'
'Then . . . prepare!'

— 40 —

'You're shaking, Apollo!'
  'You're rattling, amigo!'
  'Rock 'n' rolling, mate!'
  'Ya-ya!'
  'Watch this, my Brovs!'
  'Gosh! We're lifting!'
  'Hovering, amigos.'
  'Floating, mates.'
  'Ya-ya!'
  'And now, my Brovs . . .'

'Higher!'
'Higher!'
'Higher!'
'Ya-ya!'
Gosh! We're moving away from the hill.
'The ground's getting lower, amigos!'
'The sky's getting closer, mates!'
'Ta mooo . . . ta mooo.'
'You see, BigBrov? Everything's safe.'
'I know, Apollo. Very safe!'
'It's incredible, amigos!'
'It's Elvissy, mates!'
'Gosh . . . we're swooping!'
'Holy macaroni!'
'Stars 'n' bars!'
'Ya-ya!'
'Look at the houses, amigo!'
'So small, mate! And the supermarket!'
'It's like a tiny box full of fairy lights, Mem.'
'Oh, look how beautiful the street lights appear from up here —'
JOLT!
'Apollo! What happened?'
'Everything OK, amigo?'
'You've never jolted like that before, mate.'
'I know, my Brovs. And I don't know what's causing —'
JOLT! JOLT!
'Aha! Now I know, my Brovs! Look! Over there . . .' Apollo swoops
lower. 'You see it? Ahead of us. Beside the pile of plastic trees. Oh, it
has fallen over. It is on its side. Oh, look! You see? You see?'
'Gosh!'
'Holy macaroni!'
'Stars 'n' bars!'
'Ya-ya!'
'Exactly, my Brovs . . . it is a trolley!'

— 41 —

The trolley has a dent in one side (as if someone heavy has been using it as a seat) and two of its wheels are severely buckled. Inside are empty cans of drink (mostly beer), a few empty takeaway pizza boxes, screwed-up newspapers and lots of cigarette butts.

Apollo lands –

Gosh! So smoothly!

– and wheels up alongside.

Eeeka-eek-clicka-click . . .

'Poor trolley, eh, mates?'

'Trollee inn snooo,' says Newt.

'Yes, little brov. The poor trolley has been left in the snow.'

'Poor snooo trollee . . . poor snooo trollee . . .'

'Who could do such a thing, amigo?'

Eeeka-eek . . .

'My Brovs, this trolley has been used as a . . . *rubbish bin!*'

'Holy macaroni, I'd like to get my hands on whoever did this!'

'Me too, mates!'

'It's . . . it's trolleyphobia!' spits Nabil.

'They need to have someone sit on them!' cries Zip.

'They need to have pizza boxes thrown in them!' cries Memphis.

'Ya! Ya! Ya!' cries Newt.

'My Brovs! Please! Stop! No anger! All we can do now is . . . try to help this poor trolley — Wait! Danger! Something bad is getting near!'

'Gosh, what?'

'What, amigo?'

'What, mate?'

'Wha?'

'Look, my Brovs! There! A black van is heading this way!'

'I see it,' says Zip. 'It's got ... something written down the side. It says ...'

'TROLLEY SEARCH!' cries Nabil.

'It's from the supermarket, mates!'

'They're after you, amigo!'

'Fly, Apollo, fly!'

'Quick, mate! It's getting closer!'

'Apollo?'

'Apollo, amigo?'

'Apollo, mate?'

'Apple-loo?'

But Apollo doesn't move.

'Oh, no!' gasps Zip. 'Apollo is frozen!'

— 42 —

The van crunches to a halt beside them.

For a moment it waits there, engine throbbing, steam rising from its front, like a wild animal about to pounce.

Who's driving? I can't see –

'Zi-Zi!'

'Don't be scared, little brov.'

Clunk!

The van door is opening!

A black boot appears . . .

Another black boot . . .

Oh, no! No!

Dark glasses!

Bald head!

It's Guard Krick!

My Brovs are so scared. I can feel their fear. I want to help them. I want to speed them away somewhere safe. And yet . . . I cannot move. No matter how hard I try. I cannot move!

'We meet again, misterzzz,' says Guard Krick, his dark glasses glinting, his gold teeth glistening, his bald head gleaming. 'Kids! Nothing but trouble. They lie. They cheat. They steal.'

'We ain't stolen anything, mate!'

'Gosh, no!'

'Nah!'

'Noo!'

'If you didn't steal anything, misterzzz . . . what's this?' Guard Krick points at the fallen trolley. 'And this?' Pointing at Apollo. 'Are they Scotch mist? Are they vagrant offspring of the duck-billed platypus? No, misterzzz, they are not! They are supermarket trolleys. And who *owns* these supermarket trolleys?'

'Gosh, no one should *own* trolleys!'

'These are *free* things!'

'Stars 'n' bars! *Free!*'

'SHUT GOBS, MISTERZZZ! These trolleys belong to the supermarket! Now, you might've been able to get away with sneaking them out before. But not any more, misterzzz. I have persuaded the supermarket management to change its policy. Yes! Me! Guard Krick. I told the management, "You don't understand the ways of trolleys. You don't understand the ways of children. You don't understand the ways of trolleys and children together. But I do! And I am telling you, management – I am *warning* you, management – DO NOT ALLOW TROLLEYS OFF THE PREMISES!" – And, I'm glad to say, the management heeded my words.'

'Told you, mates!'

'SHUT GOB, MISTER . . . Or is it *Miss*?'

Oh, no!

Oh, no! Guard Krick is prowling round Memphis. He is nodding and grinning. Look at his gold teeth flashing.

'You ain't no *mister*, mister!'

'I *am*!'

'Do you think I'm a fool?'

'Well, I think we should take a vote on it!' mutters Nabil.

'SHUT GOB, MISTER. Otherwise I'll take that rat off your shoulder and turn it into a draught excluder.'

'It ain't a rat! And if you dare hurt one whisker –'

'DON'T YOU DARE THREATEN ME!' He stands in front of them, his dark glasses reflecting their four terrified faces. 'You're too undisciplined to threaten me! All of you are too snivelling, too weak, too spoilt. A cold shower is what you need! Boiled string to eat. No popcorn when you watch telly. Nothing fizzy to drink. Just water. Warm water. Warm water with maggots floating in it. Five hours' sleep a night. Dreaming not allowed. And you know why you need all these things? Because you need to be saved, you pathetic little puppies. You need to be saved from getting too soft. Because if you get too soft, you start wanting affection. Listen to my words. Do not get close to things. And especially not . . . TROLLEYS!!'

He's grabbed hold of the fallen trolley!

'Leave that trolley alone!' yells Zip.

Oh, my brave BigBrov!

'SHUT GOB, MISTER!' Guard Krick strides over to the

black van, holding the trolley above his head. 'This trolley is going back to the supermarket and there's nothing you can do to stop me!'

'But – gosh! – it's injured. I mean, damaged.'

'SHUT GOBS, MISTER!' Guard Krick opens the doors at the back of the van. 'If the trolley is no longer functional I have a special way of curing them.'

'What way?' asks Zip.

'I CHOP THEM UP!' Guard Krick throws the trolley into the back of the van. 'In fact, to teach you a lesson in just how cruel and unfair the world can truly be, I think I'm gonna cure this trolley real good. And . . .' he points to Apollo '. . . *that* trolley too! You hear me, misterzzz? Both these trolleys are gonna be . . . CHOPPED TO PIECES!'

— 43 —

'No!' cries Zip. 'You can't! It's not fair!'

'It's wicked!' cries Nabil.

'It's cruel!' cried Memphis.

'Ya!'

'That's what the world is like, misterzzz.' Guard Krick strides over and gives them a shark-like grin. 'It's cruel and wicked and unfair. And the sooner you realize that the sooner you'll be able to cope. And now –'

He's grabbed me!

Apollo!

'– this trolley is for the chop too, misterzzz!'

'THAT AIN'T NO TROLLEY!' yells Zip. 'THAT'S MY FRIEND!'

'AND MINE!'

'AND MINE!'

'YA!'

BigBrov has grabbed Guard Krick round the waist. NabBrov has grabbed Guard Krick round the neck. LittleBrov is kicking Guard Krick's shin. And MemBrov —

'YEEE-HAA!' cries Memphis, striking a very impressive kung fu position. 'I learnt this from the King, mates. He liked all this stuff, mates.'

Guard Krick is spinning round and round now —

'GET OFF ME, MISTERZZZ!!'

Oh, no! NabBrov has been thrown —

'Ommpph!'

— into the snow. BigBrov is hanging on but —

'Ooompph!'

BigBrov is in the snow too. LittleBrov keeps kicking and kicking. Oh, no! Guard Krick is picking LittleBrov up with one hand —

'Leave my brother alone!'

'Leave amigo alone!'

'YEEE-HAA!'

Guard Krick drops LittleBrov —

'Ooompph!'

— into the snow. Oh, I don't want any of my Brovs to get hurt! BigBrov! Can you hear me? Apollo to BigBrov! Apollo to BigBrov!

Hear you, Apollo!

Don't put yourselves in danger — oh, no!

Guard Krick has grabbed you!

BigBrov!

He's taking you to the van!

BIGBROV!!

'APOLLO!'

'AMIGO!'

'MATE!'

'APPLE-LOO!'

Oh, help ... help ... MemBrov is still doing kung fu movements —

'YEEE-HAA! YEEE-HAA!'

'Is that all ya gonna do, amigo?'

'It's all I know *how* to do, mate! I've never got beyond lesson two.'

I'm nearly at the van! BigBrov!

'Say goodbye to freedom, trolley,' sneers Guard Krick.

What can we do, Apollo? What? Guard Krick is too strong for me and Newt. Mem knows how to pose a kung fu kick but not how to use it. Oh, what can we do? What? What?

Don't panic, BigBrov. I have an idea — RUDI! CAN YOU HEAR ME?

Twitch!

Yes!! Rudi can hear me — RUDI! YOU'VE GOT TO DISTRACT GUARD KRICK! DO YOU UNDERSTAND?

Twitch!

THEN RUN UP HIS LEG! NOOWWW!!

And suddenly, Rudi is running!

Running towards Guard Krick ...

'Baby!' cried Nabil. 'What ya doing?'

'AAAAAHHHH!! THE RAT IS ON ME!!'

This is your chance, BigBrov! Quick!

'This is our chance, everyone!' cries Zip. 'Quick!'

MemBrov must push me!

'Mem! Push Apollo!'

'You got it, mate!'

MemBrov has got hold of me! Oh, how safe I feel with MemBrov's hands on my push bar — Call NabBrov, BigBrov!

'Nab! Come on! Quick!'

'I'm not leaving without Rudi,' says Nabil, watching as the ferret scarpers down one of Guard Krick's sleeves.

'Get the rat off me! I hate rats! All soldiers hate rats! AAAHHHHH!'

Apollo! Nab will never make a run for it without Rudi!

I will call Rudi away from Guard Krick, BigBrov. Get ready to run!
Okey-dokey.
RUDI! GO TO NABBROV! NOW!
Twitch!
Rudi scarpers away from Guard Krick.
'My baby!'
Twitch!
'Run, Nab! Mem – push!'
'Here we go, mates!'
Eekaeekaclickaclick.
'I'M GONNA GET YOU, MISTERZZZ!'
*MemBrov can run so fast. MemBrov's legs must be so strong.
But –*
'You two mates are holding me up, mates. Both of you –
in Apollo now! Quick!'
You took the words out of my metal frame.
'Come on, Nab! In we get. That's it! Budge over a bit!'
'That OK, amigo?'
'Perfect!'
Eekaeekaclickaclickeekaeekaclickaclickeeka ...
BigBrov! I don't want to alarm you but –
Gosh! Guard Krick is approaching the van!
Guard Krick is getting in the van.
'Faster, Mem!'
'Faster, amigo!'
'Fasser, Mi-Mi!'
Guard Krick has started the van!
The van's moving.
He's after us!
'Mem!'
'Amigo!'
'Mi-Mi!'
'I'm going as fast as I can, mates. But I don't know if my
strong-boy legs can outrun a van. Wrong! I *do* know! And
they *can't*! You hear me, mates! *They can't!*'

— 44 —

Apollo! Are you sure you're still frozen?
  Afraid so.
So there's no chance of rock 'n' rolling us somewhere safe?
  None.
'The van's getting closer, amigos – Faster, Mem!'
'I'm trying, mate! I'm trying!'
Turn left — here!
'Turn left, Mem!'
Eekaeekaclicka – tuuurrrnnn!
See that empty house there?
You mean the one that's not finished yet?
Exactly. Go in there!
'Go into that empty house, Mem!'
Eekaeekaclick – inntoo hoouuussse!
'But there's no windows in this house, amigo!'
'And no wall over there, mate!'
'Guard Krick will see us, amigo!'
Not if we go to the cellar.
'Not if we go to the cellar!'
'And where's that, amigo?'
'Under the staircase, I suppose. Like in our houses!'
'The staircase ain't been built yet, mate.'
'Hard to get bearings, amigo!'
That hole in the floorboard over there!
'Apollo says it's over there! The hole in the floor!'
Hurry! Guard Krick has just parked outside.

'Hurry! Guard Krick has just parked outside!'

MemBrov is carrying me down with LittleBrov still inside. Oh, it's dark and very damp down here. I will rust very quickly if left too long in these conditions —

'Zi-Zi?'

'Don't worry, little brov!'

'If he catches us down here we're trapped, amigo!'

'I know, Nab.'

Klack!

Guard Krick is in the house.

— 45 —

You still frozen, Apollo?

I'm . . . beginning to defrost.

Really?

Yes.

So you could get us out of here soon?

So long as Guard Krick don't come down here too quickly —

Klack!

Klack!

Klack!

He's right above us.

Yes.

Newt is scared!

Hold him, BigBrov.

Who's going to hold me?

Imagine I am.

Klack!
Klack!
Klack!
He's approaching the hole in the floor.
I know, Apollo.
Are we in the darkest corner?
We are — Oh, no!
KLACK!
He's at the top of the cellar steps!

My Brovs are trembling with fear. If I was made of flesh and blood I'm sure I'd be trembling too. If Guard Krick would only stay up there for another minute, I'm sure I'd be defrosted enough to —

KLACK!
KLACK!
He's coming down the steps!
KLACK!
KLACK!
KLACK!
KLACK!
KLACK!
Guard Krick is in the cellar!
Apollo?
The defrosting has stopped.
So . . . we're trapped.
In a word . . . yes.

— 46 —

Guard Krick has taken his dark glasses off!
   What scary eyes.
   Like bits of broken glass.
   KLACK!!
   He can't see us yet, can he?
   No. His broken-glass eyes need to adjust.
   'Misterzzz . . . you here?'
   I can feel BigBrov's heart thumpa-thumpa-thumpa! If I had a heart
it would be thumpa-thumpa-thumpa too!
   Oh, Apollo! You've got to do something!
   But I don't know what —
   Try anything, Apollo! Anything!
   Keep calm, BigBrov! Let me think —
   Klack!
   Think quick!
   KLACK!!
   Go away, Guard Krick! The misterzzz are not here! Say after me.
The misterzz are not here. The misterzzz are not here.
   'The misterzz are . . . not . . .'
   The misterzz are not here.
   'The misterzzz are not here!'
   He's turning around!
   So I see.
   He's going back up the stairs.
   So he is.
   You did that, didn't you?

I don't like to boast.

KLACK!
KLACK!
KLACK!
KLACK!
KLACK!
We're safe!
We are, BigBrov.
'Phew,' sighs Zip.
'Phew,' sighs Nab.
'Phew,' sighs Mem.
'Poo,' sighs Newt.
Twitch!
And that's when –
BZZZ! BZZZ!
My mobile!!

— **47** —

'MISTERZZZ!' roars Guard Krick, descending the steps again. 'So you're here after all, eh? Hiding in the dark like hunted animals. In a minute my eyes will get used to this dark and I will see you as well as smell you. And what will I see? What pathetic sight will greet my eyes? I'll tell you. Four terrified faces. Eight eyes wide with terror. Sweat will be trickling from foreheads. Sweat will be trickling down backs. Am I right, misterzzz?'

Yes.

Yes.

'Of *course* I'm right. And what else will I see? Eh, misterzzz? Oh yes, I nearly forgot ... I will see *a trolley*.' He takes a step forward. 'I bet you're all holding on to the trolley now, right, misterzzz? You're trying to protect the trolley. You think the trolley is your friend. Am I right?'

Yes.

Yes.

'And *how* do you know the trolley is your friend? After all, a trolley is just metal and plastic and rubber.' He takes another step forward. 'Well, *this* trolley can be your friend, can't it, misterzzz? Eh? And *why* can this trolley be your friend? Because ... it's *alive!*'

He knows!

He knows!

'I know what you're thinking, misterzzz. He knows! And, yes, I do know. I know everything. I know more about these trolleys than you will ever know. I've had *years* of experience. And that's why you've got to trust me in what I'm about to say ... *Do not trust your trolley!*'

What does he mean?

What does he mean?

'You think that trolley is your friend and I am your enemy. But you've got it all wrong, misterzzz. I'm trying to help you. I'm trying to save you from the clutches of that ... *thing!*' Another step forward. 'That trolley will turn you against your family! It will turn you against your friends! Trust me!'

Don't!

I won't!

'I bet you already want to be with the trolley night and day, don't you? I bet you already prefer its company to almost everyone else in the world, don't you? And this is

— 148 —

only the beginning, misterzzz. Pretty soon you won't be able to do without it. Not for one second! Nothing else will matter to you except being with the trolley.' Another step. 'Aha! My eyes are beginning to get used to the gloom now. Is that you in the corner? Is it? Eh? Oh, answer me, misterzzz. Please. Join hands with me and let us rid the world of this deceitful trolley –'

I've got to do something!

'– this deceitful trolley –'

now!!

And, suddenly, there's a flash of light.

And a whoosh of sound.

And –

'GOOOOOOOSSSSSSSHHHHHHH –'

'HOOOLLLYYYMMMACARONIIIII –'

'STAARRRSSNNNBARRRRSSSSS –'

'YAYAYAYAAYAAAYAAAYAA –'

— 48 —

'– HHHHHHHHHHHHHHHHHHHHH!!'

'– IIIIIIIIIIIIIIIIIIIIIIIIIIIIIIIIIIIIIIIIIIIIIII!!'

'– SSSSSSSSSSSSSSSSSSSSSSSSSSSS!!'

'– AAAAAAAAAAAAAAAAAAAA!!'

We're back!

'All safe, my Brovs. No one can harm us while we're here!'

'Gosh . . . I'm . . . I'm . . .'

'Breathless, amigo!'

'That was Elvissy, mates!'

Listen to my Brovs. They are buzzing with things. So excited that they can barely breathe. And they're going over every detail of what has just happened —

Wait!

One by one ... my Brovs are staring at me. 'What, my Brovs?'

'Oh ... gosh! Nothing, Apollo ...'

But it's not nothing. I know what it is. They are remembering those nasty things Guard Krick said about me. They are wondering ...

'You are wondering ... can you trust me.'

'No, Apollo.'

'Nah, amigo.'

'Nah, mate.'

'Ni-ni, Apple-loo.'

'Listen to me, please ... I do not know why Guard Krick said what he said. I do not know why he hates trolleys so much.'

'It's irrational, ain't it, amigo?'

'What's irrational?' asks Zip.

'I'll tell ya what irrational is, mate!' says Memphis forcefully. 'It's neighbours throwing bricks through windows cos they don't like the clothes you wear! It's the church you've belonged to all ya life – the very church ya very own dad preaches at – telling ya you're not welcome any more cos you're a sinner. It's ya so-called mates shutting their doors in ya face cos they don't like the sound of ya voice. It's putting nasty letters through ya letter box and scrawling nastier things on the front of your house. Even though ya ain't hurting anyone, would never hurt anyone, could never hurt anyone and ... and ...' Memphis slows down and looks round at the others. 'Anyway ... that's what irrational is, mate. Hope the explanation's helped.'

'I'm sure it's helped a lot, MemBrov.'

'Yeah, Mem. Thanks.'

'Holy macaroni! Best description I've ever heard.'

'My Brovs, please listen to me ... I would never harm any of you. I would never try to turn you away from friends or family. Please say you want me here.'

'Oh, Apollo!' cries Zip. 'Of *course* we want you here!'

'We want you here, Apollo!' cries Nabil.

'We want you here, Apollo!' cries Memphis.

'We wannoo ear, Apple-loo!' cries Newt.

Apollo says, 'And I want to be here with all of you too, my Brovs. Forever and ever!'

And, one by one, they lay their hands on the metal frame of Apollo.

'Holy macaroni, that's enough mushy stuff for one day, I think. Amigo, what about those boots you promised me? Is the offer still open?'

'Of course, Nab. It's silly you having cold feet when there's spare boots in – oh, what box? Let me think ... Mmm, yes! That one over there. The big one with brown sticky tape on.'

'I see it! Nah, you stay where you are, amigo. I'll get them ... Let's have a look ... Holy macaroni, the inside of this box smells disgusting.'

'That's the forest, Nab.'

'Forest, mate?'

'Where I used to live, Mem,' explains Zip. Then adds in a whisper, 'I don't like talking about it too much. It upsets little brov.'

'Gotcha, mate,' Memphis whispers back.

'Well, if it smells like mouldy underpants,' whispers Nabil, 'you're best not to mention it to anyone – Aha!! Boots! Mmm ... They look a bit big to me, amigo.'

'Put an extra pair of socks on, Nab. A thick pair.'

'Hang on! There's something in this boot, amigo.'

'Yeah, ya foot, mate!'

'Not that one, amigo – This one! Look! It's a letter!'

A letter?

A letter?

'Looks a bit crumpled, amigo.'

'And it ain't been opened, mate.'

Why am I nervous?

'Amigo ... you should see this.'

'Yeah, mate.'

I'm so nervous.

Look at it, BigBrov.

Zip goes over and reads:

> To my son, Zip
> From his loving Dad
> (To be opened in the event of my death)

— 49 —

Can a human being freeze? Because that's what I feel like. I can't move. I can barely breathe.

'What's wrong, mate?'

'His dad's a popped clog.'

'You mean *dead*, mate?'

Nab nods, then whispers in Memphis's ear. 'He don't like to talk about it.'

'Gotcha, mate,' Memphis whispers back.

'Amigo, come and sit down.'

Where am I? I'm sitting down on a sofa. Two people are sitting on either side of me. Who are they? Do I know them ...?

Oh yes, of course. It's Nab and Mem. They are my friends. Oh, where's little brov –?

'Newt? Newt?'

'He's right here, amigo.'

'I'll put him in your lap, mate.'

'Do you want some lemonade or something, amigo?'

'No, no . . . Where's Apollo?'

'I'm here, BigBrov.'

'My dad, Apollo. My dad wrote me this . . .'

'I know, BigBrov.'

This is my dad's handwriting.

And there's a smudge of earth.

A smudge in the shape of a thumbprint.

This is my dad's thumbprint.

'What's it doing in a boot, mate?'

'I'm not sure . . . I don't . . . Apollo?'

'I can feel that . . . your dad knew he was about to do something that . . . might be dangerous. Is that right, BigBrov?'

'. . . Yes. That's right, Apollo.'

'What was it, mate?'

'Don't ask questions!' snaps Nabil.

'Your dad didn't want to worry you by giving you this letter face to face, BigBrov. So he put this letter in your boot —'

'Where he knew I'd find it.'

'If anything happened to him, yes. He knew you would find it eventually. And if nothing happened to him —'

'Then Dad would remove it without me knowing.'

'Exactly, BigBrov.'

This is my dad's handwriting.

And there's a smudge of earth.

A smudge in the shape of a thumbprint.

This is my dad's thumb–

'Da-da, Zi-Zi!'

'Oh, Newt!' Zip wraps his arms round his brother and

kisses the top of his head. 'It's all right. We mustn't get upset, must we? Dad wouldn't want –'

THUDDD!

The back door has thumped open again and –

'SUGARPLUMS!'

'BABYCAKES!'

Gran and Aunt Ivy are standing there, arm in arm, looking brighter and bolder than ever.

'What's been keeping you, sugarplums? We've been waiting and waiting for you. Ain't we, Sis?'

'We have, Sis!'

'Waiting for what?' asks Zip.

'Didn't you get me text message?' asks Gran. 'I sent it ages ago. Didn't I, Sis?'

'You did, Sis!'

'Oh . . . gosh! Yes! I forgot to read –'

'Well, read it now, sugarplum!'

'Then do what it says, babycake!'

They go back inside the house.

Zip gets the mobile from his pocket and reads:

WE'RE HAVING A PARTY! JOIN US!

— 50 —

There is music. There is food. Gran and Aunt Ivy are dancing. They are kicking their legs and wriggling their hips. They are each holding a glass of gin and tonic in one hand and a sandwich in the other.

'Give us a twirl, Sis! Go on!'

'You give one too, Sis! Go on!'

BigBrov has tucked the letter from his dad under a sofa cushion. BigBrov says he's not ready to read the letter now anyway.

I am glad this party came along when it did. The atmosphere in here was getting a bit sad and —

Apollo! Can you hear me?

Loud and clear, BigBrov. Are you enjoying the party?

Yes. Mr Brazil is sitting on the sofa and smiling. He's not drinking anything alcoholic, I'm pleased to say. He's admiring the way Gran and Aunt Ivy are dancing —

'You two look like – Hmm? – you could still dance most teenagers off the dance floor.'

'Come and join us, sugarplum!'

'Let yourself go, babycake!'

'Oh – Hmm? – all right. Why not?'

Gosh! Mr Brazil is dancing with Gran and Aunt Ivy.

So I see. Most amusing.

Missy is coming out here to the kitchen now —

'What are all you young lambs doing out here?'

'I – well, gosh – I like watching you all enjoying yourselves, Missy.'

'I'm always in the kitchen at parties, amigo.'

'I go where my mates go, Missy.'

'Ya! Ya!'

'Well, so long as you're all having a good time, lambs. That's the main thing. Oh, Zip, lamb. Your gran and aunt are the partiest party girls I've ever seen. From a distance and if you screw your eyes up, they look about nineteen.'

'Everyone looks nineteen if you screw your eyes up and look at them from a distance, amigo.'

'Your dad don't, mate.'

'Very true, amigo.' Nab leans towards Zip and whispers, 'You're trollepathizing with Apollo again, ain't ya?'

'How can you tell?'

'You get this odd look in your eyes. Me and Mem were wondering ... why ain't Apollo trollepathizing with us?'

'I don't know, Nab.'

'Well, *ask!*'

Apollo, did you hear –

I did, BigBrov. Please tell the other Brovs I have tried, but I cannot. I do not know why.

'Apollo says your brain's too boring to trollepathize with.'

'What!'

BigBrov!

All right, all right, I'm sorry.

'No, Nab. A joke. Apollo's tried to trollepathize with you but, so far, no luck. I'm sure Apollo will keep trying though.'

'Holy macaroni, I hope so. I'm gonna have another sandwich. Speak to you later.'

NabBrov is upset I cannot trollepathize with him.

It's not your fault.

I know. But I will keep trying. Just like you said.

Apollo? I asked Mum to join the party earlier. She ain't come down. I don't know whether to go up and ask again or not.

Mum is sitting at the top of the stairs, BigBrov.

She's left the bedroom!

Yes.

Another step in the long journey.

She is listening to the music and the sound of everyone enjoying themselves. Go to her again, BigBrov. But do it very ... casually.

What do you mean?

Don't make a big thing of it. Don't put her under pressure. You understand?

I understand.

BigBrov is walking out of the kitchen and into the hall and ... oh, very well done! BigBrov's just glanced up and seen Mum as if by accident –

'Oh! You okey-dokey, Mum?'

'Yes, love. Sounds like you're all having a good time down there.'

'It's the new neighbours. All the grown-ups are dancing – well, not Missy. She's pregnant.'

'Pregnant! Oh! I *loved* being pregnant. Your dad and me were going to ...' Tears well in her eyes and she turns her face away. She takes a few deep breaths, then looks back at Zip and attempts a smile. 'Your dad loved dancing. Remember, Zip?'

'Yes, Mum.'

'I remember one solstice ...'

Solstice?

Oh! It's an ancient festival. There's two. In winter and summer. They celebrate the longest and shortest day of the year. We used to stay up all night and sing and ... and dance. And then we'd watch the rising sun.

It sounds glorious.

It was.

Mum's talking again –

'It was the solstice I was pregnant with Newt. A summer solstice. Midsummer night. I watched your dad dance all night. He took his shirt off and rubbed earth and leaves all over his skin. He put flowers in his hair. You remember that night, love?'

'... Yeah.'

'Didn't your dad look wonderful? Like a creature from dreams. A magical creature. And now he's gone ... now he's gone and ...' She sighs deeply and brushes tears from her cheek. 'There's no magic any more, Zip. That's why I can't face the world ...'

I ... I don't know what to say.

Ask her something.

'Fancy a sandwich, Mum?'

Not quite what I was thinking.

'What's in them, love?'

'Oh ... er ... chicken and pickle. But I could take the chicken out.'

'I don't think I've got the appetite for a ... pickle sandwich.'

'I can make you something else.'

'I'm fine, love.'

'I can make you anything you like.'

'Don't push me, Zip!'

'I'm not!'

'You are! And ... and I can't do it yet! I'm sorry ... oh!'

Mum is rushing back to her room. I want to rush after her –

Don't, BigBrov.

Did I do something wrong, Apollo?

She just needs more time –

Ding-da-ding!

The front door!

Oh, no!

What?

I ... can't work out what she wants.

Who?

But I know we've got to face whatever it is sooner or later.

Oh, it's not The Powers That Be, is it? If The Powers That Be see Mum in this state they're bound to take me and Newt away and –

No, no, BigBrov. It's not The Powers That Be.

Then who is –?

Just open the door.

But –

Go on, BigBrov!

Zip opens the front door.

'Good evening, Customer Zip.'

'Roz! What you doing here?'

'I was coming home from work and I heard the party so –'

'You're not invited!'

'I don't want to join the party, Customer Zip. I want to talk to you about the trolley you –'

'Now's not a good time!'

'Listen! I want to talk to you and your friends. Somewhere private. You hear me? And I'm not going until I do!'

Apollo?

Take her to the hideout.

— 50 —

Roz is sitting on the sofa. BigBrov is standing by the box that had the boots in. NabBrov and MemBrov are standing in opposite corners. All of them are very wary of Roz.

'Where's that little brother of yours, Customer Zip?'

'Gran is putting him to bed. It's past his bedtime.'

'He's so cute –'

'What do you *want*, Roz?' snaps Zip.

Don't lose your temper, BigBrov.

Sorry.

Roz takes a deep breath. 'You all think I'm the enemy, don't you? But I'm not. I've been trying to explain that but, for some reason, you won't give me the chance. Perhaps ... perhaps if I can tell you something about myself you might change your mind about me. Can I do that?'

Apollo?

Let her talk.

'Go ahead,' says Zip.

Roz whacks her left leg as hard as possible with her walking stick.

Crrraack!!

Ouch!

Ouch!

'Don't worry, Customers. It's fake. You see? I lost it in a car crash when I was twelve years old. I was trapped in the twisted metal for hours. They had to cut me out. Unfortunately, to cut me out they had to ... cut my leg off.'

'Where's it cut off exactly?' asks Nabil.

'Above the knee.'

'Can I see the stump?'

'Nab!' gasps Zip. 'Honestly, you're so rude sometimes.'

'He's not rude at all, Customer Zip. I much prefer people to say what they're thinking than pussyfoot round the subject.' Roz looks at Nabil and smiles. 'It's a bit awkward to take my leg off at the moment, Customer Nabil, but I will show you another time if you like. The surgeon did a wonderful job with the flap of skin and –'

'Enough!' cries Zip. 'I don't want to hear the gruesome details.'

'I do, amigo.'

Tell her to carry on with her story.

'Carry on with your story, Roz.'

'My parents were both killed in the car crash,' she continues. 'I went to live with my grandmother. Her name was Nollie. It's short for Noelle. Nollie didn't bother with me much at all. She kept comparing me to my mum, who was very beautiful, and then bursting into tears. Nollie used to say to me, "You've got ya dad's looks. Unfortunately. And they won't do you much good in life. Especially when you've only got one leg."'

'Gosh ... how nasty.'

'Oh, that was nothing, Customer Zip. Things were far worse at school. My classmates thought it great fun to snatch my crutch and hurl it across the playground. How they used to laugh to see me hop after it.'

Hop? Didn't she have a false leg?

'Didn't you have a false leg?'

'Good question, Customer Zip. And the answer is, yes, I did have a false leg. But, for some reason, I just couldn't get on with it. I tried and tried, but I couldn't keep my balance. And it made my stump so sore.'

'Did you get blisters?'

'I did, Customer Nabil.'

'Did you burst them?'

'Nab! Please!' cries Zip. Then looks at Roz and, very calmly, says, 'Ignore him and carry on with your story.'

'The only place I felt truly safe,' Roz continues, 'was beside the canal. It was my own private place. It was at the back of the supermarket and, to be honest, was little more than a rubbish tip. Old washing machines. Old furniture. There was even a burnt-out car I seem to remember. But for me it was . . . oh, it was quite, quite beautiful.'

Beautiful?

'Beautiful?'

'I know it sounds odd, but it's true. The rust on the old metal glistened like gold. The green slime of the canal glistened like emeralds. The cracks in the pavement were like pieces of modern art. I used to sit there for hours and hours drawing in my sketchbook.'

'I've got a sketchbook too!' Zip can't help blurting out.

'Really! What do you draw, Customer Zip?'

'Not much since I left the forest. Although last night I did do a drawing of –'

BigBrov!

Ooops. Sorry. My big mouth. Nab and Mem are shooting me warning looks too.

Tell her to carry on.

'Carry on, Roz.'

'It was by this canal that I made my first friend. I started talking to her one day and ... well, it was like we'd known each other all our lives. You ever felt that, Customers?'

'Yes.'

'Yeah.'

'Yeah.'

Oh yes.

'My friend's name is Mary. She teaches me how to walk with my false leg. It's tricky to keep balance at first, of course, but I hold on to Mary. She supports me. She holds me up. And Mary keeps on encouraging me. "You can do it, Roz!" she says. "You can do anything you want to! Oh, what a brave and wonderful girl you are!" And she makes me believe it too. I know I can do it! I take one step ... after another. It takes days and days and days. But Mary doesn't lose patience with me once. Not once. And slowly but surely ... oh, Customers, I throw away my crutch! I am walking, Customers. And all because of Mary.'

What a friend Mary is.

'What a friend Mary is!'

'Oh, she was, Customer Zip. The best friend anyone could ever want. She advised me on how to apply my make-up. What clothes to wear. How to do my hair. She changed me from an ugly duckling into ... well, if not exactly a swan, then at least a prettier duckling. We went everywhere together. We were inseparable. Inseparable. And then ... oh!' Tears well in Roz's eyes and she dabs them away with a tissue. 'This is going to be so difficult to tell ... so difficult ...'

Encourage her, BigBrov.

'Please tell us, Roz.'

'Yeah, amigo.'

'Yeah, mate.'

'There was a boy!' says Roz. 'His name was Vinnie. His dad owned the local junkyard. A junkyard for cars. Where they crush cars. You know? And this Vinnie took a shine to me. Don't ask me how or why. I'd certainly given him no encouragement. None! I didn't even know he existed until Nollie said a boy had called for me and wanted to take me on a date. Of course, I said no. I didn't want dates with anyone. Mary was all I needed. But Nollie insisted. She said it was time I grew up and stopped hanging around with Mary. "You ain't gonna get many chances, my girl," she said to me. "Not with one leg."'

'I don't like this gran of yours at all, mate.'

'Nor me, amigo.'

'Nor me.'

Nor me.

'Oh, it gets worse, Customers. Nollie and this Vinnie start plotting together. Plotting how they can get me away from Mary. They blamed Mary for everything. They blamed Mary for me not being interested in Vinnie. And then one day ... oh ... oh.' She wipes away more tears. 'They kidnap Mary from me! They kidnap Mary and take her to the junkyard and they ... they put her into one of those car-crushing machines and they – oh, I'm not gonna cry! I won't! – they crush my Mary, Customers! *They crush her!*'

'What!' gasps Zip. 'They ... what?!'

'Before I carry on, Customer Zip, I feel it only fair to show you a drawing I made of my Mary. I treasure it. Here! Look!'

'Gosh!'
    'Holy macaroni!'
    'Stars 'n' bars!'
    'Yes, Customers. Mary was a trolley.'

— 51 —

I never guessed!
    I did.
    Why didn't you say something?
    And spoil the surprise? — Roz is about to speak.

'I've missed her all my life, Customers. I've done everything I could to meet another living trolley. That's why
I got jobs in supermarkets. But so far ... I've never seen
another trolley like Mary. Until now ...'

Roz is coming over to me.

She's kneeling in front of you.

Roz is running her fingers through my metal frame.

'Oh, Apollo ... You know, I haven't drawn a picture,
not one, since my Mary was ... taken from me. It's like
all my inspiration was ... crushed along with her.'

Oh ... Roz ...

'Apollo ... I know it's difficult for you ... I'm a
grown-up and, if you're like Mary, you find it impossible
to move in front of grown-ups. But ... oh, Apollo. Will
you try to do the impossible for me? Please, Apollo, I want
you to ... *be my friend too*!'

*Roz is resting her head against Apollo. The garage is very still.
Look at Nab and Mem! They're barely breathing ... Apollo?*

Hear you, BigBrov.

What shall I tell Roz?

Tell her ... I will try.

'Apollo's going to try!'

'Oh, thank you, Apollo!'

'You can do it, amigo!'

'We're willing ya on like mates, mate!'

*My Brovs and Roz are all staring at me. Roz is clutching my metal
frame. I am concentrating very hard but —*

Nothing's happening!

I know.

The radio's not even crackling.

I know.

We're all listening and waiting ...

Do more than that! Encourage me!

'Come on, everyone. Encourage, Apollo!'

'Yes! Come on, amigo, you can do it!'

'Come on, mate! I know you can!'
'It would mean so much to me, Apollo.'
I must do this.
'I need to be friends with a trolley so much, Apollo.'
Roz needs me.
'Come on, Apollo . . .'
'Come on, amigo . . .'
'Come on, mate . . .'
'Speak, Apollo . . .'
Nothing is impossible.
Nothing is —
'Hello, Roz,' says Apollo, wheeling forward a little.

— 52 —

Roz is gently weeping, gently laughing, gently saying, 'Apollo . . . Apollo . . . Apollo . . .'

Eeeka-eeka . . .

'Are you all right, Roz?'

'All right? Oh, Apollo, I'm more all right than I've been since . . . well, you know when.'

'I know, RozSis.'

'RozSis!' gasps Roz.

'You're part of our Family now, Roz. You're one of The Friends of Apollo.'

Roz wraps her arms around Apollo's metal frame and kisses the push bar. 'Oh, thank you, Apollo. Thank you. Thank you.'

'This is all getting a bit mushy for me, amigos.'

'Yeah. It's a bit too girlie.'

'Roz,' says Zip, taking the drawing he'd done of his dream from his jacket pocket. 'Did this mean anything to you? Not the tree necessarily. But the shape it's in.'

Roz gazes at the drawing a moment. 'Why ... yes. Yes, it does – Did you dream this, Customer Zip?'

'Yes.'

'And it's a dream you had before? Only before ... the tree was not shaped like this? Am I right?'

'That's right! Exactly! Roz, did you have a similar dream when you were with Mary?'

'I did, Customer Zip. Goodness, I'd forgotten all about it until now.'

'What was it, RozSis?'

'Well, I used to have a recurring dream. It was of my mum and dad. They were standing on a hill and waiting for me with open arms. I knew where the hill was. It was a place we used to have picnics some Sunday afternoons. Not surprising I used to have a dream like this, of course. Not after ... what happened to them.'

'A double popped clogging,' says Nabil.

'Nab! Don't be so ... so ...'

'The word is "honest", amigo.'

'Customer Nabil's right. He's just being honest. It was a ... double popped clogging. And I used to see my popped-clogged parents waiting for me on a hillside. Their arms used to be open as if waiting for me to run into them. And then ... after I met Mary ...'

'The dream changed.'

'That's right, Customer Zip. My parents no longer had their arms open, ready to embrace me. They were facing each other with their arms outstretched. On each other's shoulders. You know? My mum's hands were on my dad's shoulders. And my dad's hands were –'

— 167 —

'Like the branches joining the two halves of the tree in this drawing!'

'Exactly.'

'The mystery thickens, mates.'

'Roz,' says Zip, 'did you ever discuss this with Mary?'

'Oh, many times. And Mary was convinced the shape was something to do with her.'

'She was changing the shape of your dreams?'

'She was, Customer Zip. Just as, by the looks of it, Apollo is changing the shape of yours.'

'But did you ever find out ... what the shape meant?'

'Well ... at first Mary had no idea. All she knew was that –'

'She wanted to go through the shape?'

'Yes! You too, eh, Apollo?'

'Yes, RozSis.'

'And was that all Mary knew, Roz?'

'Not quite, Customer Zip. As time passed and Mary and I had the same dream more and more often, Mary became convinced the shape meant something very special. Not just to her. But to all trolleys.'

'*What*, Roz?'

'It meant ... no shopping.'

'Gosh!'

'Perhaps I would've found out more from Mary, but the day after she told me, she ... she was crushed ... oh!' Roz turns away, her voice breaking. 'It's so, so difficult to talk about. After all these years.' She looks towards the garage door and says in the brightest voice she can muster, 'Ooo, voices on the street! It sounds like the party's finished.'

'Yes, RozSis. Everyone is saying their goodbyes.'

'They all sound like the friendliest neighbours I've ever heard. And ... Ooo, I should go too, Customers. I've got work to get to in the morning. I can introduce myself to all your relations on the way out. Thank you, Apollo. Thank *all* of you. So much. This is one of the happiest days of my life – Oh! One more thing before I go. It will help you understand something a bit more. That boy I was telling you about. Vinnie.'

'The tyrant who crushed your Mary, amigo?'

'Exactly, Customer Nabil. The tyrant who crushed my Mary. Afterwards – and this takes some beating – he still said he loved me. Honestly! Of course I told him to ... well, words I wouldn't like to repeat now. Vinnie said he had a broken heart and joined the army to forget me.'

'Good riddance to bad rubbish, mate!'

'Not quite, Customer Memphis. Because he couldn't forget me. He left the army after a couple of years and started following me all over again. Now, no matter where I go or what I do, Vinnie always pops up!'

'So you're expecting him to pop up here, Roz?'

'Oh, I'm not *expecting* it, Customer Zip. It's already *happened*. He's here and he's working at the supermarket.'

'You mean –? Oh, gosh!'

'Exactly! Vinnie is Guard Krick!' She looks round each of them in turn, then says softly, 'Goodnight, all.'

— **53** —

It is gone midnight now. BigBrov is sitting alone on the sofa. He's been there for over an hour. Everyone else is in bed and asleep and BigBrov should be in bed and asleep too. But he cannot go to bed yet. He has too much on his mind.

'Oh, Apollo . . .'

Oh, what a sad sigh. BigBrov is holding the letter from his dad. He cannot decide whether to open it or not. First BigBrov looks at the front of the envelope. Then the back of the envelope.

'Oh, Apollo . . . why do people die?'

'I do not know, BigBrov.'

'Where do they go when they die?'

'I do not know.'

'Can they still see us?'

'I do not know.'

Another sad sigh from BigBrov. He is clutching the letter tighter and tighter. It looks like his eyes might start leaking again at any moment.

'Apollo . . . why do bad things happen to good people?'

'I don't know the answer to that either.'

'My dad was a good person, you know. He was the best person I've ever met. He liked to help people. He helped animals. Plants. Everything.'

I wish I had arms to hold you, BigBrov.

'It was so glorious in the forest, Apollo. Really. My dad – he started this whole community there. He was the leader of it, I guess. When Dad got fired up about something – oh, gosh, he was so exciting! His face became like . . . something burning. You just did whatever Dad asked you. He made you feel like you could do anything. Anything at all . . .'

Don't stop, BigBrov.

'We lived in wooden huts. We grew our own vegetables. My dad taught me the names of all the birds. All the plants. I know how to roast chestnuts by digging a hole in the ground and lighting a fire and . . . and . . . oh, so many things! Dad told me, "Listen up, Zip!" – when Dad wanted to get my attention he always said "listen up" – "Everything's connected, Zip. Never forget that. Everything on the planet is all part of the same thing. We are one entity. If you hurt one person or one thing, then you hurt everyone and everything. If you pollute the seas, then fish die, and the creatures that eat the fish die, then birds die, then shorelines die, communities die, the future dies. You see? It just goes on and on." Oh, he was something special, Apollo, my dad. I wanted to be like him so much . . .'

'Keep talking, BigBrov.'

'There was such a glorious oak tree, Apollo. An ancient tree. It was at the centre of the forest. The Powers That Be wanted to cut this tree down. Dad said that would be a sin. He said the tree was wise and wonderful. He said the tree knew secrets and if it was chopped down, then all those secrets would get chopped down with it. All those secrets would be lost forever. Oh, Apollo . . . if you could've seen this tree, then you'd understand what Dad was talking about. I used to spend hours and hours just looking at it. It was like my best friend. I told it things. Some nights . . . I would sleep under it. When I looked up I'd see these branches above me. Like arms. The tree was this giant protecting me. I felt so safe. Nothing could hurt me while that ancient oak was there . . . Nothing could . . . hurt . . . me . . .'

'Climb in me, BigBrov.'

'Eh? Why, Apollo?'

'Don't argue.'

'Gosh, of course. Whatever you say.' Zip climbs into the trolley. 'But . . . are we going somewhere?'

'Yes, BigBrov. I'm taking you back there!'

'Back there?'

'To the forest!'

— 54 —

'But, Apollo ... it's late! It's dark!'
  'Perfect!'
  Vmmmmmm ...
  'What if someone sees us?'
  'Everyone's asleep.'
  'But –'
  'Do you want to see the forest again or not?'
  'Of course I do!'
  'Then hold tight.'
  We're wheeling out of the garage.
  We're wheeling down the main road.
  Eeeka-eeka-clicka-click ...
  'Apollo airlines ready for lift-off.'
  Eeekaeekaclickaclickeeekaeekaclickaclick –
  We're taking off ...
  We're flying ...
  Higher ...
  Higher ...
  'Apollo! We're ... we're leaving New Town behind ...
and – oh, look at it down there. All those flickering lights.
Like a hive of fireflies. And it's getting smaller ... and
smaller ...'
  'Shall we go even higher, BigBrov?'
  'Yes!'
  *There is so much space all round me. To my right – twinkling
distant lights. City lights. To my left – the motorway twists like*

a glittering amber river. And – oh, look! I can see through the wire mesh beneath my legs.

So high and getting higher ...

'Higher, BigBrov?'

'Yes, Apollo! Higher!'

Clouds!

They swirl above me. So thick. Thicker than any early morning mist in the forest. And ... we're getting closer to the clouds ...

Closer ...

'Want to go in the clouds, BigBrov?'

'Yes!'

'Then get ready ... Here come the clouds!'

Gosh! The clouds are all around me.

'It's glorious, Apollo.'

'Glad you approve, BigBrov.'

'Can we go still higher? Please!'

'Whatever you want, BigBrov.'

Higher ...

Higher ...

And now ... oh, we burst through the top of the clouds. Like a dolphin jumping out of the ocean. And ... starlight! Moonlight. Been so long since I saw them. So much space and colour and everything ... everything is so sharp and in focus. Like I've just been given a new pair of glasses and they've taken away every blurred thing.

'Apollo ... what's that light over there? You see it. It's flashing and ... oh, it's not a UFO is it? Look! It certainly looks like –'

'No, BigBrov. It's not a flying saucer. It's a plane. I've cut most of the sound out otherwise it would deafen you. But I suggest we trollepathize if we want to get any closer.'

BigBrov to Apollo!

Hear you, BigBrov!

Closer to the plane, Apollo, please.

Of course . . .

Gosh, it's huge!

Gigantic, BigBrov.

Like a whale – Oh, Apollo!

What?

Make sure no one sees you.

Most of them are sleeping.

Even so . . . I don't want one of the grown-ups waking up and you freezing and plummeting to the ground.

I don't think that will happen but, don't worry, I will be careful.

Oh, Apollo . . . I wonder where they're all going? All those people with other lives. Other stories to tell. Family and friends will be waiting for them at airports. Husbands waiting for wives . . . Daughters waiting for mothers . . . Sons waiting for fathers . . .

I'll get closer.

You sure?

Yes.

We are flying alongside the plane.

I look through the windows . . .

A boy! He's about seven years old. And –

Oh! Apollo! A boy!

I see him.

He's not asleep.

I know.

But he might –

Too late!

He's seen us!

— 55 —

The boy stares at Zip and Apollo.
  He rubs his eyes and shakes his head.
  He can't believe that he's seeing Apollo.
  Wave to him, BigBrov.
  I'm waving!
  For a moment . . . the boy does nothing.
  He just stares, mouth open, eyes wide.
  And then –
  He's smiling!
  The boy's smile gets wider and wider and –
  He's waving back!
  So he is.
  Can we get closer, Apollo?
  I think so, yes.
  Oh, gosh, we're getting so close I can see peeling paint.
  The boy presses his face against the window.
  The boy's breath mists the glass.
  The boy's nose gets squished.
  Gosh! Look at him, Apollo!
  He's happy to see us, BigBrov.
  Can we get even closer?
  I'll get as close as I dare.
  I could pick the paint off we're so close.
  The boy's trying to show you something.
  What?

He's done a drawing.

What is it of?

A bird, I think.

No . . . it's not a bird. It's an angel.

Show him you like the drawing.

'It's glorious!' Zip calls out to the boy.

He can't hear you, BigBrov. Smile.

I'm smiling.

You see! The boy is smiling back.

I'm reaching out to touch the glass. Oh – look!

The boy is reaching out to touch the glass too.

I'm laughing.

He laughs.

I laugh more and – oh, look! The boy's mum!

She is waking. We must go.

Okey-dokey . . .

We're pulling away from the plane.

I wave and wave to the boy.

The boy waves and waves to me.

I wave and wave until the plane is just a small speck.

BigBrov . . . we are descending now . . .

Are we getting near the forest?

'I believe so, yes.'

— 56 —

'Oh, we're back to talking out loud now, are we?'

'Well . . . there's no plane noise now . . . And it is more private for you this way. No chance of me hearing something you don't want me to hear.'

'I've got no secrets from you, Apollo.'

'Thank you, BigBrov — Now, keep your eyes open for something you recognize. The forest should be starting any moment now ... We're getting lower ... and closer ... closer ...'

'Yes! Apollo! This road. I remember that roundabout over there. It leads right into the forest. It hasn't snowed here. Everything's just as I remember it. Though, of course, I've never seen it from up here – Oh, Apollo! We're close! So very close! We'll be seeing it any second. I know we will!'

'I can't wait, BigBrov.'

'Nor me, Apollo.'

I get lower and lower ...

'Apollo ... where are all the trees? There should be trees by now.'

'Yes. I know.'

'Can you get any lower, Apollo?'

'Of course.'

Lower ...

Lower ...

'Gosh, it's ... very flat. Perhaps I'm wrong. Perhaps the forest is further up.'

'I don't think so, BigBrov.'

Lower ...

Lower ...

Lower ...

'Apollo! Look! There's chopped stumps of trees everywhere. Oh, Apollo ... you see? The white circles of wood are gleaming in the moonlight. It's like a game of draughts with only white pieces below us.'

'I see, BigBrov.'

'There's a space over there. Can you land?'

'Of course.'

Lower ...

Lower ...

Lower ...

Gently, Apollo's wheels touch the earth. They roll for a moment, then come to a halt.

Zip looks all around him.

'Oh, Apollo ... they didn't waste much time, did they? Soon as we were gone they must've got the chainsaws out and ... They've chopped down everything! Everything! Oh, Apollo ... *my glorious forest has gone!*'

— 57 —

It's ... it's like a huge hurricane has blown everything away.

It's like a huge fist has punched the land flat.

'Apollo ... I'm getting out.'

'Be careful, BigBrov.'

I'm walking over the black earth.

No grass. No flowers. No fallen leaves.

'Apollo ... they've destroyed everything. The whole forest. I didn't ... I didn't realize they were going to do this. I thought ... I thought it was just the oak tree and some of the surrounding trees. But not ... oh, Apollo, not everything! Not *everything!*'

'BigBrov, perhaps we should go.'

'No!'

'But you're getting upset —'

'What happened to the animals? What happened to

the foxes and hedgehogs? The forest was full of them. Where'd they all go, Apollo? Where?'

'I don't know, BigBrov. I wish I did. I wish I'd never brought you here.'

'Apollo . . . I'm going to look over there . . .'

'I'll be right behind you, BigBrov.'

BigBrov is walking faster and faster.

'Be careful, BigBrov!'

'Where *is* everything? What's the point of you bringing me here when there's nothing to see? When you can't even tell me where everything has gone? Eh? How come you know some things but don't know others? Eh? What's the point of that? You're useless, Apollo! *Useless!*'

BigBrov stumbles and falls.

BigBrov is just lying there trying to get his breath back.

I can feel Apollo getting closer . . .

I can feel Apollo beside me . . .

I just lie still . . .

'BigBrov?'

'Oh, Apollo . . . I'm . . . I'm sorry . . .'

'Nothing to be sorry for.'

'There is! I said you were . . . useless.'

'It's how I feel right now.'

'But you're not. You could never be – Apollo! Look! Look!'

BigBrov is pointing beneath him.

BigBrov has fallen on a tree stump.

It is the largest circle of tree stump in the forest.

Oh, no . . . no . . .

Oh, no!

'It's the oak.' Zip is running his fingers across the bright wood beneath him. 'It's all that's left of the glorious oak . . . Oh, no! NOOOOOOO!!'

— 58 —

There is nothing I can say.
  There is nothing I can do.
  Except watch.
  And listen.

'My dad ... he must've known The Powers That Be were going to do all this ... but he didn't want to upset me any more than I was. But ... oh, that's why he fought so hard to save it!'

My BigBrov is still slumped on the stump.
My BigBrov is still wracked with tears.
My BigBrov is shaking all over ...

'My dad ... he said to me, "It might get a bit dangerous tonight, Zip ..." It was ... the last night ... the police were everywhere ... They all had plastic shields and helmets on ... This was the night they'd decided to cut the tree down ... Tonight ... And there were people with cameras ... and a telly crew ... and there was me and Dad and Mum and everyone ... and we were all chanting, "Save the tree! Save the tree! Save the tree!"'

BigBrov is sitting up now.
BigBrov wipes tears from his face.
BigBrov is getting his breath back ...

'My dad said, "What's that you're holding, Zip?" ... And I ... I showed him. It was a ... banner I'd made ... Red paint on a white sheet ... It said, "SAVE ME". I said to Dad, "I wanted to put it ... on the tree ..." But

I couldn't get to the tree now ... Police had surrounded it ... No one could get to the tree ...'

BigBrov has got his breath back.
BigBrov makes no more tears.
BigBrov looks at me ...

'My dad said, "Give it to me, Zip." And I give him the banner. And before I know what's happening – before anyone knows what's happening – Dad has pushed through the police and he's running for the tree. The police chase after him. And me and Mum and all of us are cheering, "Go for it! Do it! Do it!" And Dad gets to the tree ... And Dad starts to climb the tree ... And I cry out, "Put it right at the top, Dad. So everyone can see it!" And Dad climbs and climbs ... None of the police can climb like him ... They just watch ... Dad gets higher and higher ... And, when he reaches the top, he looks down at me ... and everything sort of goes quiet and calm ... like the air sometimes gets before a big crack of thunder ... And Dad smiles and waves at me ... It's such a happy smile ... And that's when the branch breaks. Dad – he takes forever to fall. I see it all in slow motion. I hear every branch snap and split ... I can still hear them ... And I can still hear the sound of my dad hitting the ground. I'll always hear that sound ... We rush over to him ... Mum is screaming and screaming ... My banner is wrapped round Dad ... Dad's face is scratched by the tree ... Dad's legs are sticking out all the wrong way ... I say, "Dad! Get up, Dad!" But Dad don't move. Dad is ... dead.'

'Oh, BigBrov ...'

'How can that happen, Apollo? Eh? So quick! One moment Dad's here. He's alive and running and smiling and the next ... it's all gone! That can't be possible. Can it? There can't be a world without Dad. He can't be here one second and gone the next. I never had a chance to tell him ... so much. There's still stuff I want to tell him ...'

'BigBrov?'

He's not answering.

'BigBrov?'

Still nothing.

'BigBrov! Listen to me!'

'... What, Apollo?'

'Climb on board, please.'

'Are we ... going home?'

'I want to show you something first.'

'What?'

'Climb in and see ... That's it. Now ... Watch the circle of wood, BigBrov?'

'But why, Apollo, why – Hang on! The circle of wood! It's glowing gold!'

'Yes, BigBrov.'

'But what –?'

'Just watch, BigBrov! Watch!'

The glow – it's becoming brighter and brighter.

This glow – it seems to have a life of its own.

Like a million fireflies swarming round the wood.

'It's getting bigger, Apollo!'

'Taller, BigBrov!'

'Like a ...'

'Tree!'

The golden glow is like liquid. Liquid flowing up. And it's so bright. Like sunlight.

It grows up ... up ...

A tree trunk!

'Apollo!'

'Watch!'

Golden branches are growing now.

Golden twigs on the golden branches.

Golden leaves on the golden twigs on the golden branches.

'Oh, Apollo ... it's getting bigger and bigger and –!'

'Watch!'

The branches are spreading above me.
The leaves are rustling and sparkling.
The truck is twisted and gnarled.
And now —
'The oak tree!'
'Yes, BigBrov.'
'But . . . it's not real, is it?'
'No. I am creating it.'
'Like a . . . a ghost of the tree.'
'In a way, yes.'
'But how did you know what it looked like?'
'Because I saw it in your mind, BigBrov.'
Zip looks up at the glorious, golden, ghostly oak.
The radiance blazes in Zip's eyes.
The radiance blazes on Apollo's metal frame.
'Ain't it something, Apollo?'
'Indeed it is, BigBrov.'
'Thank you, Apollo. Thank you for letting me see it
again. Even though it's not real.'
'I haven't finished yet, BigBrov.'
'What now?'
'Watch!'
What's that? Something is moving away from one of the
branches. Something small and floating.
Like a . . . like a golden bumblebee.
But it's not a bumblebee.
It's a —
'An acorn!'
'An acorn it is, BigBrov.'
'Where's it going?'
'Shall we find out?'
'You mean . . .?'
'Yes, BigBrov . . . Let's follow it!'

— 59 —

Gosh!

We're flying up . . . up . . . up . . .

The acorn is speeding away fast.

'There it goes, Apollo!'

'I can see it!'

'Follow!'

'Follow!'

The acorn slows down for a moment, then whizzes off again, first to the left . . . then to the right . . . then up . . . down . . . up again . . . as if caught in the current of a wild and twisting river.

'Where's it going, Apollo?'

'Wait and see, BigBrov.'

'It's disappeared in the clouds.'

'So it has.'

'I can still see it glowing – There!'

'I see it too.'

'It's like a golden stain in the sky – Look!'

'It's coming out of the clouds.'

'Getting lower.'

'Lower.'

The acorn lands in the middle of a vast expanse of earth. It shines on the dark soil as bright as a light bulb.

Apollo lands nearby . . .

'What's happening now?'

'Keep watching, BigBrov.'

'The acorn . . . it seems to be . . . wriggling.'

'It does, yes.'

'It's burying itself!'

'It seems to be, yes.'

'And look! A golden shoot.'

'Oh yes.'

'Apollo! Another tree is growing!'

Once more, the ghostly gold grows.

Again . . . a golden trunk.

Again . . . golden branches.

Again . . . golden twigs.

Again . . . golden leaves.

'Oh, Apollo! It's another oak tree!'

'Do you like it, BigBrov?'

'It's glorious! Glorious!'

'Now . . . WATCH THIS!'

And suddenly, oak trees are growing everywhere.

A hundred ghostly, golden trunks.

Thousands of ghostly, golden branches.

Millions of ghostly, golden twigs.

Zillions of ghostly, golden leaves.

'Apollo! It's another forest!'

'I suppose it is.'

'Gosh . . . it's so bright.'

'Let me fade the light a little . . .'

'Apollo! You're making the leaves fall!'

'Do you like it, BigBrov?'

'Oh, it's glorious!'

'Try to catch one.'

'Okey-dokey . . . Ha!
My fingers go right through it!
Oh, Dad would've loved this.
Autumn was his favourite time of year.
He loved it when the leaves changed to red and
started to fall.'

'This is like the king of all autumns, eh, BigBrov?'

'It is! Oh, look! The branches of the trees.'

'What about them, BigBrov?'

'They're not looking so golden any more.'

'No?'

'No. As the leaves are falling . . .
the branches of the trees look more like wood.'

'And the trunks, too.'

'Yes!'

'All the leaves have nearly fallen now.'

'The leaves are dissolving into the earth.'

'Just like they dissolved into your fingertips.'

'And the golden light is gradually fading.'

'The golden light is almost gone.'

'Oh, Apollo! These trees are real!'

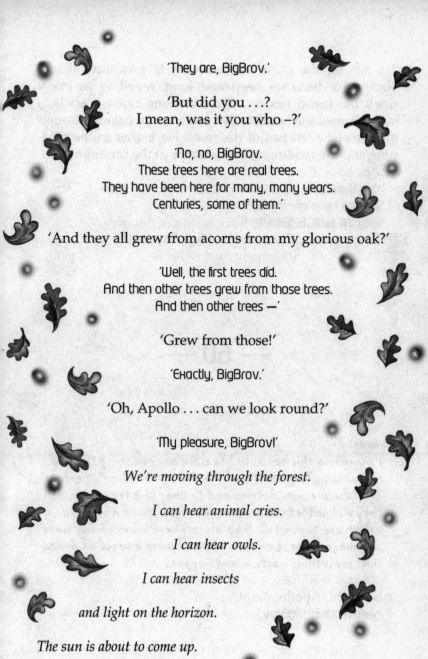

'They are, BigBrov.'

'But did you ...?
I mean, was it you who –?'

'No, no, BigBrov.
These trees here are real trees.
They have been here for many, many years.
Centuries, some of them.'

'And they all grew from acorns from my glorious oak?'

'Well, the first trees did.
And then other trees grew from those trees.
And then other trees —'

'Grew from those!'

'Exactly, BigBrov.'

'Oh, Apollo ... can we look round?'

'My pleasure, BigBrov!'

We're moving through the forest.

I can hear animal cries.

I can hear owls.

I can hear insects

and light on the horizon.

The sun is about to come up.

Zip sits on the grass and runs his fingers through the blades. He breathes deep and long, revelling in every smell the forest has to offer. He leans against Apollo's metal frame and watches the sky change colour through the skeletal branches of the trees. He listens to the bird-song and the rustling of tiny animals in the undergrowth.

'Apollo . . .?'

'Yes, BigBrov.'

'Please take me back!'

'Why the rush, BigBrov?'

'I have to read Dad's letter. I have to read it *now*!'

— 60 —

Dearest Zip,

I'm writing this because I feel we are reaching the end of our long, long Battle of Ancient Oak. The Powers That Be are now determined to chop this tree down and they will not let us stand in their way. More and more police are turning up. The atmosphere is becoming more and more tense. I cannot help but have a sense of dread that something nasty might happen.

'And it did, Apollo, it did.'

'Keep reading, BigBrov.'

I hope you don't feel bad about the kind of life I've given you. I know you've never gone to school — and you've missed out on having schoolmates and all that sort of stuff — but I've tried to teach you the things that I think are important. I've tried to teach you how to appreciate the glory and the wonder of the world. I've tried to teach you how to be a good human being, not fill your head with useless facts. You can pass all the exams under the sun, but it doesn't mean a jot if you're not filled with joy at the sight of a sunset. You can earn lots of money, have a big house, a car, anything you want . . . but what does this matter if you are not happy to sit down and think your own thoughts? Oh, Zip, I hope you understand me!

'Oh, I do, Dad, I do.'
'Read on.'

Zip, if anything does happen to me over the next twenty-four hours, I want you to know I am prepared for it. Of course, I hope it doesn't. The last thing I want to do is leave you and your mum and little Newt — who probably won't remember any of this by the time he's your age (a scary thought for me) — but some things . . . some things you just cannot let happen without a struggle. And I cannot let The Powers That Be destroy this glorious oak without struggling to my very last breath (especially as I don't believe The Powers That Be when they say they only want to chop down a little bit of the forest. They want it all, Zip. I know it!) I hope you understand this, Zip.

'You were right, Dad.'
'Read on . . .'

You know, Zip, I don't believe in life after death at all . . . but I've always liked what the ancient Egyptians had to say on the subject. They believed that, after you die, your soul travels to the gates of the afterlife and there you are asked two questions. And only if you are able to answer yes to both questions will you be allowed to pass through the gates. The two questions are, 'Did you find joy?' and 'Did you make joy?' All I can say is that, if I were an ancient Egyptian, those doors would open like a shot. Because in you, my glorious Zip, I both found and made all the joy a man could want.

Because of you, my son, I will live forever.

I will always love you
Dad
xxxxxx

'I'll always love you too, Dad.'
'There's a PS, BigBrov.'

PS I'm enclosing a drawing of a place I visited when I was about your age. It was this place that got me interested in all the things that were to fill the rest of my life. In a way, my journey here to save the Ancient Oak started when I did this drawing. It's one of many such structures all over the country. They were built — as far as anyone can tell — to celebrate the rising sun. Especially at solstice. Never forget the solstice, Zip. The longest and shortest day of the year. Remember? Celebrating the solstice is one of the oldest rituals known to mankind. I always think these stone structures look like doorways. Doorways to where? Who knows? Perhaps, one day, you'll find out, Zip.

'Gosh . . . where's the drawing?'

'It's fallen to the floor — there!'

'I see it.' Zip picks the photo up and looks at it. 'Oh . . . my . . . gosh!'

'What is it, BigBrov?'

'Look!'

'BigBrov! Are you thinking what I'm thinking?'

'I think I must be!'

'This is the same shape —'

'As the oak tree in our dream.'

— 61 —

BigBrov is getting very excited. He's rushing round and round the hideout. He's jumping up on the sofa ... off the sofa ... climbing over piles of boxes ...

'Gosh ... oh, gosh ... gosh, gosh.'

'Keep calm, BigBrov.'

'I *can't* keep calm! We dreamed the oak tree had been changed into a different shape. And my dad – my very own dad – had *seen* this shape. It was something that changed his life. Oh, gosh! Oh, gosh, oh, gosh – what does it all mean – oh, gosh, oh, gosh – Apollo, ain't you a little bit excited?'

'I am, BigBrov, but if the two of us spin round the hideout we'll never think about this clearly. We need to keep calm. BigBrov! You listening?'

'Yes ... of course.'

'Good. Now ... sit down.'

'Okey-dokey ... okey-dokey ...'

'Deep breaths.'

'Okey-dokey ...'

'Feel calmer?'

'Yes ... yes ... I'm calmer. Right! Gosh ... gosh ... Let's think this thing through.' Zip points at the drawing his dad had made. 'This shape is important to you. It came from somewhere inside your metal frame and rubber wheels and plastic push bar.'

'Correct, BigBrov.'

'And you feel you want to wheel through it.'

'It pulls me like a magnet.'

'And Roz's Mary saw this shape too.'

'And she felt it had something to do with a place without shopping.'

'And my dad ... he thought this shape was a doorway.'

'He did, BigBrov.'

'A doorway to ... a place without shopping!'

'Oh ... yes, BigBrov. Go on, go on!'

'And you want to wheel through it. And so did Mary. So perhaps ... all trolleys want to wheel through it.'

'To get to this place with no shopping! Oh yes! BigBrov, what a glorious place this must be! Freedom! Freedom!'

'Okey-dokey, now we're getting somewhere! Oh, gosh! So this shape is a doorway for trolleys to get to a place without shopping – oh, gosh! Of course! It's all falling into place now. It's all making sense!'

'What, BigBrov?'

'It's all in Dad's letter! Don't you see? Dad had the answers all along! Listen, Apollo! Listen! The shape works twice a year. On the solstice.'

'The longest and shortest day of the year!'

'Exactly. On the sunrise of the longest and shortest day of the year, the rays of the sun will shine through this shape.'

'And if a trolley goes through it at that very moment —'

'No more shopping!'

'So ... perhaps ... what we've got to do is get to one of these ... structures, BigBrov! What do you think?'

'I don't think ... that's necessary, Apollo.'

'What do you mean?'

'I think all that's important is ... well, the shape. That's why, in our dreams, it was made out of all sorts of things. Trees. Roz's parents. Or even – as in Dad's drawing – stone. No, it's not what it's made out of that's important.'

'Just the shape?'

'Exactly! And the ability to see sunrise through it.'

'So we can build the shape anywhere, BigBrov!'

'Exactly. Anywhere and out of anything. Why, we can build it out of the cardboard boxes in this very hide-out. We can build it outside in the street. The sun rises at the end of the main road. It will be the perfect place – Oh, gosh! Oh, gosh!'

'Oh, gosh, oh, gosh, oh, gosh!'

'Now *you're* getting excited!'

'I can't help it!'

'Nor can I!'

'When is the next solstice, BigBrov?'

'Hang on! There's Dad's diary. It'll tell us the sunrise times and then we'll know when ... let's see ... Here! Mmm ... yes ... yes ... oh!'

'What?'

'OH!'

'What? What?'

'Apollo! The next solstice is tomorrow!'

'Tomorrow!'

'Gosh! Oh, gosh! I've got to phone Nab! And Mem! And Roz! What's the time? – Yes! They should be up by now. Even if they're not, I'm gonna wake them – oh, Apollo! Don't you see what this means? We're going to build the shape – No! Not the shape. The Doorway! That's what we'll call it from now on. The Doorway is going to be built right outside here. A Doorway made of cardboard boxes. We'll build it so the rays of the next rising sun will shine right through it. And when that happens ... oh, Apollo! You will wheel through it. You hear me? When the sun next rises ... *you will be free!*'

— PART THREE —

— 62 —

'Top of the morning, everyone, and – oh, gosh, I'm so excited I can barely speak! Welcome to the ... well, the first emergency meeting of The Friends of Apollo, I guess. If we can begin – purely for the record – by announcing ourselves, my name is Zip Jingle and I am a Friend of Apollo.'

'My name is Nabil Brazil and I am a Friend of Apollo.'

'My name is Memphis Lemonique and I am a Friend of Apollo.'

'My name is Roswell Shepherd and I am a Friend of Apollo.'

'Ma nimmy Noo-Noo nam yam freend Apple-loo.'

'My name is Apollo and I am ... well, Apollo.'

'Okey-dokey, Friends. Now, I'm sure you've all managed to piece together what's going on by now. After all, me and Apollo ain't stopped talking about it since you got here.' Zip checks his watch, then continues. 'In about twenty hours we will build a Doorway in the main road. Right outside the hideout here.'

'Build it out of what, mate? I missed that bit.'

'So did I, Customer Zip.'

'We'll make it out of the cardboard boxes in here. There's loads of them! Look! All different shapes and sizes. We'll use them like bricks. And then the rays of the morning sun will shine through the Doorway and Apollo will wheel through and –'

'But . . . where to, amigo?'

'To . . . to a place without shopping, of course.'

'Just like my Mary said, Customer Nabil.'

'I think it's pure Elvissy, mates.'

'Gosh, yes, Mem. Elvissy it is!'

'Ya! Ya! Ya!'

'Amigos! Stop! Wait! Hang on! Slow down! Cool it!' Nabil holds his hands up and looks at them with bewildered eyes. 'If I might be allowed to interject a tiny pinch of sanity into your big bowl of doolally.'

'Go ahead, NabBrov.'

'Apollo! Amigo! No one wants you to be free of shopping more than me. I want *all* things to be free of shopping. You know that.'

'I know.'

'But what happens . . . when you go through the Doorway? Do you . . . just disappear? I mean . . . where is this place where there ain't no shopping? Another planet? Another dimension? I just want to know . . . *what blooming happens*?'

'NabBrov . . . I don't have the answer to that. Nor does BigBrov. Perhaps no one does. Only those trolleys that have already gone through the Doorway know what it's like.'

'If any trolleys have,' says Zip.

'Exactly, BigBrov. We don't even know that for sure.'

'Holy macaroni! We don't know *anything* for sure!'

'Oh, no, NabBrov. There you are wrong. I know I need to go through the Doorway. How do I know? I have no idea. But I know!'

'It's like the kingfisher, Nab.'

'Eh? What? Have I missed something?'

'It's a bird. There was a beautiful one in the forest and –'

'Oh, no! Don't get all happy clappy on me, amigo. That's all I need!'

'Tell us, Customer Zip.'

'Yeah, what's a kingfisher look like, mate?'

'It's got bright blue feathers on its breast and wings. The one in the forest built a nest by the river. Now, how did it know it had to do that? Or even how to do it? After all, it never went to How To Build A Nest classes. The kingfisher just knew. And then ... another surprising thing happens.'

'Oh, spare me, spare me.'

'Carry on, Customer Zip.'

'The kingfisher lays eggs in the nest. Now, wouldn't that surprise you if it's never happened before? It would certainly surprise me. But does it surprise the kingfisher? Not a bit. It ain't surprised in the least. It just sits on them and keeps them warm. How does it know how to do this? It's never been to How To Hatch Eggs classes –'

'Holy macaroni, I'm gonna puke in a minute.'

'Listen, Nab! The kingfisher watches the glorious eggs until they crack and little kingfishers appear. And these little kingfishers – do they look anything like the big kingfisher? No. They're featherless and pink. Their wings are almost non-existent. But is the kingfisher surprised or confused? Not a bit. It just goes off in search of food.'

'OK, OK, enough! This is blooming torture.'

'And then one day,' continues Zip, louder and more vigorous, 'the little kingfishers make their way to the edge of the nest and ... jump! Now they've never done this before. They might fall into the river and drown.'

'I hope they do!'

'But they don't worry about any of this. They just know something is making them jump. Something they don't understand, just feel. And so they don't ask questions. They don't wonder why ... they just fly!'

'Don't wonder why, just fly!'

'That's beautiful, Customer Zip.'

'Elvissy, mate!'

'Ya!'

'All right, all right, I get the point – Apollo, amigo, I'll do whatever you want. You know that. Without question.'

'Thank you, NabBrov.'

'Thanks, Nab,' says Zip, reaching out to give Nabil's arm a squeeze. 'We're going to save Apollo from any threat of being used as a shopping thing ever again. Apollo will never end up like that poor trolley we found in the snow.'

'Oh, don't remind me, Customer Zip.'

'Guard Krick is probably chopping the poor thing up as we speak, amigos.'

'No, NabBrov. The snow trolley is still in one piece. I can feel it.'

'But for how long? Eh, mates?'

'Please, Customer Memphis! Please! I can't bear to think of –'

'Glorious!' exclaims Zip, jumping up in the air with excitement. 'Why didn't I think of it sooner? It's so obvious! Of *course*! Of *course*!'

'Would someone mind telling me what's going on now?' sighs Nabil.

'No idea, mate.'

'Nor me, I'm afraid, Customer Nabil – Customer Zip, would you mind explaining what –?'

'It's staring us in the face! Gosh, of course! That's why we've got twenty hours ahead of us. Don't you see?'

'Amigo, I am a non-violent human being. But if you don't explain what you're jabbering on about pronto, I will be forced to give you a slap round the chops!'

'We've got time to do it, Nab!'

'Do *what*, Customer Zip?'

'Rescue the snow trolley, of course!'

— 63 —

BigBrov and me are making plans. We've been trollepathizing non-stop for almost thirty minutes. We have asked RozSis many questions about the supermarket. Now BigBrov is standing on the armchair and —

'Listen up, everyone! The plan is simplicity itself!'

'I hope it doesn't involve running, amigo.'

'It does, Nab. But not by you.'

'Me, mate! My macho-boy muscles can outrun Guard Krick any day. So long as he's not in the van, of course, mates. I'll run in that supermarket and snatch it from under his nose and run out again before he has a chance to say, "Misterrr!"'

'Well, that's half of the plan,' says Zip with a chuckle. 'But there's just a little more to it than that. Now ... according to Roz, Krick would've taken the snow trolley down to the basement.'

'Well, that's where he takes all damaged trolleys, Customer Zip.'

'Yes, RozSis. I feel the trolley is there too.'

'But, amigo – and I'm not doubting anything, this is just a question, so no sugary stories of fluffy bunny rabbits or tweeting birdies, if you don't mind – are you suggest- ing we ... what? Just saunter into the supermarket and stroll down to the basement without Guard Krick noticing us?'

'I *want* Krick to notice us, Nab.'

'Customer Zip! What're you saying?'

'Listen up! The only way we're going to get down to the basement is to keep Krick distracted.'

'And – holy macaroni – how do you intend to do that?'

'*I'm* not going to do it. *Rudi* is.'

'My baby?'

'How, mate?'

'Krick has got it in for Rudi. You've all heard him. "I'm gonna get that rat!" So, Nab, you walk into the supermarket with Rudi on your shoulder. When Krick catches sight of you, Rudi will run off your shoulder. Krick will chase after Rudi. And Rudi will lead Krick a merry dance all over the place, while I rush down to the basement and rescue the –'

'Hang on! Slow down! Stop!' Nabil holds Rudi to his chest and kisses the top of the animal's head. 'Now, far be it from me to be a juicy maggot in your peach of a plan, but ... Amigo! Be reasonable! This ain't some cutesy Hollywood kiddie movie with forest animals doing the housework and making dresses for wannabe princesses. Rudi here – he's an intelligent beast – but you can't expect him to know where to run and how to –'

'Rudi won't *have* to know, NabBrov.'

'Eh?'

'Apollo will tell him, Nab.'

'Holy macaroni! You're gonna trollepathize with my baby!'

'Exactly, NabBrov.'

Rudi scarpers out of Nabil's hands, across the floor, and up on to Apollo's push bar.

'Well ... looks like my baby is eager to get started.'

'No harm will come to him, NabBrov. Trust me.'

'Of course I do, amigo.'

'Okey-dokey, everyone, listen up. This is the plan. Me, Nab, Mem and Rudi will go to the supermarket –'

'Meee too, Zi-Zi!'

'Of course, little brov. I wouldn't leave you out.'

'Ya-ya, Zi-Zi!'

Is it wise to take LittleBrov on such a dangerous mission?

I've got no choice.

I could look after him here.

But what if Gran or Aunt Ivy comes in? All they'll see is that I've left Newt alone.

Yes. I understand.

'Okey-dokey. Listen up. When we get to the super-market, me and Nab will go inside. Mem, you will wait outside with Newt.'

'You got it, mate.'

'Ya-ya, Zi-Zi!'

'Nab, you will make sure Krick sees you and Rudi.'

'Sure thing, amigo.'

'Once Krick starts chasing Rudi, I will make my way to the basement –'

'Make sure you use the lift, Customer Zip. It's much quicker.'

'Thank you, Roz. And I'll need the lift to get the snow trolley back up, of course. Carrying it up stairs would take forever.'

'Not if I'm doing the carrying, mate!'

'There's no point two of us risking getting caught down there, Mem. Besides, you'll be where you're needed most. Because as soon as you see me rush out of the supermarket with the trolley – grab it from me and run!'

'All the way back here, mate?'

'Fast as you can!'

'You got it!'

'And me, Customer Zip? What can I do?'

'Roz, just do your job at the till as if nothing is happening.'

'That's going to be very tricky.'

'But it's very important you do it, RozSis. If Guard Krick sees you act as normal, he will not suspect anything is amiss.'

'Of course, Apollo. I'll do my best.' She checks her wristwatch. 'And, on that note, Customers, I must make a move. My shift starts in twenty minutes.'

Roz stands and heads for the door –

'Before you go, RozSis, I just want to say how proud I am of you. All of you. No trolley could have found a more loving and supportive Family.'

Vvvmmmmmmmm . . .

'Goodbye, Customers – Good luck.'

'See you later, amigo – Good luck.'

'See you later, mate – Good luck.'

'See you later, RozSis — Good luck.'

'See la-la, Ri-Ri – Gooey duck.'

— 64 —

I am in the hideout. I can see my Brovs as they cross the car park on their way to the supermarket. Their breath is like smoke. They are shivering. More with nerves than cold I think —

'Gosh! We're here. Ready to do your stuff, you three?'

'Raring to go, mate.'

'As ready as I'll ever be, amigo.'

'Ya-ya, Zi-Zi!'

I'm more nervous than I've ever been and yet . . . I love it! Every bit of me is tingling. I can hear my blood rushing. I feel so . . . alive! BigBrov to Apollo! Come in, Apollo!

Here, BigBrov.

Me and Nab are about to enter the supermarket.

So I see.

Vssshhhhh . . .

We're in the supermarket!

You don't have to keep telling me what's going on, BigBrov. I can see everything, don't forget. Oh, there's RozSis at her checkout.

She looks worried.

So do you.

With reason.

Everything will be just fine.

Where's Krick?

Over by the toiletries.

Has he seen me and Nab come in?

Of course.

Is he heading this –?

Klack!

Klack!

Does that answer your question?

What shall we do?

Tell Nabil to walk to the centre aisles; biscuits and sauces. Guard Krick will see him there.

'Nab! Walk to biscuits and sauces.'

'You got it, amigo.'

Quick! Tell him to put Rudi on his shoulder.

'Nab! Rudi. Shoulder. Krick's got to see him.'

'Come on, my little baby. Up here – that's it.'

Twitch!

Nab's heading for the central aisles.

You keep telling me what I know.

Sorry!

Wait for Guard Krick to make eye contact with them! Then run to the back of the supermarket.

But I won't be able to see Nab and Rudi once they've walked into the aisle.

You'll hear the moment. Wait for it! Three ... two ... one —
'MISTERZZZ!'
Contact!
Run!
Past the fresh bread?
Yes!
And the cakes?
Yes! Now ... you see that silver door?
Yes!
That's the lift to the basement.
Is this the button to call the —?
Yes.
I'm pressing it.
I know.
Sorry.
Clunk!
There's the lift! Get in!
I ... I can't open the door.
Don't push! Slide it!
Chunk-skreeek!
Inside. Quick!
In!
Press the button marked Basement.
There ... is no button marked Basement!
What? Oh, let's see ... Lower Lower Lower Ground Floor! That's it!
Pressing! ... The doors ain't closing!
You have to do it by hand! Slide the —
'MISTERZZZ!'
'Leave my pet alone, you capitalist pig!'
Klack!
Klack!
Klack!
Sounds like Krick's chasing Rudi to the other end of the store.
He's certainly trying to, BigBrov.
As far away from us as possible, eh?

Exactly. And at the moment, if I may say so, Rudi is following my instructions a bit quicker than some I could mention.

What d'you mean?

Close the lift door!

Oh! Gosh! Sorry –

Skreeeeek-chunk!

Press the —

Yes, yes.

Zssshhhmmmmm ...

Lower Lower Lower Ground Floor here we come.

It's a very slow lift.

What's Nabil doing?

Waiting by the main doors as we planned.

I bet he's worried about Rudi.

He needn't be.

What's Roz doing?

Watching everything from her checkout.

Bet she's worried about Rudi too.

RozSis is worried about all of us — Aha! We're here! Slide the —

I know!

Chunk-skreeeech!

Welcome to the basement.

It's ... it's so dark. I can't see a thing. Not a single – oh, Apollo! How am I ever going to rescue the snow trolley in complete darkness?

— 65 —

There's a light switch.
  Where?
  By the staircase.
  I can't see the blooming staircase.
  Turn to your right, BigBrov.
  Okey-dokey.
  Now start walking forward.
  I'm worried about tripping over something.
  I won't let you do that.
  Can you see as well in the dark as in the light, Apollo?
  Apparently.
  And when did you find out you could do this?
  Just now — Stop!
  What now?
  Lift your left hand . . .
  Like this?
  Higher . . . Stop! Now . . . move it forward . . .
  Aha! What's this?
  The light switch. Press!
  Lots of fluorescent lights flickering on in the basement
and – there's Krick chasing Rudi down the breakfast cereal aisle
in the supermarket. Look how fast Rudi is running! Hang on! –
Apollo!
  BigBrov!
  Did you see that?
  I did!

I just had a flash of what's going on upstairs in the supermarket!

So it appears, BigBrov.

How did that happen?

No idea.

Let's see if I can do it again ... Yes! I can see Rudi running and ... I can see Krick chasing and –

'I'M GONNA CATCH YOU, YOU RAT!!'

– I can hear him too!

So you can!

It's like having a television set in my head. I know I'm down here in the basement, but when I focus on what's going on upstairs, I can see that in part of my brain too. Oh, gosh. It's like being in two places at the same time.

Or having two minds at the same time, BigBrov.

Two minds?

It appears we have become so close, you are now in my mind as much as I am in yours.

Gosh!

There's no time to dwell on it now.

The snow trolley! Where is it?

You see those big boxes at the other end of the basement?

It's behind them. Right?

Right!

Look at the size of this place, Apollo. It's huge.

It is, BigBrov.

What's that?

You mean that wire mesh cage?

Yeah.

That's where Guard Krick lives.

But it's like a ... a ...

Prison cell?

Yeah. Just a bed and a sink. And some weights to build his muscles up with. And – oh, there's a book! What is it?

THE SOLDIER'S HANDBOOK OF SURVIVAL!

Typical! But . . . oh, Apollo! Don't you think living like this –
Is a bit sad?
Yeah.
I do.
Do you think Guard Krick is very –
Lonely?
Yeah.
I do.
There's nothing in his life, Apollo. Nothing except this prison
cell and hatred for trolleys and – Wait! Apollo! Krick is catching
up with Rudi, I can see it!
Rudi! Run towards the fish counter . . . NOW!
Twitch!
Rudi's running.
And Guard Krick is chasing.
Klack!
Klack!
Klack!
Rudi's looking –
A little tired, yes. We have to –
Rescue the snow trolley! Quick!
Behind that big box.
I'm looking.
See it?
Yes. Oh, it looks so sad.
It's been alone for over a day.
And Krick has been threatening it, I bet.
Undoubtedly.
I'll just grab it and wheel it to the lift and we can – oh, no!
It's tied to the radiator!
With rope.
So many knots.
The most complex I've ever seen.
Can you untie them, BigBrov?
Mmmm, let's see . . . if I pull this bit of rope here – oh, no!

The knots are getting tighter.
I'll pull this bit here – oh, no!
They're getting tighter again!

Oh, gosh! I remember now ... Dad taught me these knots once ... They're the most difficult to untie.

But can you do it?

I don't know.

— 66 —

You'll just have to try, BigBrov.

I am!

... How's it going?

Not good.

Can you remember the time your dad taught you how to untie this knot?

I ... I'm not sure.

Think harder! You're back in the forest ...

Yes.

Is it day or night?

Day.

Sunshine?

Yes. But ... wait!

What?

Rain has come and gone ... That's it. We've just gone through a storm. Dad has tied something to a tree so it won't get blown away. Now he's showing me how to untie it.

What did you untie?

I can't remember ...

Think! You're untying something. Your dad is beside you. Imagine the scene ...

I can hear ... Dad breathing.

And?

A river! That's it! We're beside the river. We're untying a ... a ...

Yes? Yes?

A raft!

Very good! Now ... You're back there! Imagine it! Imagine your dad's voice. This knot is easy to untie, son. All you do is —

Pull this bit of rope here.

That's it. And now you —

Pull this through this and —

'A TROLLEY!'

That's Krick's voice!

I know.

He's stopped chasing Rudi.

Keep still, Rudi. Await instructions.

Twitch!

Guard Krick is just staring at Rudi.

I know, I know.

'Wait a minute! You're not just running away from me, are you, rat? Eh? Oh, no. It's like you're *leading* me on. *Playing* with me. Rats ain't clever enough to do that. Not all by themselves ... Mmmm ... what's going on here? Eh? What's going on?'

BigBrov, untie that rope as fast as you can! Quick!

Why the sudden panic?

Something has happened I didn't prepare for.

What?

Guard Krick is beginning to suspect.

'Someone's telling you *where* to run, ain't that so, eh, rat?'

Twitch!

Oh, no!

Oh, no!

'Someone or some*thing*!'

Twitch!

Oh, no!

Oh, no!

'And could that thing be . . . a *trolley*?'

Twitch!

'It *is*!'

Oh, no!

Oh, no — Untie that rope. Quick! Quick!

I'm going as fast as I can! Pull this bit of rope through this loop here . . . What next, Dad?

'Now why would a trolley want to keep me occupied chasing a rat, eh? . . . Mmmm, there's Roz watching me from her checkout . . . I bet she knows something . . . And there's that kid who owns you, waiting by the doors . . . And there's the mister who ain't a mister waiting outside in the car park . . . Mmmm, it looks like some kind of plan to me.'

Oh, no!

Oh, no!

'And where's the kid with the dreadlocks, eh? I saw him come in with you. But I can't see him anywhere now . . . Of course! How could I have been so stupid! You're here to rescue that trolley I saw you with in the snow yesterday, ain't ya?'

Twitch!

Oh, no!

Help!

Klack!

Klack!

Klack!

BigBrov! You've got to free the snow trolley as soon as possible!

You don't have to tell me! Krick is —

Heading for the basement!!

I'll pull this bit of rope here . . . What next, Dad?
    Give it a pull.
    It won't work yet!
    Quick!
    Nab has seen Guard Krick heading for the basement.
    Klack!
    Klack!
    Klack!
    NabBrov is signalling to MemBrov.
    They don't know what to do.
    Nor do I.
    You're filling me with confidence.
    NabBrov is about to say something to MemBrov —
    'Amigo! Something's gone wrong!'
    'Guard Krick has stopped chasing your Rudi, mate.'
    'He's gonna catch Zip in the act of stealing!'
    'Stop him, mate!'
    'Ya!'
    'OI! YOU CAPITALIST ROBOT!'
    Oh, Nab is being so brave!
    He's running after Guard Krick.
    'STOP, YOU IMPERIALIST –'
    'SHUT GOB, MISTER! The game's up! I know what's
going on. That criminal-in-the-making friend of yours is
downstairs!'
    Klack!

Klack!
Klack!
I pull this through this . . . Oh, I see, Dad. Yeah! Apollo!
You've done it.
Yes!
Well done, Brov!
Well done, Dad, you mean.
Push Snow to the lift as quickly as possible.
Chunka-chunka-clonk-clonk-clonk . . .
Oh, gosh! Another wonky wheel!
Two wonky wheels actually.
It makes pushing it very difficult.
Chunka-chunk-clonk-clonk-clonk . . .
'SHUT GOB, MISTER! I'll call your friends anything I like. You are all a bunch of weirdos. A bunch of thieving weirdos! And I'm about to catch one of you red-handed. And you know what that means? Police! Prison! Ha!'
Klack!
Klack!
Klack!
Chunka-chunka-clonk-clonk-clonk . . .
I've reached the lift.
So has Guard Krick.
I'm pressing the green button.
So is Guard Krick.
Oh, no!
Zssshhhmmmmm . . .
The lift is going up to him.
What can I do? It'd take me ages to walk up all those –
I know, I know. Let me think!
Think quickly!
Aha! Got it!
What?
Listen!
Zssshhhmmmmm – KRA-CHUNKA!!

What's that?

I've stuck the lift!

Good thinking! Look! Guard Krick is kicking the door to the lift. Look how angry he is. I think he's going to burst a blood vessel in a minute. Listen to him —

'STUPID LIFT! COME ON UP HERE! STUPID LIFT!'

Kick!

Kick!

He's heading for the stairs.

We'll have to time this perfectly.

Bring the lift down to me.

Here it comes!

Zssshhhmmmmm . . .

Klack!

Klack!

Klack!

I can hear Krick on the stairs.

He's got another couple of flights to go yet.

Can't you —?

Speed the lift up? No.

Zssshhhmmmmm . . .

Nab is looking really worried now! He's looking around for Rudi too.

Rudi's safe, BigBrov. Over by the chocolate. See?

He should go to Nab.

Of course . . . Rudi! Run to NabBrov! Now!

Twitch!

'My baby! There you are!'

NabBrov is pleased to see Rudi.

But he's still worried about me.

So is MemBrov.

And Newt! Oh, I hate to see Newt so worried and —

Get ready.

For what?

Clunk!
Aha! The lift!
Open the —
I know!
Chunk-skreeek!
Klack!
Klack!
Klack!
Close the —
I know!
Skreeek-chunk!
Klack!
Klack!
Press the —
Apollo!
Sorry.
Zssshhhmmmmm . . .
We're on the way up.
Guard Krick is in the basement.
He's wondering why the lights are on.
I think he's guessed.
Come on, lift! Come on!
Zssshhhmmmmm . . .
Guard Krick is making his way to where he tied Snow . . .
Klack!
Klack!
Klack!
'MISTER? YOU HERE?'
Zssshhhmmmmm – Clunk!
We're here!
Open the —
Gosh, stop saying the obvious!
Chunk-skreeek!
I'm pushing Snow as fast as I can towards the main doors.
Guard Krick has seen Snow is missing.

— 217 —

'MISTERRR!!'
Klack!
Klack!
Klack!
'Amigo! What kept ya?'
'I'll explain later, Nab! Quick! Run!'
Guard Krick is heading for the stairs.
I'm waving at Roz. How relieved she looks –
'Run, Customer Zip!'
Viiissshhhhh!
'Mate!'
'Zi-zi!'
'Mem! Grab the trolley!'
'You got it, mate!'
'To the hideout! Quick! See you soon, Newt!'
'Ya!'
Klack!
Guard Krick's at the top of the stairs!
'Nab! You got Rudi safe?'
'In my pocket, amigo.'
'I just hope Mem gets the trolley across the footbridge
before –'
Klack!
Klack!
Klack!
'You go too, Nab. I can distract Krick alone.'
'I'm not leaving you, amigo!'
'But there's no point in two of us –'
'Well, *you* go, then. It's more dangerous for you. If The
Powers That Be –'
'I'm not leaving you alone!'
'And I'm not leaving you!'
'Oh, Nab . . . you're such a good friend!'
'Don't get mushy!'
'STOP RIGHT THERE, MISTERZZZ!'

Where's Mem?
On the footbridge.
Klack!
Klack!
'Who, *us*, Guard Krick?'
Ooo, you sound so innocent.
That's the general idea.
'I KNOW WHAT YOU'VE BEEN UP TO!'
'You do, Guard Krick? And – gosh – what's that?'
'STEALING!'
'That's slander, amigo!'
'Where's your proof?'
MemBrov is on the other side of the bridge.
They can't be seen by Krick?
No.
Phew!
You can think that again.
Phew!
Don't get clever.
'You think I'm an idiot, misterzzz!'
'We don't think, amigo!'
'We *know*!'
'SHUT GOBS, MISTERZZZ! I know what's gone on here! There's a trolley behind all of this. It's that other trolley, ain't it? Eh? The trolley I saw you with. The one you rushed off with. The one you were hiding with like hunted animals in the cellar. The one you . . . *disappeared* with!'
'*Disappeared, amigo?*'
'You sure you haven't been drinking too much, Guard Krick?'
'Hallucinating, amigo?'
'You don't want to be telling the police fairy stories like that, Guard Krick. They'll laugh in your face. Like we are – Ha! Ha!'
'Ha! Ha!'

'HA! HA!'
'HA! HA!'
Don't push your luck, BigBrov.
'Come on, Nab. Let's get back home. I'm sure Guard Krick's got work to do. Charming to talk to you, as always, Guard Krick. Until we meet again.'
'Oh, we'll meet again, misterzz! You can bet your life on it! WE'LL MEET AGAIN! YOU HEAR ME? WE'LL MEET AGAIN!'

— 68 —

My Brovs are back in the hideout. I'm so relieved to have them here. They are safe. Oh, look at them! They are buzzing with what has just happened. They are talking so fast their words tumble over each other —

'And I was waiting outside, mates. I was getting so worried, mates!'
'*You* were getting worried, amigo! What about *me*?'
'*You* two were getting worried? Gosh – what about *me*?'
'Mee, Zi-Zi!'
Oh, look at LittleBrov! He's happy to be back in the hideout. Safe and sound. His face is glowing with joy and pride. If I had a face, it would be glowing with joy and pride too.

'And my little Rudi did such a wonderful job!'
'He did, mate!'
'Gosh, yes!'
Twitch!

'Ya!'

My Brovs have started acting out bits from the rescue now. BigBrov is showing them how he burnt the rope through with the blowtorch. NabBrov is showing them how he tried to see what Rudi was up to. MemBrov is showing them how hard it was to push the snow trolley home with two wonky wheels tugging in different directions — Wait! Roz is approaching the hideout ... Apollo to BigBrov!

What's up, Apollo?

Roz is going to knock on the garage door ... Now!

Knock!

'Holy macaroni, who's that?'

'Don't worry, Nab. It's Roz. Apollo, the –'

Vvvmmmmm ...

'Did Apollo tell you it was Roz in your mind, mate?'

'Yes, Mem.'

'Holy macaroni, amigo, I *do* wish the two of you would refrain from all that trollepathy malarkey when others are in the room. I'm beginning to think it's a touch rude.'

'Sorry, Nab. You're right.'

'We won't do it again, NabBrov!'

We probably will.

I know.

'Oh, Customers! I've had to leave work early. I've got such a migraine. Guard Krick has been shouting and storming round the place. I've never seen him in such a bad mood – Oh, I've got to sit down.'

'Would you like some cool lemonade, RozSis?'

'Thank you, Apollo. And some headache tablets if you've got any.'

'Gosh, you shouldn't take those chemicals, Roz. Here – I'll massage your shoulders. It's probably just tension.'

'*Just* tension! It's *all* tension, Customer Zip! Guard Krick's yelling has made me tenser than the cables on a suspension bridge – Ooo, that feels nice, Customer Zip.'

'Dad taught me.'

'Here's your lemonade, RozSis.'

'Thank you, Apollo – Ooo, delicious!'

'You shouldn't let Guard Krick get to you, amigo. We laughed in his face, didn't we, amigo?'

'We did, Nab.'

'Listen, my Brovs. Don't underestimate Guard Krick.'

'Holy macaroni, that capitalist robot don't scare me!'

'Stars 'n' bars, nor me!'

'Well, he should! If he catches you with me and the snow trolley, then he will have the proof he needs to cause any amount of trouble. Especially for BigBrov and LittleBrov.'

'Apollo's right, Customers. I've never seen Vinnie like this. He can't prove anything yet – and he knows if anyone asks me I'll tell them I saw you all leave the supermarket without a trolley – but ... oh, his pride has been wounded today. And there's nothing more lethal than a wounded wild animal.'

'You're right, Roz,' says Zip softly. 'We were all getting carried away with the success of our mission.'

'We will all stay in the hideout.'

'Gosh, yes. We've got no reason to leave the hideout until sunrise. Krick won't be around then. How's your head feeling, Roz?'

'Ooo, I'm feeling less tense by the second. You've got magic hands, Customer Zip. And I must say, despite all the tension, all the worry, all the shouting and anger of Vinnie, it was worth it to save this poor, mistreated trolley here.'

I am looking at the snow trolley. There is rust near the base of the metal frame. One of the wheels is surely beyond repair.

Snow looks sad, Apollo.

I know, BigBrov.

It's strange to have a trolley in the hideout that's not moving and talking.

I agree.

If it was alive we could tell it not to be sad any more. We could explain that we're going to build a Doorway and – oh, Apollo! I've got an idea.

I know you have.

Is it possible?

I don't know.

But we should try, shouldn't we?

Of course.

'Everyone! Me and Apollo have just had an idea!'

'Holy macaroni, they've been trollepathizing again!'

'That's not very matey, mate!'

'Listen up! We're going to try to bring the snow trolley to life!'

— 69 —

My Brovs and Sis are kneeling round the snow trolley. I have wheeled so close, the corner of my metal frame is touching the snow trolley's metal frame. I'm trying to feel if there's any life in there — at all —

Is there?

I believe so.

How do we unlock it?

No idea!

You must have!

Why?

It unlocked in you.

But I've no idea how.

You must remember something about it.

Why? Do you remember your birth?

No, of course not. But ... well, I know how *it happened ... Come on, Apollo! Think hard. Remember that day. You're in the supermarket. Little brov grabs hold of you ... He pushes you towards the newspapers and magazines ... Anything?*

All I can vaguely remember is ... hearing the voices of you and LittleBrov.

Talk! Okey-dokey!

'Let's talk to it, everyone.'

'Oh, Customer Zip, I really don't want to be – as Customer Nabil once so eloquently put it – the juicy maggot in your peachy plan, but ... well, don't you think I haven't tried to do this before? I've talked to so many trolleys since I lost my Mary. Over and over again. And never – not once! – have any of them so much as squeaked a wheel.'

'Sounds to me like it ain't got anything to do with a trolley being spoken to by mates, mates.'

'Perhaps a trolley decides all by itself whether to live or not, amigos.'

'You know what I think, Customers? Perhaps not all trolleys have the potential for life.'

'Perhaps you're right, amigo.'

'Perhaps! Perhaps! Gosh, everything's perhaps. None of us knows for sure about anything. But if we let all the perhapses get in the way, we'll never discover any certainties. Now, I don't know if talking to the snow trolley is going to work or not. But, in the absence of any better ideas from you lot, I'm prepared to give it a try. And I hope, as fellow Friends of Apollo, you'll all try along with me ... Well?'

'Sure thing, amigo. We'll try anything. Won't we, amigos?'

'You got it, mate.'

'Ya-ya, Zi-Zi.'

'Of course, Customer Zip.'

BigBrov is leaning very close to the snow trolley —

'Hello, in there . . . we are all your friends . . . we would never hurt you . . . Hello?'

'Nothing's happening, amigo.'

'You try, Nab.'

'Er . . . I'm as big an enemy of the global conspiracy of supermarkets as you are . . . none of us here would put any capitalist shopping in you. Holy macaroni, we wouldn't put any shopping in you at all . . . Holy macaroni, come on, squeak a wheel!'

'Nothing, mate.'

'You try, amigo.'

'Wotcha, mate . . . Come on, rock 'n' roll! The world is a wonderful Elvissy place . . . Wake up and jive to the music!'

'Not a tremor, Customer Memphis.'

'You try, mate.'

'Oh . . . please come alive, dear trolley. We're building a Doorway tonight so you can be free at sunrise. Imagine that! . . . Hello? Hello?'

'Nothing, RozSis.'

'You try, Apollo.'

'I am like you. I am a trolley. I know that somewhere inside you, life is waiting. I can feel it pulse through your metal frame and rubber wheels and plastic push bar. There is no reason to keep it hidden. There is no reason to be afraid . . . Live! Live!'

'Oh, gosh, still nothing. What are we going to –'

'Zi-Zi!'

'Oh, sorry, little brov. You haven't tried yet, have you – Wait! I've just had an idea. Why don't we recreate with this trolley exactly what we were doing when we first met Apollo? We might've been doing something significant without realizing it.'

'Good thinking, amigo.'

'Gosh . . . so, let's think! Yes! I was pushing the trolley

and – Yes! Little brov was riding in the trolley! Come on, Newt. Up you get . . . There! You're a spaceship again.'

'Apple-loo to moon!'

'Well, this trolley ain't called Apollo, is it, little brov?'

'Nooo . . . it Snoo.'

'What? Oh yes, of course. It's Snow.'

Chunka!

'Oh, gosh! Gosh! Did you see that?'

'I did, amigo.'

'I did, mate.'

'I did, Customer Zip!'

The trolley moved!

— 70 —

'It's alive!' cries Zip.

'But how, amigo?'

'What did we do, mate?'

'It must be . . . yes! It's the name! Gosh, everyone, don't you see? It's *naming* the trolley that gives it life – Welcome, Snow.'

'Gosh, yes! Welcome, Snow!'

'Wotcha, Snow, mate.'

'Hello, Snow, amigo.'

'Top of the afternoon to you, Snow.'

'Welcome, Snow.'

'Ya-ya, Snooo!'

Chunka-chunka!

It's moving again!
'It's looking at us.'
'Where's my mobile – oh, gosh!'
'Here! Use mine, mate.'
'Thanks, Mem.'
Touch.
Where am I?
'You're safe in my garage.'
'In our hideout, mate.'
Who are you?
'We're all your amigos, amigo.'
'We're all your mates, mate.'
Where is all the tinned food and fresh fruit and –?
'There's no shopping here, amigo.'
Then how will I be filled with items?
'Oh, gosh! We don't want you to *shop*, Snow.'
'No way, amigo.'
'No way, mate.'
'Ni-ni, Snoo.'
'That's right, Snow. The Customers and me don't want
you to shop ever again.'
   **But . . . you are soft and warm things. I have a memory . . .
Yes! Soft and warm things want me to shop.**
   'No, Snow. These soft and warm things are our friends, not our
masters.'
   No! No! No!
Chonka-chonka-clonk-clonk-clonk . . .
Snow's starting to spin round!
Snow's scared.
Calm the poor thing, Apollo. Can you do some trollepathy?
'I'll try' . . . *Apollo to Snow! Can you hear me?*
. . . *Yes*
Please calm down, Snow.
   *I don't want to calm down! I don't want to be here! Take me back
to . . . to where I was before.*

The supermarket?

Yes. I was . . . safe there.

But you're safe here.

It does not feel safe. It feels . . . different. I don't like different.

But you were treated so badly in the supermarket!

I don't care! It felt safe! I don't care! I don't care! HELP! HELP! HELP!!

Chunkachunkaclonkclonkclonkchunkachunkaclonk clonk –

Silence!

'Wh . . . What's happened, Customers?'

'Holy macaroni . . . Snow's just stopped moving!'

'Like someone pulled a plug, mates.'

'Gosh! It looks like . . . Snow's frozen.'

'It usually is, amigo.'

'No time for jokes, Nab!'

'Sorry, amigo.'

'Apollo? What's happened? Is it fear done this to Snow? . . . Apollo? *Apollo?*'

'Stars 'n' bars! Apollo's frozen too.'

Apollo!?

I'm sorry, BigBrov. I got so distracted with Snow, I let my guard down –

'Babycakes!'

'Sugarplums!'

It's Gran and Aunt Ivy. They're standing at the back of the garage.

I'm sorry . . . I'm sorry . . .

How long have they been there?

Fifteen seconds.

Who's that woman with them?

Haven't you seen her before?

She does look a little familiar, yes.

I'm sorry . . .

'Oh, babycakes, you've no idea what joy it gives us to see you all play with your toys like this. Ain't that right, Sis?'

— 228 —

They didn't hear you speak, or see –
No, no, of course not.
Then there's no problem.
Oh, there is, BigBrov.
What?
'Zip, babycake, surely you remember Nicci Crib? She decided to pay us all a surprise visit.'

Oh, no! I remember now. It's Nicci Crib from –
The Powers That Be.

— **71** —

Nicci Crib takes a step into the hideout and looks round. She is wearing a neat, two-piece, grey suit, with a string of pearls round her neck. Her hair is blonde and pulled in a tight bun at the back of her head. She is holding a clipboard on which she makes continuous notes.

'Hello, Zip. Hello, Newt. Don't mind me having a little snoop round, do you? ... Oh, you've made it so cosy in here, I must say. What a charming rug. Brand new by the looks of it. A sofa and armchairs too. I hear this style is coming back in fashion. Goodness, what a lovely place to hang out with your friends, eh, Zip?'

Answer her.

'Er ... yes, Miss Crib.'

'I must say, I'm so impressed at all the changes that have happened in your family since I last saw you all. Look at your gran. Like a new person.'

'I am, sugarplum!'

'And I even heard little Newt laughing earlier, if I'm not very much mistaken. That's a sound I've never heard before. He looks so well and happy. You both do. Are you and your brother both well and happy here, Zip?'

Answer her!

'Oh . . . yes, Miss Crib.'

'Are you looking forward to starting your new school – why, your *first* school, I believe – next term? Eh?'

Answer.

'Er . . . yes, Miss Crib.'

'I only wish your mum was here so I could congratulate her on the wonderful things she seems to have achieved.'

Mum! Oh, Apollo! Mum's still in her bedroom and –

Keep calm, BigBrov. Gran and Aunt Ivy lied. They said Mum is shopping in the city and will not be back till late.

Good lie!

Go along with it. Say something!

'Mum will be sorry for missing you too, Miss Crib. She has been looking forward to it for so long. Hasn't she, Aunt Ivy?'

'Oh yes, babycake.'

'It's all she talks about, sugarplum.'

'But Mum just had to get some shopping, didn't she, Gran?'

'Oh yes, sugarplum. Vital shopping from the city.'

'That's right, mate! Your mum went with my Missy.'

Memphis is such a natural liar!

Good!

'And you must be . . . Memphis?'

'That's right, mate. Mate's gran and aunt tell you all about me big-boy muscles, did they?'

'They told me something, yes. And this Missy who's gone with Zip's mum to the city, that's your mum, I take it?'

'She is. And Missy and mate's mum went to the city to get some shopping together. They're great mates. They do everything together. Like mates do. Ain't that right, mates?'

'That's right, amigo. I saw them. I waved them goodbye. I said, "Don't give the capitalist pigs too much of your money!"'

'You must be Nabil?'

'Nabil – Enemy of the Global Conspiracy.'

'And what conspiracy is that?'

'Who knows? That's why it's a conspiracy.'

'And you live in New Town, do you?'

'Well, considering the nearest other place is about twenty miles away, I should think that's a very likely assumption. Unless, of course, I jumped on my own private helicopter and flew here to hang out with my amigos.'

'You're a sarcastic boy, aren't you?'

'I try me best, yeah.'

'I'm not the enemy, you know, Nabil,' says Nicci, softly and coolly. 'I'm here to make sure that Zip and Newt get the best life possible.'

'They've got the best life possible!' exclaims Nabil, stamping his foot. 'They're with the best family and the best amigos. That's all they need. Right, amigos?'

'Right, mate.'

'Right, Customer Nabil.'

Nicci looks at Roz and smiles. 'You must be the one-legged girl from the supermarket?'

'Hang on, let's check.' Roz feels her legs. 'Yep! One of 'em's false all right, so I must be her.'

'And tell me,' continues Nicci with her smile fixed firmly on her face. 'Is that why these two trolleys are here?'

Oh, no!

— 231 —

Don't panic!
She's touching you.
She's touching Snow too.
If she thinks we've stolen you and Snow from the supermarket ... oh, Apollo, The Powers That Be will take me and Newt away –
Just think of an excuse why we're here.
Easier trollepathized than done.
But you've got to!
I know!

'Well ... yes,' stammers Roz. 'Of course! The supermarket trolleys are here ... because ...'

Gran says with a laugh, 'Oh, little Newt loves playing in them, don't you, sugarplum?'

'Ya!'

'What?' wonders Nicci, still smiling. 'Play in *two* at the same time?'

Think of something.

I'm trying!

'Besides,' continues Nicci, 'wanting to play with a trolley is no excuse for not returning it to the supermarket. In fact, I thought the local supermarket had introduced a new policy where no trolleys are supposed to be taken beyond the car park. So, if that's the case, why ... the mere fact that they're here at all could be considered ... stealing.'

'Stealing!' gasps Gran.

'Stealing!' gasps Aunt Ivy.

Think!

I can't!

'We're *helping* the supermarket, mate,' says Memphis, stepping forward. 'Ain't that right, mates?'

'Er ... gosh, yes, of course.'

'Er ... exactamundo, amigos.'

'Er ... of course you are, Customer Memphis.'

— 232 —

'Er ... Ya-ya, Mi-Mi!'

What's Mem getting at?

I'm not sure yet.

'And how are you doing that exactly, Memphis?' asks Nicci, still smiling. 'Do tell.'

'Well, mate ... A lot of people round here take trolleys out of the supermarket and then don't return them. It's a terrible problem.'

'I thought New Town was practically empty of people,' says Nicci, still smiling. 'In fact, I wouldn't be surprised if almost the entire population of New Town is in this garage right now.'

'The workmen!' exclaims Memphis. 'The ones building the houses and stuff. They take the trolleys from the supermarket. They fill them with their lunches and ... and stuff. I know there ain't been many workmen here since the snow started, but ... well, they certainly left a lot of trolleys behind. And so ... well, Roz, here, mate, asked us to help out and find them and bring them back to the store. And ... well, these are the first two we've found.'

What a liar.

What a friend.

Say something, BigBrov.

'Gosh, yes! We were going to return them on our next trip to the supermarket.'

'Yeah, amigo, we were gonna return them as soon as we could.'

I'm proud of you all!

'Well ... in that case,' says Nicci, 'I'll have to give you the benefit of the doubt, won't I, eh? But make sure the trolleys are back where they belong by the next time I see you. You promise?'

'Gosh, of course, Miss Crib. No one wants to get them where they belong more than us.'

'It's time I was on my way,' says Nicci with a big, bright

smile. 'The motorway's going to get chock-a-block if I leave it any later. But I must see Mrs Jingle before I can make any final assessment. You do understand that, don't you?'

'Of course, babycake.'

'Of course, sugarplum.'

'Gosh, yes, of course, Miss Crib.'

'So will you tell Mrs Jingle I'll see her in the morning. It's got to be extremely bright and early, I'm afraid, because I need to get all this wrapped up before the holiday season hits.'

'That's fine by us, babycake. We're all early risers in this house. Ain't that right, Sis?'

'Oh, the earlier the better, sugarplum.'

Apollo! What about Mum?!

I know, BigBrov.

She's pottering around the house and stuff now, but ... oh, Apollo, she'll never be totally back to her old self by morning.

She'll have to try.

But how? We mustn't force her, you said.

I know, I know.

One step at a time, you said! What are we going to do? What are we –?

I haven't got any answers at the moment, BigBrov, but I will try to think of some — Wait! Aunt Ivy is about to say something to Nicci Crib —

'Here, love. It's quicker to go out through the garage door. I'll get the door for you.'

Vvvmmmmm ...

Nicci stands with her back to the opening door and says, 'So ... until the morning. Zip, make sure your mum's here to see me, won't you?'

'Yes, Miss Crib.'

A vehicle pulls up outside the garage door.

Oh, no!

Oh, no!

'I'm making it your responsibility, Zip. Your mum must be here, otherwise ... well, I don't like to think of the consequences, really I don't.'

Someone gets out of the vehicle.

Klack!

No!

No!

'See you in the morning,' says Nicci.

A figure appears in the doorway.

'Well, what luck I was passing,' says Guard Krick. 'I've been looking for these two trolleys everywhere.'

— 72 —

I can't believe this is happening. It's like a dream. It's not real.

I can't believe Krick is walking into the hideout.

'Oh! Hello!' says Nicci. 'You must be from the supermarket. Am I right?'

'You are correct. Miss ...?'

'Crib. Nicci Crib. The children were just telling me how they've collected the trolleys to return to the supermarket. You've saved them a trip ... Mr?'

'Krick. Guard Krick.'

I can't believe Gran is smiling.

I can't believe Aunt Ivy is smiling.

I can't believe –

BigBrov!

Apollo! What are we going to do?

Nothing, BigBrov. You must not make a fuss in front of The Powers That Be. This Nicci woman can take you and LittleBrov away from Mum and Gran and Aunt Ivy. You know that!

But we've got to —

No!

'Well, Guard Krick,' says Nicci, flashing her eyelashes at him. 'You can start loading the two trolleys on to your van, can't you?'

'Indeed I can, Miss Crib.'

I can't believe this is happening.

This can't be happening.

Guard Krick can't be picking up Snow and —

CLUNK!

— hurling Snow trolley into the van.

'Zi-Zi!'

Newt is crying.

Pick him up.

I am but . . . oh, I don't know how to comfort him.

'Oh . . . Zi-Zi . . . Zi-Zi . . .'

'How strong you are, Guard Krick. Do you work out?'

'I train with weights, Miss Crib.'

'I must say, it shows.'

'A disciplined body and a disciplined mind. That's what I believe.'

'How right you are, Guard Krick.'

Guard Krick is heading for me.

'Amigo?' whispers Nabil.

'Mate?' whispers Mem.

I shoot them a pleading look! They know there is nothing we can do. We've got to keep our mouths shut and watch.

Yes. They understand, BigBrov.

Krick has grabbed you!

'Ni! Ni! Apple-loo!'

Gran says, 'Oh, look at Newt, the poor lamb. Don't cry. They're only trolleys.'

'He gets so attached to things,' says Gran. 'His mum says he was like this in the forest. He thought a hedgehog was his best friend once.'

'Children have such imaginations, don't they?' says Nicci Crib.

Guard Krick has lifted me into the air!

'So strong, Guard Krick.'

'Many thanks, Miss Crib.'

Gran strokes Newt's hair. 'Don't worry, love. I'll buy you a bike instead. Would you like that?'

'Na!' cries Newt. 'Na!'

Guard Krick is taking me to the van.

Klack!

Klack!

'NO!' cries Zip. 'NO!'

My hand is on Apollo.

My hand is clutching Apollo.

'YOU'RE NOT TAKING THIS ONE!'

Guard Krick grins and bends to whisper in Zip's ear, 'So this is the special one, is it? Thank you for making that so clear to me, mister. I'll make sure this one gets . . . very *special treatment*.'

Zip glares at Guard Krick.

'I'm not scared of you, Krick!' hisses Zip.

'Quite a little rebel, ain't ya, misterrr?'

'Gosh, I blooming hope so!'

'Zip, babycake, what's got into you?'

BigBrov! Don't do anything!

I'm not letting him take you, Apollo.

You must!

Roz steps forward and says, 'It's the radio! That's all. Zip wants to remove the radio from the front of the trolley before you take it.'

Memphis says, 'Oh ... er ... good thinking, mate. That's my radio and I ... er ... wouldn't be able to listen to Elvis broadcasts without it.'

'Allow me, mister,' says Guard Krick, tugging the radio from Apollo.

No, no, no, no, no, no, no.

'Your strength amazes me, Guard Krick.'

'It's only string, Miss Crib. You should just see what I could do to one of these trolleys. Why, with my bare hands ... I could crush one to the size of a dice!'

Roz gasps.

I still can't let go.

You've got to.

'Let go of the trolley, mister.'

I can't!

'Oh ... I think Customer Zip is a little tired,' says Roz, prising Zip's fingers from the push bar one by one. 'All the excitement of the snow has got to him. Let go of the trolley, Customer Zip.'

No, no, no –

'Let go ...'

No, no.

'That's it!'

All the fingers have been prised away and –

Guard Krick is grabbing hold of Apollo.

'GOTCHA!'

Guard Krick is taking Apollo to the van.

Klack!

Klack!

No, no, no, this can't be happening!

Please don't be upset, BigBrov.

Guard Krick hurls Apollo into the back of the van –

CLUNK!

NO, NO, NO, NO –

BigBrov ... are you listening to me? BigBrov?

I'm listening . . .
Thank you for what you tried to do . . . I will always be grateful . . .
Guard Krick slams the back of the van shut.
Guard Krick says, 'Goodbye, all.'
'Goodbye, babycake.'
'Goodbye, sugarplum.'
'Goodbye, Guard Krick.'
Do not blame Gran or Aunt Ivy for being pleasant to Guard Krick . . .
They do not know what has been going on.
Guard Krick gets in the van.
Guard Krick starts the van . . .
Please do not get leaky eyes, BigBrov. I cannot bear it if you get
leaky eyes —
The van drives away . . .
'Apollo!' gasps Zip.
'Apollo!' gasps Nabil.
'Apollo!' gasps Memphis.
'Apple-loo!' gasps Newt.
'Apollo!' gasps Roz.
Try not to forget me, BigBrov.

— 73 —

It is dark now.
The hideout is still and silent.
Zip sits on the armchair, Newt curled in his lap.
Nabil and Memphis are on the sofa, leaning against each other, holding hands.

Roz is sitting in the other armchair, stroking Rudi.

I can't believe this has happened.

I can't believe this has happened.

It is gone midnight.

Earlier, Mum and the other grown-ups had brought in plates of sandwiches, a big bowl of popcorn and a bottle of Coke and told them all to enjoy their slumber party.

The food and drink is still on the table.

Not a mouthful has been eaten.

Not a mouthful has been drunk.

I can't believe this has happened.

I can't believe this has happened.

Memphis has managed to find a plug socket so the lamp is turned on.

But the heat . . . that went with Apollo.

The hideout is very cold now.

I can't believe this has happened.

New Town is sleeping.

Mum, Aunt Ivy, Gran – all of them are in their beds, content, dreaming dreamy dreams.

But no one in the hideout is sleeping.

No one in the hideout is content.

There are no dreamy dreams here.

Here, everyone is wide awake and discontent.

And in the middle of a nightmare.

I cannot believe . . .

I . . . won't believe!

'I won't!' says Zip, stomping his foot. 'You hear me? I won't believe this is what is supposed to happen! Not after all we've been through. All we've achieved. All we were on the brink of achieving. It makes no sense!'

'Amigo, don't look for –'

'Don't say it, Nab! Because I *am* looking for sense. In fact, I *demand* sense. And if I don't get it . . . why, if I don't get it I'm going to get really, really angry.'

'Oh, Customer Zip,' says Roz. 'There's nothing we can do. Honestly. Don't you think I haven't been going over and over it in my head? The supermarket is shut. *Sealed!* All the doors are electronically locked. There's a very high fence all round the back. The main building has alarms at every door and window. It's a fortress, Customer Zip! And fortresses are not meant to be broken into.'

'NO!' yells Zip, pushing Newt aside and jumping to his feet. 'I WON'T ACCEPT IT! NO! NO!! NO!!'

'Holy macaroni!'

'Stars 'n' bars!'

'Oh, Customer Zip!'

'Ya!'

'Listen, everyone! Apollo is in the supermarket! And I for one am not going to sit around and do nothing. And it has to be done now. This instant. This very second. Not tomorrow. Not the day after tomorrow. You heard what Krick said. He wants to teach Apollo a lesson. That means ... Apollo might not even *see* another tomorrow or day after tomorrow. Krick will take a blowtorch to Apollo and –'

'How d'you know ...?' interrupts Nabil, then turns away, mumbling, 'Oh, forget it.'

'No, Nab. I know exactly what you were going to say. How do I know Krick ain't taken a blowtorch to Apollo already? Right?'

'... Right.'

'Well, he hasn't! I *know* that! Don't ask me how. I just do. I feel it in every atom of my blood and skin and bones. Apollo is safe. At the moment. But if we sit here and do nothing, then the moment will pass and Guard Krick will grab his blowtorch and take it to Apollo and –'

'Oh, don't, Customer Zip. Please. I can't bear it.'

'Don't worry, Roz. You won't have to bear it. Because I

won't let it happen. I won't allow Apollo to be hurt! I will not *allow* us to be beaten!'

'Ya-ya, Zi-Zi.'

'I know it looks impossible at the moment, but ... but we *will* work something out. We *will* make the impossible possible again. And why? Because we won't give up. We're going to get into that supermarket tonight. We're going to break in and rescue Apollo and Snow. And, what's more, we will get both through the Doorway at solstice. Are you with me, Friends of Apollo?'

'Ya-ya, Zi-Zi!'

'Oh yes, Customer Zip!'

'All the way, amigo!'

'Mates together, mate!'

'Then listen carefully ... because this is what we're going to do ...'

— 74 —

I am in the basement of the supermarket. Oh, how I miss talking to BigBrov. I want to have his voice in my metal frame and rubber wheels and plastic push bar again. But ... oh, what's the point? I have said my goodbyes so perhaps it's best to leave it at that. After all, I have seen the blowtorch —

... Apollo!

It's BigBrov! He's trying to contact me —

Apollo?

BigBrov shouldn't do this. It will only upset him.

Can you hear me?

I mustn't answer. Why prolong the pain?

I know what you're thinking. But answering me is not going to prolong the pain. It will shorten it! It will stop it altogether! You must answer. Hear me? You must! You must!

... I'm here, BigBrov.

We're going to rescue you.

No. I refuse to let you put yourself in danger. If The Powers That Be find out you —

We'll be careful not to get caught.

But Guard Krick is bound to see you. He'll tell —

It'll be our word against his. If Nicci Crib asks any questions we'll say we were all here. In the hideout. All night. A sleepover. Roz will say she was here too. We'll each be each other's alibi.

But what if Nicci Crib doesn't believe —

The decision's been made, Apollo! That's it! No argument! We're getting you out and that's that! Now ... see us! Come on. I need your help for this to work. See us! Quick!

All right ... Oh! I can see you all. You are standing in the middle of the rose rug. LittleBrov is kneeling at your feet, NabBrov is standing next to MemBrov by the sofa. RozSis is sitting in the armchair. Tell them all I miss them so much already.

'Apollo misses you all!'

'We miss you too, amigo.'

'Too right, mate!'

'Ya-ya, Apple-loo!'

'Oh, Apollo, sweet Apollo.'

Okey-dokey. That's all the mushy talk out of the way. On with business. Show me where you are ...

Here! Look!

The basement! I should've guessed! Where's Snow?

Beside me.

I see, yes ... And Krick?

In his cage.

— 243 —

Aha! There he is. Flopped out on his bed.

He's been drinking.

Is he drunk?

He was.

Well, that's lucky for us, I guess. It stopped him doing any damage to you and Snow.

He was threatening to.

What did he say?

I don't want to fill your head with such horrible images.

Now, listen up, Apollo. Keep calm and don't let Snow start panicking. We'll have you both out of there soon. I promised to set you free. And I will.

Oh, BigBrov! Please. I beg of you. Don't do anything that puts you or LittleBrov at risk. Breaking into a supermarket is a crime. Taking trolleys out of a supermarket is a crime. I would never forgive myself if The Powers That Be found a reason to take you and LittleBrov away from Mum and —

Over and out for now.

But —

Shut up!

— 75 —

Zip searches through some boxes.

'What are you looking for, Customer Zip?'

'There!'

'What, amigo?'

Zip throws them some camouflage jackets and a tin of

black shoe polish. 'Put the jackets on and cover all visible skin with polish.'

'Mate? What's going on?'

'We used this stuff in the forest. Wear the jackets over your clothes – Nab, you might have to take the fur coat off. It's a bit bulky. But don't worry. The jackets are very warm. Once you've got these on it will be more difficult to see you at night, even with infrared binoculars. Black shoe polish on the skin is good camouflage at night too, no matter what shade your skin. Believe me, I know what I'm talking about. And now – here!' Zip takes a tool kit from another box and opens the lid. 'Here's the stuff we need! Dad's penknife! This will come in useful. And here're the torches! Enough for one each, I think. Yes.'

'I wann torshh, Zi-Zi.'

'Of course, you can have a torch, little brov!' Zip gives Newt a torch, then looks in the box again. 'And ... Aha! Yes! Balaclavas!'

'Balaclavas!'

'Balaclavas!'

'Balaclavas!'

'Black lavs!'

'Our hair will reflect light no matter how dark it is!' explains Zip. 'Especially hair with wet-look gel in, Mem!'

'But, mate ... a balaclava will mess my quiff!'

'No time for vanity, amigo!'

'But –'

'Do it, Mem!'

'Stars 'n' bars!' mutters Memphis, pulling the balaclava on.

'Okey-dokey! Now for the most important thing! *Stink bombs!*'

'Stink bombs, amigo?'

'Dad made them. We used to throw them in

demonstrations against The Powers That Be in the forest. If Guard Krick gets a whiff of one of these ... well, he won't be any trouble to us, believe me ... Now listen up, everyone. This is the plan. We'll get in through the back lot of the supermarket and –'

'But, Customer Zip, that's where the high fence is.'

'*I'll* climb it.'

'*You, amigo?*'

'I've been climbing trees for most of my life, Nab. Trust me. A fence is easy.' Zip looks at Roz. 'Once I'm over the fence, Roz, what's the way to get the main gates open so Nab and Mem can join me?'

'Let me think, Customer Zip ... Yes! There's a control booth. There must be something in there that operates the gates to the back lot.'

'Will the control booth be locked?'

'I'm ... not sure.'

'Then I'll face that problem when I get to it. Okey-dokey, let's say I'm in the back lot. How do me and Nab and Mem get into the supermarket, Roz?'

'Well ... there's a back door.'

'Okey-dokey!'

'But it'll be alarmed, Customer Zip.'

'Then I'll have to cut the alarm wire!'

'Stars 'n' bars!'

'Holy macaroni!'

'Listen up! Once me and Nab and Mem are in the store, we'll make our way to the basement. We'll have to use the stairs for surprise. There's three floors. Make sure you're fast, but quiet as fieldmice.'

'What do we do once we're in the basement, mate?'

'We ... rescue, Apollo.'

'No ... detailed plan, amigo?'

'Not really, Nab. It's tricky to make a detailed plan for something we can't forsee. All I can say for sure is this:

we'll throw stink bombs and hope the resulting stink renders Krick useless.'

'If it don't, mates, I'll give him one of my kung fu kicks where it hurts most.'

'No violence, Mem! You hear? That was something Dad was always very strict about. Wasn't he, little brov?'

'Ya!'

'We can ... restrain him. But nothing that harms him in any way.'

'Much as we'd all like too, of course, amigo.'

'That's a base and animal instinct you must learn to control, Nab. Although, I have to admit, it's base and animal and perfectly understandable.'

'Customer Zip? What will I be doing while all this is going on?'

'You and Newt will wait outside keeping watch.'

'Zi-Zi! Wanna comm helll yooo!'

'You will be helping me, little brov. I need you to keep watch outside. No one has eyesight like you. Remember how you saw the badgers when no one else could?'

'Ya ... But wanna comm –'

'And you've got another important job to do as well. You've got to keep little Rudi tucked in your jacket at all times. His fur is far too bright for what we've got to do. Think you can manage these important tasks, Newt?'

'Ya-ya, Zi-Zi!'

'That's my little brov!'

'I have a question, amigo.'

'Fire away, Nab.'

'The stink bombs ... they're revolting, you say?'

'Pure skunk and essence of pig poo.'

'So ... what's gonna stop us getting all ponged up along with Guard Krick?'

'These!' cries Zip, rushing to another box. He rips open the top and removes 'Gas masks!'

'Holy macaroni!'

'Stars 'n' bars!'

'Ooo!'

'Ya!'

Zip throws one each to Nabil, Memphis and Roz. 'Tie them to the belt of your camouflage jackets,' he tells them. 'When the stink starts, put them on!'

'Your dad was prepared for everything, wasn't he, amigo.'

'He was, Nab.'

'Mate!' says Memphis, picking up the radio. 'We should take this! After all, we want Apollo talking to the mates again, don't we, mates.'

'Good thinking, Mem,' says Zip, taking the radio and squeezing it into one of his pockets. 'Now, are we all ready?'

'Yeah, amigo.'

'Yeah, mate.'

'Ya-ya, Zi-Zi!'

'Yes, Customer Zip.'

'And don't forget! We've got to do it quickly. Apollo needs to be going through the Doorway at sunrise and that's only ...' Zip looks at his watch. 'Two hours away.'

Apollo to BigBrov.

What is it, Apollo?

Guard Krick is waking up! Hurry! HURRY!!

— 76 —

I can see them! Five figures creeping out of New Town. Roz is holding LittleBrov. They are dressed in camouflage jackets and balaclavas. Their skin is darkened with boot polish. How bright their teeth and eyes look. Gas masks hang from their belts and they're holding torches. And there's Rudi! I just caught a glimpse of him tucked in LittleBrov's puffa suit. They have reached the footbridge.

Is it safe to cross, Apollo?

Let me see ... Yes! NOW!

'Okey-dokey. Cross now!'

'Lucky, not much traffic, eh, amigo?'

'Always quiet this time of night, Customer Nab.'

'And the snow has made motoring difficult, amigo.'

'My head is itching in this balaclava, mates.'

'Ha-ha, Mi-Mi!'

'No talking in the ranks,' hisses Zip. 'Concentrate!'

What's Krick doing?

He's sitting on the edge of his bed.

Is he still drinking?

Yes.

Perhaps he'll pass out again.

I don't think so. He keeps looking over at me. There is such hatred in his eyes.

We've crossed the footbridge.

Let me see if it's safe for you to cross the car park ... Yes! Run now!

'Run now!'

Make sure you creep round to the back of the supermarket as quickly as possible, BigBrov.

I know, I know! . . . Right! There's the back lot.

That's a very high fence.

I've seen higher.

Can you climb it?

Easy!

What did I tell you? A hero!

'Roz, you're sure none of the security cameras are working yet?'

'Positive, Customer Zip.'

'Good!' Zip looks round at everyone. 'Now, don't forget, all of you wait here while I climb over the fence and get into that control cabin over there so I can open the gates for –'

CRASHHHH!!

Apollo! What's that?

Guard Krick has thrown his whisky bottle! Start climbing!

You've got it!

Oh, look at BigBrov grab hold of that wire fence. He's so strong and — oh! Up he goes.

'Holy macaroni, look at the amigo go!'

'He's like a spider, mates!'

'Ooo, he's so agile!'

'Ya!'

BigBrov has reached the top.

Just getting my balance . . . There!

BigBrov is swinging his leg over.

Now . . . down the other side.

'Zi-Zi!'

'Don't worry, little brov. Everything's just fine.'

Oh, no! Guard Krick has got to his feet!

I'm nearly in the back lot, Apollo!

Guard Krick is walking towards me.

Klack!

Klack!
Guard Krick is about to talk —
'There was once a boy,' says Guard Krick. 'And all this boy did was hate. Hate everything and everyone. He hated the whole world ... And do you know who this boy was?'
Help us, BigBrov!
'This boy was ... ME!'

— 77 —

I'm in the back lot.
'Well done, amigo.'
'Nothing to it, Nab!'
'Customer Zip,' whispers Roz. 'The control booth is over there.'
'I see it,' Zip whispers back, staring at them through the wire fence. 'Now, keep your eyes peeled. If you see anyone coming, make an owl noise.'
'An owl noise, amigo?'
'Don't think I can, mate.'
'Newt can. Go on, little brov. Give us a hoot!'
'Hooot-hooot!'
'Glorious! And don't forget ... keep little Rudi tucked in your jacket.'
'Ya!'
Twitch!
Apollo? How's things?
Can't you hear?

'When I was a boy I hated the morning, hated people at bus stops, hated the sound of people eating, hated the way old people took ages to cross the road, hated the way babies cried, hated the afternoon, hated cotton wool, hated all pop songs, hated the night . . .'

I'm creeping across the back lot.

You've reached the control booth.

It is made of wood and it's got . . . two windows.

One window is on the door and the other at the front.

I'm trying the door.

Locked?

Yes.

How are you going to get into —? Oh, no, Guard Krick is breathing his whisky breath all over me. I wish I had a nose to hold.

'And, as well as hating, I *did* lots of hateful things. I smashed things and smashed and kicked things. And no matter how hard or often I smashed and hit and kicked, I never felt any guilt. Nothing at all. And I hated feeling nothing. And the more I hated feeling nothing, the more I smashed and hit and kicked.'

He gets doolallier and doolallier.

Just get me out of here.

I will. But I need to open the door to this cabin first!

Well, think of something.

You're a great help!

'One day I saw a girl sitting by a canal. I watched her from a bridge. She didn't see me. She was drawing a supermarket trolley. She was so calm and peaceful. Just watching her made me not want to smash things. I went to the bridge to watch her every day. It got to the point where the only reason I got up in the morning was to watch the girl by the canal.'

I've got an idea!

What?

Surely you know.

Yes. But it's too noisy.
You got a better idea?
No.
Then there's no choice.
Well, be careful you don't cut yourself.
If I kick the window in with the sole of my boot, it'll break —
I'm not sure I like this.
I've seen my dad do it, Apollo. I won't get hurt.

'One day, I followed her home. I stood in the street and watched her at her bedroom window. I felt like I'd known her all my life. I felt she belonged to me. Finally, I went up to the front door and knocked. I spoke to her. She said her name was Roz.'

Okey-dokey . . . I'm going to boot the window in now —
Wait! I'll see if I can do some mind control on Guard Krick so he won't hear.
Good thinking!
Guard Krick! You won't hear any smashing glass . . . You won't hear any —

'WHAT YOU DOING, TROLLEY? TRYING TO GET IN MY MIND, EH? I CAN FEEL IT! YOU EVIL TROLLEY! YOU EVIL TROLLEY!'

BigBro! Quick! He's shouting. Boot the —
I know!
SMASHHH!!
'I WON'T LET YA DO IT, TROLLEY!'
He didn't hear.
Your mind control worked.
Not in the way I'd planned, though.
It doesn't matter.
Be careful when you —
Put my hand through the broken window, I know.
Well, broken glass can be very —
Dangerous! I'm not a two-year-old, Apollo. Now . . . I've got to feel for the handle to open the door . . .

Left a bit ... down a bit ... There!
Do I turn or push?
Turn!
It's opening.
Go inside.
I am – oh, look at that control panel!
I've never seen so many switches and buttons.
Any ideas which one opens the gates?
No.
How come you know some things but not others?
That's one of the things I don't know — Oh, no!
What?
Can't you see?
Guard Krick has grabbed the blowtorch!

— 78 —

'But Roz wouldn't have anything to do with me. Why? A trolley had turned her against me. That's why. That same trolley I'd watched her draw. It had poisoned Roz's mind against me. Like all trolleys poison minds.'

Charming!

He's one hundred per cent doolally.

Oh, no!

Guard Krick is approaching Snow!

You've got to open the gates quick, BigBrov! Just press a button.
Any button.

Any button?

Yes.

But –

Do it!

Zzzzttmmmmm . . .

'Gosh! The gates are opening!'

Guard Krick is lighting the blowtorch!

I'm signalling to Nab and Mem to join me.

You've got to move quick, BigBrov.

I know, I know.

'Amigo!'

'Mate!'

'Welcome to the back lot, you two.'

'Holy macaroni, we got so nervous when you smashed the –'

'No time for that now. Krick's about to start using the blowtorch on Snow! To the back door! Come on!'

He's still ranting and raving. Listen to him —

'I loved Roz so much. I begged her to stop talking to that evil trolley and marry me. But Roz just went into the garden shed and refused to listen to a word I said. That's where she kept her trolley. The garden shed. One day I watched them through the shed window. Roz was laughing and chatting away to the trolley. She never so much as smiled when she was with me.'

I'm not surprised.

We're at the back door.

There's the alarm up above.

The red box?

Yes.

'Gosh! It's pretty high.'

'What is, amigo?'

'The alarm. See it? Red box.'

'Get on my shoulders, mate!'

'You took the words out of my mouth, Mem!'

Guard Krick is aiming the blowtorch at Snow's push bar!

Tell Snow to be brave.
Be brave, Snow ... Be Brave!
I'm on Mem's shoulders.
You're taking the penknife from your pocket.
I'm opening the penknife.
You're reaching for the alarm wire ...

'Gosh ... I can't ... quite ... reach ...'

'I got rid of that spiteful trolley of hers! I snatched it away from her and crushed it to the size of dice! And since then, I've hated every trolley. And that's why ... I'M GONNA BURN YOU, TROLLEY!'

BIGBROV!

I know, I know.

'You'll have to lift Zip higher, amigo!'

'How, mate?'

'Climb on that window ledge there, amigo!'

'You got it, mate!'

'I'll help you keep balance, amigo.'

You're being lifted higher.

I'm stretching for the wire ...

'BURN!'

BIGBROV!

I KNOW!

Stretching ...

Cut!

Yes!!

'You've done it, amigo!'

NOOOOO!

Apollo! What?

Can't you see? Look!

Oh, no! Krick is burning Snow!

'BURN, TROLLEY, BURN!'

Be brave, Snow.

The back door's locked, Apollo.

Then knock it down. I'll distract Krick's mind again. Just hurry!

'We've got to knock the door down!'

'But, amigo, Guard Krick will hear!'

Guard Krick! You will not hear a door being knocked down ... You will not hear a door being knocked down ...

'YOU'RE DOING IT AGAIN, YOU EVIL TROLLEY!'

'Krick won't hear! Apollo's distracting him so –'

'Out the way, mates!'

'Eh, amigo?'

'I do believe my kung fu kick is needed – YEEE-HAAA!!'

CRASHHH!!

The doors open.

'Well done, Mem!'

'Well done, amigo!'

'I've progressed to the third lesson now, mates!'

Apollo? Did Guard Krick hear?

Not a thing. But hurry. Snow's push bar is on fire!

'Quick, Friends!' yells Zip. 'Follow me!'

We're rushing inside.

The plastic on Snow's push bar is melting!

'Torches on, everyone!'

Click!

Click!

Click!

'SUFFER, TROLLEY, SUFFER!'

Snow is melting.

We're approaching the stairs.

Be brave, Snow.

We're rushing down the stairs to the basement.

Run faster.

What's that smell . . .? Oh, no!

Burning trolley!

We're at the bottom of the stairs.

'Gas masks, everyone!'

'I'm gonna enjoy chopping you up, you pathetic trolley! I'm gonna scatter you all over the motorway! Cars will crush you flat as coins . . . They will crush you and crush you for weeks and weeks. HA-HA-HA-HA!! – Hang on! What's that noise? Someone's in the basement! Who's there? Eh? Eh?'

'Stink bombs at the ready – Now!'

We're holding stink bombs.

Blooming throw them!

'Throw stink bombs – NOW!'

Whoooosh!

Whoooosh!

Whoooosh!

They're gonna land at Krick's feet!

Good!

PPPHHUUTT!

PPPHHUUTT!

PPPHHUUTT!

The stinks bombs are exploding with smoke.

And essence of skunk and pig poo!

'Arrrghuuughhh . . .' goes Guard Krick.

Guard Krick has dropped the blowtorch.

He's coughing and spluttering.

Quick, BigBrov!
'FRIENDS OF APOLLO TO THE RESCUE!!'

— 80 —

BigBrov is rushing into the basement. He is shrieking and yelling from inside his gas mask. All my Brovs are shrieking and yelling from inside their gas masks. If I didn't know who they were, I'd be very scared by such a sight. BigBrov is turning off the blowtorch. NabBrov and MemBrov have jumped on Guard Krick —

'GET OFF ME,' – Cough! Splutter! – 'MISTERZZZ!'
NabBrov and MemBrov have pushed Krick to the ground.
'Hold him still, Nab! Mem!'
BigBrov is struggling with Guard Krick.
'I'm gonna hurt you, misterzzz!'
BigBrov! Be careful!
You don't say?
His eyes are watering.
He's coughing all over me – Ugh!
Whisky breath. Told you.
'Stop struggling, Krick!'
'THE VOICE OF THE HIPPY MISTERRR!' Splutter!
Cough! Splutter! 'YOU WON'T GET AWAY WITH
THIS!' Cough!
'Shut up, you capitalist robot!'
We need to tie him up.
My thoughts exactly.
Where's the rope?

On the bench behind you.

'Mem! Sit on Krick and hold him as still as possible!'

'You got it, mate!'

BigBrov is rushing to the bench and gets the rope.

Krick's wriggling too much to tie him.

Threaten him with another stink bomb.

'Keep still ... or it's more stink for you, Krick!'

'GET OFF ME,' – Struggle! Cough! Struggle! – 'MISTERZZZ!'

BigBrov's taken another stink bomb from his pocket.

'I'm warning you, Krick!'

'STINK DON'T SCARE ME! YOU'LL NEED TO DO' – Cough! Splutter! – 'BETTER THAN THAT!'

BigBrov has dropped the stink bomb —

PPHUTT!!

'Ahhgggaaagggyuukk ... I feel sick ... no more stink! No more stink!'

Ha!

Ha!

'Keep still, Krick!'

'Yeah, keep still, imperialist storm trooper!'

'Yeah, keep still – or I'll kung fu kick you where it hurts!'

'Mem!'

'Sorry!'

He's stopped struggling.

He can barely breathe in the stink.

He can't see anything either.

Tie him quick, BigBrov. Then I will try to clear the air as quickly as possible.

How will you do that?

I don't know yet.

'Okey-dokey! Mem! Hold Krick's hands together.'

'You got it, mate!'

'Krick! I'm tying you up with the same rope you tied

trolleys up with. How does it feel, eh? – Mem! Hold his feet together!'

'You got it, mate!'

More knots your dad taught you?

Yes.

'You're tying his knees together too, amigo?'

'I want to make sure he's secure, Nab.'

I don't think he'll ever get out of those.

'Okey-dokey! Let's carry him over to his bunk!'

'Holy macaroni! He's heavy!'

'That's solid' – Cough! Splutter! – 'muscle, mister!'

You should tie Guard Krick to the bunk, BigBrov.

That's what I intend to do.

I thought so, yes.

Have you thought of a way to –?

Clear the stink and smoke away? Yes.

Then please –

Do it? Right away.

'Okey-dokey, put him down! Nab – you tie his feet to the bunk. Mem – tie his hands. I'm going to Apollo.'

'With pleasure, amigo!'

'You got it, mate – Hey! Where's all the smoke going?'

I'm sucking it out through the air shafts.

'Apollo's sucking it out through the air shafts.'

'Can we take our gas masks off now, mate?'

Yes.

'Yes.'

BigBrov takes his gas mask off and breathes deeply. The others do the same. BigBrov is coming over to me. He takes the radio from inside his camouflage jacket and starts tying it to the front of my metal frame.

I know you and I don't need this any more, but –

The others need to hear my voice.

Exactly. How's Snow?

I'll ask ... Snow? Are you all right?

My push bar is melted . . . my push bar is melted . . .
Snow's in shock, I think, BigBrov.
I'm not surprised.
Here come NabBrov and MemBrov.
'The robot of nastiness is tied securely, amigo!'
'He'll never escape from all those knots, mate!'
'I'm sure he won't, my Brovs!'
'Amigo!'
'Mate!'
'It's good to have you near me again!'
'Likewise, amigo!'
'Yeah, mate, totally.'
'Okey-dokey, let's keep it moving. Nab, Mem – take Snow up to the store. Use the lift. It's over there.'
'I'll go and bring Roz and Newt in, shall I, mate?'
'Good thinking. Make sure you close the lift doors so me and Apollo can get up!
'Sure thing, amigo.'
MemBrov has grabbed hold of Snow and he and NabBrov are heading for the lift.
Chunka-chunk-chonk-chonk-chonk . . .
NabBrov has pushed the button to call the lift —
Zssshhhmmmmm . . .
How are little brov and Roz doing, Apollo?
They're very worried. Here. Look.
Oh, Newt is in Roz's arms. He's trying to keep Rudi inside his puffa jacket. He looks so anxious. Roz is biting her bottom lip.
'Zi-Zi . . . Zi-Zi . . .'
'Don't worry, Customer Newt. I'm sure everything is fine.'
Krunk-skreeeek!
NabBrov and MemBrov are pushing Snow into the lift —
Chunka-chunka-clonk-clonk . . .
My . . . push . . . bar . . . is . . . burnt . . .

Skreeeek-krunk!

Zssshhhhmmmmm . . .

They're going up.

Let's go over to the lift and wait to call it down and –

'YOU WON'T GET AWAY WITH IT, MISTERRR!'

Wait here a moment, Apollo.

Where are you going?

I want a word with Krick.

Ignore him!

I can't.

— 81 —

'Misterrr . . . you ain't gonna get away with this!'

'It's not important I get away with it, Krick. What's important is that I just *do* it! Do it because I believe it's right. You see, I have principles. That's something you will never understand.'

'I understand this much, misterrr. When I tell Miss Crib what you've been up to, she'll take you away from your family so fast you won't know what's hit you. They'll take you away and that little brother of yours. Your little brother will cry and cry without his mum, won't he, eh? Can you imagine the sound of him going boo-hoo-hoo? Go on! Imagine it. Boo-hoo-hoo!'

'Shut up!'

'Oh, you don't like that, do you? But that's what's gonna happen, misterrr. Your brother will sob his heart out. Your mum will sob her heart out. Your gran will sob her heart out. Your aunt. Everyone. That's all the world will be from now on. One big place of tears. And all because you had to steal two trolleys –'

'It's not *stealing*! I'm . . . I'm *liberating* them!'

'You expect The Powers That Be to believe that? Eh? They'll laugh in your face. Just like you laughed in my face earlier. Remember that? Oh, I do. I'll never forget it. That's why I'm going to have great pleasure in explaining to The Powers That Be how you broke into my super-market –'

'It's not *your* super–'

'And *stole*! Like common criminals! And theft is theft, misterrr. Don't forget that! It don't matter if it's two trolleys or a hundred. It's still a crime. Punishable by law! You hear me? Eh?'

'I hear you, Krick. And you know something – you're right!

'Beginning to regret your actions, eh, misterrr?'

'Just the opposite. Listening to you rant with such anger and spite – it's reminded me of all the things in life Dad taught me to battle against. Ignorance! Selfishness! Prejudice! That's all I see when I look at you. All I hear whenever you open your ugly mouth. So, no, I don't regret a thing. In fact, you've given me an idea!'

'Where you going, misterrr? Come back here! I haven't finished with you yet.'

'Well, I've finished with you, Krick!'

BigBrov! Don't let him wind you up —

He hasn't! He's fired me up! Come on! Let's get up to the store.

Krink-skreeek!

Eeeka-eeka.

Skreeek-krunk!

Zssshhhhmmmmm . . .

What's this idea he gave you?

The most obvious thing in the world! Didn't you hear? To rescue two trolleys is the same as rescuing a hundred. Or two hundred. So ...

You mean...?

Exactly!

— 82 —

Zssshhhhmmmmm.

We're here!

Krunk-skreek!

'Zi-Zi!'

'Amigo!'

'Mate!'

'Oh, Customer Zip! Apollo! Thank goodness! Come on, let's get out of this place as soon as poss–'

'Not so fast, Roz!'

'But we've got to –'

'Listen up! Everyone!'

BigBrov has jumped up on to a freezer!

'We've done good work tonight. Glorious work. But it's not over. In fact, it's barely begun.'

'I mean ... WHAT ABOUT THOSE?' yells Zip, pointing at the rows of trolleys by the main entrance. 'Look at them! See how their metal frames sparkle in the orange light from outside. How beautiful they look. Tell me ... are you prepared to leave these poor trolleys here to be kicked and shouted at? Will you be able to sleep at night knowing what Krick might be doing to them?'

'No, amigo!'

'No, mate!'

'Oh, certainly not, Customer Zip!'

'Ni-ni, Zi-Zi!'

'Of course not! So listen up! The plan for tonight has just got bigger. Bigger than any of us ever imagined. The plan's become what it should have been from the very beginning. We're not just going to rescue Apollo tonight. We're not just going to rescue Snow. We're going to rescue every trolley in the store! And more! We're going to bring every single one . . . to life!'

'Holy macaroni!'

'Stars 'n' bars!'

'Oh yes, Customer Zip! Yes!'

'Ya! Ya! Ya!'

'Okey-dokey! Listen up! There's no time to lose. We've only got – let's check my watch – one hour and thirty-two minutes before sunrise. Now, you all know what to do.'

'Name a trolley, amigo.'

'Exactly. If a trolley proves difficult, move on to the next. We can come back to it later –'

BigBrov!

What, Apollo?

It's too dangerous.

Don't you want to rescue all these –?

Of course I do! But sneaking a whole supermarket's worth of trolleys out of the store and across the footbridge and into New Town is a lot riskier than sneaking just me and —

We've got to do it, Apollo!

But BigBrov! What if you're seen? Your alibis won't help you much if you're caught with all these! Oh, BigBrov! Think of you and LittleBrov! The Powers That Be will —

My mind's made up!

'Friends – to the trolleys!'

BigBrov is rushing to a trolley. BigBrov is talking to it. BigBrov has called it a name. The trolley moves!

Apollo?

Yes, BigBrov?

Calm the trolleys as they come alive. This is going to be a strange experience for them.

It's a strange experience for me.

Well, it's not something I do every day either.

And I still think it's very dangerous.

Well, so do I. But we're still going to do it.

BigBrov is bringing more and more to life. NabBrov has not had any success with a trolley yet. Nor has MemBrov. Nor has LittleBrov or RozSis. They are naming trolley after trolley, but so far, not one of them has squeaked a wheel.

'Customer Zip! It's not good! I can't do it.'

'Nor me, amigo!'

'Nor me, mate!'

'Noomi, Zi-Zi!'

'You have to think of a name that has something to do with the trolley. Like where it's found. Or . . . if it's got any markings on it. Or just how it looks to you. Anything. It's easy!'

'For *you*, yes, amigo!'

'But not for *us*, mate!'

'No, Customer Zip, it's not easy for us at all.'

'BigBrov! Everyone! Listen up! Don't you see? While it's true that all trolleys have the potential to come alive, not all soft and warm things can make it happen.'

'Apollo . . . you mean . . .?'

'You're the only one here who can do it!'

'Gosh!'

'You took the words right out of my metal frame.'

— 83 —

'Only the amigo! Holy macaroni!'

'Only the mate! Stars 'n' bars!'

'Oonni mee brov! Ya!'

'But, Apollo, what about me? Presumably something happened between me and Mary. If I could do it with her ... why not again?'

'Perhaps it has something to do with age, RozSis. Only young soft and warm things can do it. As you get older your ability to connect with a trolley gets less and less. Until even a trolley that is already alive will freeze in your presence.'

'Ooo ... how sad.'

'Whatever the reason,' says Zip, rushing to a trolley, 'we can't do our heads in about it now. If I'm the only one here who's got the power, then ... well, I've got a lot of work to do. Quick! Everyone! Line the trolleys up!'

'Sure thing, amigo!'

'You got it, mate!'

'Of course, Customer Zip!'

'Ya-ya, Zi-Zi!'

'That's it! Good! Now, you've all got to help me! Keep pushing the trolleys down to me. As soon as one moves – wheel it out of the way. Push the next trolley in front of me! Apollo, you –'

Calm the trolleys, yes, I know.

'Holy macaroni! It's like a production line in a factory!'

BigBrov is talking to a trolley. The trolley moves. Life! It is wheeled out of the way. I calm it.

BigBrov is talking to another trolley. The trolley moves. Life! It is wheeled out of the way. I calm it.

Another trolley. Moves —

I'm doing this faster and faster.

So I see.

'ALL THE LIVING TROLLEYS SHOULD MAKE THEIR WAY TO THE CHECKOUTS, READY TO LEAVE!' yells Zip. Then, more quietly, at Newt, 'Little brov! You keep watch at the window. If you see anything suspicious at all – you know what to do.'

'Hooot!'

'You're a star!'

BigBrov is talking to another trolley. The trolley moves. It is wheeled out of the way. I calm it. BigBrov is talking to another trolley. It moves. I calm it. BigBrov is talking to another trolley. It moves —

'You're gonna do it, amigo!'

'Yeah, mate! Nearly all the trolleys are alive!'

'I've never seen anything like it, Customer Zip.'

'Holy macaroni! You don't say?'

Gosh, listen Apollo. The supermarket is full of the sound of squeaking wheels and clunking metal frames. It's the most glorious sound I've ever heard.

Twenty trolleys to go, BigBrov.

No problem.

It's draining you of strength.

No.

It is. I can feel it.

Ten to go.

'ROZ! GET READY TO OPEN THE DOORS!'

'Right away, Customer Zip!'

Seven to go!

'NAB! MEM! GET READY TO GO THROUGH THE CHECKOUTS WITH THE TROLLEYS!'

'Sure thing, amigo!'

'You got it, mate!'

Three to go.

Forty-five minutes to sunrise.

'IS IT CLEAR OUT THERE, LITTLE BROV?'

'YA -YA, ZI-ZI!'

Three to go.

Forty-four minutes.

'ROZ – OPEN THE DOORS!'

'With pleasure!'

Vvvsssssshhhhhh!

One.

Forty-three.

That's it!

'I'VE DONE IT!'

'Well done, amigo!'

'Well done, mate!'

'Well done, Customer Zip!'

'Weee dun, Zi-Zi!'

'OKEY-DOKEY, EVERYONE! LISTEN UP! APOLLO AND ME ARE GOING TO LEAD THE WAY!'

Climb aboard.

'LITTLE BROV – YOU RIDE HERE WITH ME!'

'Ya-ya, Zi-Zi!'

'ROZ – YOU RIDE IN A MIDDLE TROLLEY TO KEEP AN EYE ON THINGS THERE!'

'Anything you say, Customer Zip!'

'NAB – YOU RIDE IN A TROLLEY AT THE BACK TO WATCH OUR REAR!'

'Sure thing, amigo!'

'MEM – YOU BEST PUSH SNOW! ITS WONKY WHEELS MIGHT HOLD US UP!'

'You got it, mate!'

'SINGLE FILE, EVERYONE! THAT'S IT! WE'RE LEAVING THE SUPERMARKET ... NOWWW!!'

— 84 —

We're moving across the car park. The lights of the motorway are blurry in the early morning mist. BigBrov is standing up in me —

'KEEP MOVING! NO STRAGGLERS AT THE BACK!'

BigBrov's eyes are blazing.

Look at them all behind us, Apollo!

I see them, BigBrov.

Like a . . . a silver river.

We're approaching the footbridge.

Is it safe to cross?

There's a big gap in the traffic . . . ΠOW!

'COME ON, EVERYONE! ACROSS THE FOOT-BRIDGE! NOW!'

We're moving up the ramp. Oh, there's so much joy and energy in BigBrov's face.

'EVERYTHING OKEY-DOKEY WITH YOU, NAB?'

'Never better, amigo.'

'MEM?'

'Elvissy!'

'ROZ?'

'Ooo, so happy!'

'What about you, Newt? Happy?'

'Ya! Ya! Ya!'

Thirty minutes to sunrise.

Let's move a bit faster.

Eeekaeekaclickacliclick ...

'NAB? MEM? ONCE WE'RE IN NEW TOWN WE'LL HAVE TO WORK FAST. AND – DON'T FORGET! – KEEP YOUR VOICES DOWN! WHISPERS ONLY!'

'Sure thing, amigo.'

'You got it, mate.'

'Of course, Customer Zip.'

We're here, BigBrov.

'Shhhhh, everyone ... We're entering New Town.'

— 85 —

We've come to a halt outside Home.

'Okey-dokey! No time to lose! Nab, Mem, Roz – we need to build the Doorway ... Here! Yes! The sun will rise at the other end of the main road and shine through it. Perfect! Get the cardboard boxes from the hideout and start building!'

'Sure thing, amigo!'

'You got it, mate!'

'We'll have it built in no time, Customer Zip!'

'Good. Because no time's about all we've got. Apollo – get the garage door for them, please.'

Of course.

Vvvvmmmmm ...

'Little brov! Make sure you keep watch! Okey-dokey?'

'Ya!'

'And what do you do if you see anything suspicious?'

'Hooot-hooo!'

'Glorious!'

NabBrov and MemBrov and RozSis have started building a pile of boxes. They are moving very quickly and very quietly —

'That's it! Good! Start building the other pile about ... here! That should give each trolley more than enough space to wheel through.'

'Sure thing, amigo!'

'You got it, mate!'

'The perfect gap, Customer Zip!'

BigBrov is making sure the two columns of boxes are safe and sturdy. He shuffles them into place.

This look right to you?

Perfect ... Twenty-five minutes to sunrise.

We're doing fine.

The sky's getting brighter.

Is Mum still asleep?

Yes.

And Gran and Aunt Ivy?

Yes.

Keep watching them, Apollo. Everything will be ruined if anyone wakes up —

'The two columns are built, amigo.'

'Gosh! Well done. We just need something to go across the top.'

'There's no boxes long enough, mate.'

'You sure?'

'We've checked everything, Customer Zip.'

'Mmm, let me think ... Got it! The rug! That's it! Roll up the rose rug and put it across the top.'

'Holy macaroni, yes!'

'Good thinking, Customer Zip.'

'I'll get it, mate!'

Twenty minutes.

Apollo — line the trolleys up in front of the Doorway.

Right away, BigBrov.

'Here's the rug all rolled up, mate!'

'Lift me up on your shoulders, Mem. I'll put it on top ... That's it ... A little higher ... Nearly there ... Good! Oh, gosh!'

Oh, BigBrov!

We've ... we've built it, Apollo.

The Doorway ...

It looks so ... so ...

Glory rush?

Glorious, indeed, Apollo. Look at all the different cardboard boxes. All different shapes and sizes.

With different patterns and writing on them.

And some are torn.

And some are nearly crushed.

And yet they all fit together.

Fit together perfectly.

Like they were ... meant to be.

'Ooo, you've done it, Customer Zip!'

'We've *all* done it, Roz!'

'Yeah!'

'Yeah!'

'Ya!'

'Okey-dokey, the sun's gonna rise any minute! Apollo? The trolleys ready?'

Not exactly, BigBrov.

What do you mean?

They won't move.

They won't ... what?

Snow has been trollepathizing with them behind my back. Snow has convinced them all that they are wrong to leave the supermarket. Snow has persuaded them all to —

'Amigo! What's happening?'

— 274 —

'The trolleys are turning round, mate!'
'The trolleys are heading out of New Town, Customers!'
Apollo!?
They're going back to the supermarket!

— 86 —

'STOP!' yells Zip, rushing to stand in front of them. 'YOU MUST NOT GO BACK!'

'Amigo! Why are they doing this?'

'They're scared, Nab!'

Chunka-chunka-clonk–

'No, Snow! Stop! Please! – Oh, Apollo! *Do* something!'

I've tried, BigBrov. They will not listen to me!

We must get back to the supermarket.

Snow! I can . . . I can hear you in my head now!

Good! Then listen to me, Zip! To be outside the supermarket . . . it's too . . . too different . . . it's too confusing . . . We're scared! — FOLLOW ME, TROLLEYS! WE'RE GOING BACK!

Chunka-chunka-clonk-clonk-clonk . . .

'NO! STOP! LISTEN UP . . . TROLLEYS! I KNOW EXACTLY HOW YOU FEEL! BELIEVE ME! OF *COURSE* YOU'RE CONFUSED! DIFFERENT THINGS ARE ALWAYS CONFUSING ! WE . . . GET USED TO THE WAY SOMETHING IS . . . AND THEN WHEN THAT SOMETHING IS TAKEN AWAY IT . . . IT SCARES US. THAT'S ONLY NATURAL. BECAUSE

SOMETIMES WE CAN'T SEE THE SENSE OF IT. WHY SHOULD THINGS CHANGE? WHY? AND BECAUSE WE CAN'T SEE THE MEANING OF THE CHANGE, WE ... WELL, WE WOULD RATHER GO BACK ... BACK TO HOW THINGS WERE. BECAUSE WE THINK GOING BACK WILL TAKE AWAY THE CONFUSION. TAKE AWAY THE SCARED FEELING. SO IT'S ... WELL, IT'S ONLY *NATURAL* YOU ALL WANT TO GO BACK TO THE SUPERMARKET. BUT YOU'RE WRONG. YOU HEAR ME? WRONG!'

Oh, very good, BigBrov.

'Amigo's quite a speechmaker, amigos!'

'Mate should have a congregation, mates.'

'Customer Zip's a natural leader, Customers!'

'Zi-Zi isss ma brov!'

'YOU'RE *ALIVE* NOW, TROLLEYS! *ALIVE!* AND YOU KNOW WHAT I'VE LEARNT? TO BE ALIVE ... IT'S TO HAVE THINGS *ALWAYS* CHANGING. SOMETIMES THE CHANGES ARE GOOD. SOMETIMES THE CHANGES ARE BAD. BUT HOW WE *DEAL* WITH THOSE CHANGES – *THAT'S* WHAT BEING ALIVE IS ALL ABOUT. SOMETIMES ... THE CHANGES HAPPEN ALL OF A SUDDEN. WE LOSE A PLACE WE LOVE. WE LOSE A ... A PERSON WE LOVE. AND WE THINK ... WE THINK ALL THE MAGIC HAS BEEN TAKEN OUT OF THE WORLD AND NOTHING WILL EVER MEAN ANYTHING EVER AGAIN AND WE THINK WE'LL NEVER BE HAPPY AGAIN. BUT THEN ... THEN WE FIND MAGIC IN THE NEW THINGS ALL AROUND US. WE FIND MEANING IN THE NEW THINGS. AND THE OLD THINGS – THE THINGS WE'VE LOST – WE REALIZE THAT ... THAT THEY AIN'T GONE. NOT REALLY. THEY ARE PART OF US. AND THEY

HELP US FIND THE MAGIC IN THE NEW AND ...
AND ... Oh, I'm messing this all up.'

No, BigBrov.

'You're explaining things just fine, amigo. Go on.'

'Yeah. Go on, mate.'

'Go on, Customer, Zip.'

'Ya-ya, Zi-Zi.'

'TROLLEYS ... WHAT I'M TRYING TO SAY IS ...
SOMETIMES ... TO BE ALIVE IS TO BE SCARED. TO
AVOID BEING SCARED IF YOU'RE ALIVE IS ...
WELL, IT'S NOT POSSIBLE. SO ... YEAH! YOU
CAN GO BACK TO THE SUPERMARKET. YOU
CAN FEEL SAFE AGAIN. BUT IT'S NOT REALLY
SAFETY YOU'RE FEELING. IT'S NOTHING! IT'S
NO FEELING AT ALL. NO MAGIC. NO FRIEND-
SHIP. NO LOVE. AND THAT'S NOT LIFE. OH,
TROLLEYS! TROLLEYS! PLEASE, *PLEASE* RISK
BEING SCARED. RISK BEING ALIVE. BECAUSE
SOMETIMES, BY TAKING THE RISK, WE DIS-
COVER THE MOST WONDERFUL AND MAGICAL
THINGS EVER! OF COURSE, I CAN'T *PROMISE*
THAT YOU WILL FIND THEM. BUT I CAN
PROMISE YOU ONE THING. IF YOU DON'T TAKE
THE RISK, YOU WILL *NEVER* FIND THEM. AND
SO ... THAT'S ALL I'M ASKING YOU TO DO,
TROLLEYS. BE ALIVE. DARE TO BE SCARED AND
HOPE TO FIND ... MAGIC.'

'The trolleys – they're not moving, amigos.'

'They must be thinking, mates.'

'Wait, Customers! Snow is wheeling forward!'

Chunka-chunka-clonk-clonk-clonk ...

Zip ...

Snow?

Your words ... the way you speak ...

Yes?

They make my metal frame tingle.

Is it a good feeling?

Yes. It's a . . . thrilling feeling.

If you go back to the supermarket . . . you will never have that feeling again. True, you will never be scared. But you will never be thrilled. Do you want to miss the chance of having your metal frame tingled again . . . Well? Do you?

No.

Then you know what you've got to do!

Yes . . . being alive can be scary. But it's wonderful too. You can't have one without the other . . . TROLLEYS! WE ARE GOING THROUGH THE DOORWAY!

BigBrov! The trolleys are turning round again!

'You've done it, amigo!'

'You've done it, mate!'

'You've done it, Customer Zip!'

'Yooo doughnut, Zi-Zi!'

'Come on, everyone! All trolleys! Sunrise is gonna happen any second – How many seconds exactly, Apollo, eh? . . . Apollo? . . . Apollo, what's up?'

I'm so sorry, BigBrov. It's all my fault. I should have . . .

What?

Warned you.

About what, Apollo? What?

'Zip, love?'

Oh, no!

Mum's looking out of her window.

— 87 —

'Mum . . . I – gosh!'
Mum is closing her window.
She's coming downstairs.
What am I going to say?
I've no idea!

'Zip!' Mum rushes out of the house, clutching her dressing gown around her. 'What's all this about? Eh?'

'I . . . I can explain, Mum!'

'Well, you'd better start! What's that on your face?'

'Dad's boot polish.'

'Wipe it off! Now! And what're you wearing camouflage jackets for? Eh? And – oh, look, Zip! The trolleys! Oh, love, what have you done?'

'It's not what it looks like, Mum.'

'Well, I hope not. Because it looks to me like your idea of having a slumber party is to . . . steal trolleys from the supermarket!'

'No, Mum!'

'Ni-ni, Moom!'

'No, amigo!'

'No, mate!'

'Oh, no, Customer –'

'You!' Mum glares at Roz. 'I'm surprised at you. You're an adult. You're supposed to set a good example to these youngsters. Don't you know how dangerous it is for my

children to do anything . . . like this? Eh? Miss Crib could –
oh, I don't even want to think of it!'

'Mum! Roz ain't done anything wrong!'

'Ni-ni, Moom!'

'No, amigo.'

'No, mate!'

Nine minutes to sunrise, BigBrov!

'Mum! There's no time to explain. You've just got to do
as I tell you. Go back inside the house now and don't look
at what we're doing.'

'No! I'm not moving from this spot until you explain
yourself!'

*Oh, Apollo! It's all gone wrong! Things couldn't get much
worse. .*

They just have.

What d'you mean?

'BABYCAKES!'

'SUGARPLUMS!'

Oh, no!

— 88 —

'Gran! Aunt Ivy!'

'Carol? What's going on here, sugarplum?'

'Our Zip's been stealing trolleys.'

'No! Oh, gosh! . . . Listen up! Nab! Mem! Roz! The trolleys can't move with the grown-ups here! So . . . well, we'll
just have to push them through. You hear me? Quick!

Grab a trolley and push it through the Doorway as soon as you see the sun shine through!'

'Sure, amigo!'

'You got it, mate!'

'At once, Customer Zip!'

'Wait!' Mum stands in front of the cardboard boxes. 'The madness has gone far enough.'

'But, Mum –'

'No, Zip! Oh, I don't blame you, love. Honestly. I blame myself. You've been through so much and what did I do? I hibernated in a sleeping bag and tried to make out nothing was happening –'

'No, Mum!'

'Yes! I let you and Newt down. Just when you needed me most. And this is the result. Now, do as I say! Take the trolleys back to the supermarket this instant –'

'No!'

'Yes!'

'Mum! Listen! These trolleys! They ... they're alive!'

'Oh, Zip, stop it! *Please!*'

'I know it sounds unbelievable, but it's true.'

'It's true, amigo!'

'It's true, mate.'

'It's true, Customer!'

'Stroo, Moom!'

'If I hear one more word –'

'Mum! This trolley here ... this is Apollo! Apollo is our friend, Mum. We've got to get Apollo and all the other trolleys through this Doorway of cardboard boxes. We've got to do it at sunrise. It's the solstice, Mum. You know that? You know how Dad always said the solstice was a magic time and –'

'Enough!' snaps Mum angrily. 'I'm not having you use what your dad believed in to ... to wriggle out of all this irresponsible behaviour. Inside! All of you! Now!'

Mum has grabbed Newt's hand.
'Ni-ni!'
She's pulling him into the house.
'NI!'
Apollo! Do something!
Eeka-eek . . .
You're moving!
I have to! And more than that —
'Mum!'
Apollo! You're speaking! In front of Mum.
It's hard but . . . I've got to . . .
'My name is Apollo.'
Mum is staring. Her mouth is wide open.
'Everything your son has just told you is true. I am a living super-market trolley!'

— 89 —

Mum clutches at Gran.

Gran gasps and clutches at Aunt Ivy.

Aunt Ivy gasps and clutches at Gran.

Eeka-eek . . .

Mum steps back.

'Please, Mum,' continues Apollo, 'you must not be afraid. I will not harm you. It is impossible for me to harm you. All I want you to do is realize the truth —'

Eeka —

Mum steps back again.

'Don't be scared, Mum!'

'No, Mum … please don't be scared … Listen to me. Your two sons are the bravest and wisest of children. You have brought them up well. You and your husband. I have heard much about their dad. I feel as if I have met him by listening to so many things about him. He sounds a glorious soft and warm thing. You miss him so much, don't you?'

Mum hesitates, then nods.

'Mum … I can see you and him together … It is early morning … A misty morning … You are in the forest … By a river …'

Mum gasps.

'He is holding you in his arms … He tells you to look. He says he can see a most magical animal … You look … but all you can see is mist … But he keeps on describing it … And, gradually, you start to see this creature … You see what he sees … Am I right?'

'Yes. Oh yes.'

'Have you ever told this story to anyone?'

'No. It was a moment … between me and … Oh, it was our special moment. The moment Zip started growing inside me.'

'You believe what you saw that morning, don't you, Mum?'

'Yes. He could … oh, he could make anyone believe anything.'

'You saw a unicorn, didn't you?'

Mum wipes away tears, and nods.

'If this man could make you believe in unicorns … why won't you let this man's son make you believe in me?'

Mum gazes at Apollo for a moment. Then slowly, she reaches out and touches Apollo's push bar.

Two minutes to sunrise.

'Mum,' says Zip. 'Believe it. Please.'

Mum runs her fingers over Apollo's metal frame.

'Mum …?'

One minute.

'I used to think the forest was full of such magic. Your

dad used to say, "But magic is everywhere, Carol. Not just in a forest. One day you'll find it where you least expect it." Perhaps ... this is what he meant. He was preparing me for this moment.' And then, suddenly, her eyes blaze brighter than Zip has seen them in a long time. She looks up at Gran and Aunt Ivy and says, 'What're you blooming waiting for, you two? You heard! We've got to push these trolleys through those cardboard boxes! Come on!'

'Mum!'

It's sunrise!

— 90 —

The rays of the rising sun splinter the horizon. A single beam, like a gigantic searchlight, spears down the length of New Town's main road, and into the arch formed by the cardboard boxes. It fills the Doorway with golden light. A light so radiant it's impossible to look at it without squinting.

'Gosh!'

'Holy macaroni!'

'Stars 'n' bars!'

'Ooo!'

'Ya!'

Mum tugs at Zip's sleeve. 'Come on! No time for gawping! The trolleys!'

'Oh ... gosh, yes!'

Me first, Zip.

Of course, Snow.

Zip grabs Snow and pushes as hard as he can –
Chonkachonkaclonkclonkclonk–

Snow wheels into the golden light of the Doorway. The light surrounds the trolley like a liquid and then –

Gosh! Snow's gone!

'Next trolley!' cries Mum, grabbing one and pushing. 'You too, Nabil! Memphis! Everyone! Come on! This is not a spectator sport!'

Nabil grabs a trolley and pushes it through the Doorway. Then Memphis. Then Gran and Aunt Ivy. Everyone is pushing. And cheering. And cheering and pushing.

Look at Mum, BigBrov. She's so . . . not in a sleeping bag any more.

This is what she was like in the forest! Oh, Apollo! I've got her back!

The light in the Doorway is getting brighter and brighter.

It's like a million rising suns.

And look, BigBrov! You see?

Gosh! It's like . . . there's tiny sparkles in the light.

More and more with every trolley that goes through.

They're like glowing insects.

Or tiny stars.

Yes! Golden starlight! Oh, gosh! It's a shame Missy and Mr Brazil ain't here to see this.

Don't speak to soon.

What d'you mean?

'LAMBS!'

'SON! HMM! WHAT'S GOING ON?'

How did . . .? Oh, gosh! Apollo, how come –?

Gran rang them before she came out of the house!

You didn't say anything.

What was the point?

This won't cause any more problems, will it?

I don't think so — Look!

'Morning, you two!' says Mum, striding over, her face beaming. 'We haven't met, have we? I'm Zip and Newt's mum, Carol.' She shakes both their hands vigorously. 'You must be Missy. And you must be Mr Brazil. I've heard both your voices in the house. I'm afraid I've been acting like a complete soggy cabbage and have spent most of the past few months asleep. But . . . well, as you can see, I'm awake now so everything's back to normal.'

'Normal!?' gasps Mr Brazil, pointing at what's going on in the road.

'Carol, lamb, what's . . . happening?'

'Why, I would've thought that was obvious!' says Mum. 'It's winter solstice and we're trying to get all these trolleys through the Doorway so they can be free. I would've thought a two-year-old would have gathered that much. Now, Apollo here can move, but all the others can't, so . . . well, they need a blooming good heave-ho from us.' Mum strides over to a trolley and pushes it into the golden light. Then she looks up at Missy and Mr Brazil, who are still staring with their mouths agape. 'You see? Easy! Now, what're you two waiting for? There's a lot of trolleys need pushing. Come on! Sunrises don't last forever, you know! And, by the way, I'd close your mouths. You don't want one of these little stars to fly in by mistake.'

Slowly, Missy and Mr Brazil walk over and grab a trolley each.

'PUSH!' cries Mum.

Missy pushes her trolley through the Doorway.

It blazes brighter and more tiny stars appear.

Gosh! Look at Missy!

She's smiling.

Mr Brazil has grabbed a trolley.

He's pushing.

More stars.

More light.

He's smiling too.

So are you.

So are you.

I haven't got a mouth.

You're still smiling.

I suppose I am! I'm feeling such joy, BigBrov.

There's ... twelve trolleys left.

And still the light gets brighter.

And the stars grow in number.

They are sparkling everywhere.

They look so glorious.

Seven trolleys left.

Six.

Five.

Oh, Apollo ... I've just thought of something.

I know, BigBrov, I know ... Four!

Any moment now –

Three!

– it's going to be –

Two!
– your turn!
BigBrov . . . that moment is now.

— 92 —

Everything in the street becomes very still.

Slowly, Mum, Gran, Aunt Ivy, Missy and Mr Brazil approach Apollo.

'There!' says Mum. 'I hope we were of some help, Apollo.'

'You were a great help, Mum. All of you were. Thank you.'

'You're welcome, babycake.'

'You're welcome, sugarplum.'

'Of course, lamb.'

'Hmm, yes, of course.'

'And now,' says Mum, 'us grown-ups will go inside and let you say your goodbyes to the others. Goodbye, Apollo.'

They're all going into the house. It's just me, Nab, Mem, Newt and Roz here. We're standing round Apollo. I don't know what to say. None of us knows what to say. Little brov is crying. So is Roz.

'Thank you, my Brovs, my Sis . . . I have been so lucky to find such a wonderful Family.'

'It's us who're lucky, amigo! Holy macaroni, if I hadn't met you – oh, I don't wanna cry! I don't!'

'No, don't cry, NabBrov. This is a happy time.'

'It is, mate! And I'm not gonna cry cos only girls cry and I ain't no ... oh, Apollo! Apollo!'

Mem is holding on to Apollo's metal frame.

'Apple-loo ... ta moon!'

'Yes, LittleBrov, perhaps I am going to the moon!'

Roz kisses Apollo's push bar, then takes a step back. 'I think we should let Customer Zip say goodbye, Customers. Let's move over here ... Goodbye, Apollo.'

'Goodbye, everyone.'

'Goodbye, amigo.'

'Goodbye, mate!'

'Oh ... Apple-loo!'

They're moving over to the hideout.

They are such thoughtful friends.

Apollo! Look!
There are ... so many stars now.

They're hovering round us.

Apollo ...?

What, BigBrov?

This moment – I always knew it had to happen.

But you never thought about it.

I didn't want to think about it.

Nor did I.

It never seemed real somehow.

I know.

But now . . .

It is real.

Yes.
I . . . I don't know what to say . . .

You don't have to say anything.

No! I must . . . I must . . .

What, BigBrov?

Thank you for being here for me.

We've been here for each other.

Thank you for all you've done for me.

You've done things for me —

No! Listen! Just let me speak! Please.

Speak, BigBrov.

Thank you for caring for me.
Thank you for changing my dreams.
Thank you for making me part of a family.
Thank you for giving me something fizzy when I was thirsty.
Thank you for carrying me when I couldn't move fast enough.
Thank you for keeping me safe while I slept.
Thank you for keeping me warm.

You're welcome, BigBrov.

And . . . and . . .

Yes?

And . . . I'm sorry if I ever said a nasty word to you.
I didn't mean it.
I said it because I knew I could get away with it.
I said it because . . . with you . . . I felt I could say anything.
I said it because . . . because . . .

Yes?

I love you, Apollo.

I love you too, BigBrov.

Oh, Apollo . . . I . . . I can't say goodbye.

If you want me to stay here I will.

No. You've got to go.

I will only go if you let me go.

Oh, Apollo . . .

No leaking eyes! Please!

I can't help it!

I know, I know.

Apollo . . . when you go through . . .
where do you go?

I don't know.

Will I ever see you again?

I will always be in your thoughts.

That's not what I mean!

I know.

Will I . . . will I ever be with you again?
Will I speak to you again?
Tell you things?
Things I've done.
Things I feel . . .
Because things . . .
things won't mean anything unless I can tell you about them.

Come closer, BigBrov . . .
Closer . . .
Closer . . .
What do you feel?

I feel . . . arms around me.
Arms holding me like . . . like forever.
Arms holding me like they will never let go.
Arms holding me like the safest feeling in the world.
Arms holding me like I will never be scared again.

And that embrace will always be with you, my BigBrov.
You understand?

Yes . . .

The sunrise is nearly over.

Then you must go.

You're letting me go?

Yes.
Goodbye, Apollo.

Goodbye . . . my glory rush.

Eeeka-eeka-clicka-click . . .

Apollo . . . is gone . . .

'AMIGO! LOOK OUT!'

'MATE!'

'ZI-ZI!'
What's going on –?
Oh, gosh!
A vehicle has turned into New Town.
It's heading straight for me.
It's a black van!
KRICK!

— 93 —

The van swerves up on to the pavement, its tyres screech-ing, and demolishes some fencing and several plastic trees, then skids back down into the road and aims straight for the cardboard boxes.

'JUMP OUT OF THE WAY, AMIGO!'
'MOVE, MATE!'
'Zi-Zi!'

Zip hurls himself towards the hideout, and into the arms of his friends as the van crashes into the Doorway.

The cardboard boxes crash to the ground, get caught under the wheels of the van, and send it spinning across the icy road, through yet another fence, then into the front of No. 7, Yet To Be Named Road, smashing the front door and most of the windows.

'Gosh!'

'Holy macaroni!'

'Stars 'n' bars!'

'Gooosh!'

Guard Krick clambers out of the van. His eyes are wide with rage and he is shaking.

'MISTERZZZ!' he roars. 'IT TAKES MORE THAN YOUR SILLY KNOTS TO HOLD ME! I'M A TRAINED SOLDIER! I CAN ESCAPE ANYTHING!'

Krick's coming towards us.

Klack!

Klack!

Klack!

'I SAW THAT ... BRIGHT LIGHT, MISTERZZZ! WHATEVER IT WAS! I SAW THAT LAST TROLLEY GO INTO THAT LIGHT! I BET ALL THE TROLLEYS WENT INTO IT, DIDN'T THEY, EH? I WANT YOU TO EXPLAIN WHAT'S BEEN GOING ON HERE! I WANT YOU TO EXPLAIN IT TO ME SO I CAN EXPLAIN IT TO THE POWERS THAT BE AND –'

'What's all the noise about?' cries Mum, rushing out of the house. She sees the demolished boxes and the crashed van, then fixes her eyes on Guard Krick. 'Did you do all this, you silly man?'

'DON'T INTERFERE –'

'Don't you *dare* speak to me in that tone of voice!'

'THESE CHILDREN ARE CRIMINALS!'

'Oh, I've got no time for this, you silly man. Go away.' Mum looks at Memphis. 'Love, all the excitement has got to Missy and she's started having the baby!'

'What? Oh! Oh! Stars 'n' bars!'

'Now, don't panic. It's all under control. She's comfortable in my bed and Aunt Ivy is boiling some water. But I'm sure she'd like you nearby to offer some moral support!'

'She needs a macho boy to hold her hand, don't she, mate?'

'Indeed she does. And there's none more macho than you.'

Memphis rushes into the house.

'Nabil, love, why don't you keep an eye on your dad? He's trying to help, but I'm afraid he might faint at any moment.'

'Sure thing, amigo.'

Nabil rushes into the house.

Mum glances at Guard Krick and says, 'You still here?'

'You won't get away with this. None of you will. I met Miss Crib yesterday. I'm gonna tell her everything –'

'Well, go ahead!' says Mum, stepping so close to Guard Krick her chin is almost touching his chest. 'You can tell her right now. Here she is!'

A car has pulled up outside the house and Miss Crib is getting out.

Oh, gosh.

'Zi-Zi!'

'It's all right, little brov!'

Mum hisses under her breath at Guard Krick, 'I'm not afraid of you, Krick. I've been dealing with people like you for years. I was taught how to do it by my husband. You think you can threaten my children? Eh? Big mistake! Huge!' And suddenly, Mum's mood changes and she dashes up to Nicci Crib, exclaiming brightly, 'I'm so glad you're here! What a morning!'

'Wh-What's been going on here?' asks Nicci, surveying the wreckage.

'We've had a serious case of reckless driving,' says Mum. 'My poor children were helping move some of the boxes out of the garage – oh, they've been having a slumber party! Bless! You like their fancy dress?'

'Er . . . yes, it's –'

'And then – what happens? We hear a noise! Car tyres! And this ... this man here comes driving into New Town! Faster than the speed limit! He misses my poor children by a hair's breadth! The poor loves had to drop all the boxes to run out of the way and ... well, you can see where the van ended up! Look!'

'LIES!' yells Guard Krick. 'TELL THE TRUTH! THEY STOLE ALL THE TROLLEYS FROM THE SUPER-MARKET!'

'Oh, really,' sighs Mum. 'Is that the best excuse you can come up with?'

'IT'S TRUE! THEY BROKE INTO THE SUPER-MARKET, TIED ME UP, AND BROUGHT ALL THE TROLLEYS HERE. THESE TWO AND THEIR TWO MATES AND ROZ.'

'But there must be hundreds of trolleys in the super-market,' says Mum.

'THERE ARE!'

'And you expect us to believe that three children, a toddler and a checkout girl wheeled all those hundreds of trolleys here –'

'THEY DIDN'T HAVE TO WHEEL THEM! THE TROLLEYS ARE ALIVE!'

Mum looks at Nicci and rolls her eyes, murmuring, 'The man's deranged. Totally deranged.'

'IT'S TRUE! THEY PUT THE TROLLEYS INTO THIS GOLD LIGHT.'

Mum looks at Nicci and shakes her head.

'IT'S TRUE! THERE WAS TINY GOLD STARS ALL OVER THE –'

'I've heard enough of this!' snaps Mum. 'I don't know why you've got it in for my children and this poor check-out girl. All my children have ever wanted to do is help you. They even collected trolleys for you from what I've been told.'

'Oh, they did, Mrs Jingle,' says Nicci. 'I saw them.'

'And now you come round here,' continues Mum, glaring at Guard Krick, 'and spread these stupid lies and – Oh! Your breath, man! You've been drinking! Smell it, Miss Crib?'

'I do, Mrs Jingle!'

'Well, that explains everything! You get drunk and allow criminals to break into the supermarket. Then you come round here and try to blame the whole thing on a bunch of harmless children! You get here – I hasten to add – by driving while under the influence of alcohol. A van, I hasten to add, that ain't even your property! What's more, you nearly hurt my children with your over-the-speed-limit driving. You smash all these boxes full of precious things that can never be replaced. You knock down fences and nearly demolish one of the houses The Powers That Be have been trying to build for ever-so-grateful-and-in-need people like me. And then, to top it all, you come out with some drunken fantasy about living trolleys and golden light and tiny stars! Honestly, Miss Crib, I hope you intend to tell the supermarket what's been going on and make sure this man is dismissed from his job. He should never be allowed to work in a supermarket again, and I hope you will see that he is not allowed, by law, to come anywhere near me and my family ever again.'

'I will, Mrs Jingle.'

Oh, glorious, Mum! Well done!

Guard Krick glares at everyone for a moment, then starts marching towards the van.

'I think you should leave that exactly where it is!' Mum calls after him. 'The police will want that for evidence! Right, Miss Crib?'

'Right, Miss Jingle.'

Guard Krick glares once more, then points at Zip, 'YOU

LISTEN! I'M NEVER GONNA GO AWAY. NOT
COMPLETELY. NO MATTER WHAT YOU DO. I
KNOW THE TRUTH ABOUT THE TROLLEYS. AND
I WILL FIGHT YOU UNTIL THE END OF THE –'

'Threats too!' says Mum, nudging Nicci. 'Another
criminal offence if I'm not mistaken.'

'Indeed, yes, Mrs Jingle. Quite shocking. When I met
Guard Krick yesterday I thought he was so charming.
How wrong I was!'

Guard Krick lets out a roar of frustration –

'RAAAGGGHHHHH!'

– then marches out of New Town –

Klack!

Klack!

Klack!

— 94 —

'Now, Miss Crib,' says Mum, smiling and grabbing Nicci's
hand, 'can I just say how sorry I was to miss you yesterday. Lots of shopping to do. A mother's work is never
done, you know. And now ... well, you've arrived at the
perfect moment. Missy is in labour with her baby and an
extra pair of hands will go down a treat.' She pulls Nicci
towards the house.

'But I ... oh ...'

'Now, don't worry! I'm in control of everything. I
delivered lots of babies in the forest. Why my Newt was

born beneath an oak tree. You just help us with this and then I'll make us all some lovely breakfast – Oh, Zip, love, will you and Newt put all these boxes away, please?'

'Yeah, Mum!'

'Ya!'

Mum and Nicci go into the house.

'Well ... gosh! That's all I can say!'

'Goosh!'

'You too, eh, little brov? Mum's really something when she gets going, ain't she, eh?'

'Ya-ya, Zi-Zi!'

'And I think it's fair to say The Powers That Be won't be a problem any more – Okey-dokey! Let's get these boxes back into the hideout!'

They work in silence, Zip carrying all the larger boxes, leaving the smaller ones for Newt. The only sounds are the occasional moans of Missy and the encouraging noises made by Mum and the others. Zip keeps an eye on Newt, making sure none of this is disturbing him, but –

It's like Newt can't hear what's going on in the house at all. He's so wrapped up in his thoughts. He keeps looking at the spot where Apollo disappeared. And every time he walks into the hideout, his eyes look all over the place. It's like he expects Apollo to wheel out of the shadows and say, 'Hello, LittleBrov!'

Zip sets about clearing up the remains of the smashed boxes caused by Guard Krick's reckless driving.

'You stay there, little brov. I'll do this. It won't take long.'

Newt sits on the kerb and, for a while, watches Zip, then his eyes look up, up towards the sky. The clear blue sky of this frosty New Town morning.

That's it! All cleared away! Oh ... little brov, I know what you're thinking.

Zip sits next to Newt and puts his arm round his

shoulders. 'He's not gone, Newt,' he says gently. 'Just because he's not here . . . don't mean he's gone. He loved us. We loved him. That goes on and on forever. Without end. You understand that, don't you?'

'Ya-ya.'

Zip wraps his arms round Newt and holds him tight. He kisses the top of his brother's head and says, 'Love you, little brov.'

'Loo-yoo, Zi-Zi.'

And then a high-pitched cry comes from the house –

'Waaagggghhhhhh!!'

'Gosh! Listen to that! Sounds like Missy's had her baby! Everyone's clapping and cheering! Can you hear that?'

'Ya!'

'Come on! Let's get inside.' Zip picks Newt up and heads for the house. 'Let's go and say hello to this newborn thing, shall we?'

'Knee burn.'

'No, no, little brov. Not knee burn. *Newborn.*'

'*Newborn.*'

'Oh, glorious.'

Philip Ridley

had his own theatre group when he was 6, completed his first novel at the age of 7 and had his first solo art exhibition at the age of 14. At 17, he began a degree in Fine Art at St Martin's School of Art in London and at the age of 19 had his first novel published. Let's find out more.

'Children now are more visually literate than ever before. They can cope with incredibly complex sequences of imagery and I'm trying to reflect that in my stories, where I try to maintain the pace of a film or a computer game rather than that of a traditional novel'
– Philip Ridley